WHITE HEAT

WHITE HEAT

Paul D. Marks

Published by Timeless Skies Publishing

WHITE HEAT

Published by Timeless Skies Publishing

Visit Paul at: www.PaulDMarks.com
www.whiteheatnovel.blogspot.com

Book and cover design by Timeless Skies Publishing.
Cover photo © by Paul D. Marks

Timeless Skies Publishing

For

Amy

and

Norma and Norm

Author's note:

Some of the language in the novel may be offensive. But please consider it in the context of the time, place and characters.

This place [Los Angeles] was a lot friendlier and a lot nicer when I came here twenty-six years ago. There are still pockets of civility here, but they are rapidly disappearing as neighborhoods and ethnic groups get more and more polarized, and as the city gets more and more crowded. I think the violence and the ruthlessness is going to increase...

—Don Henley
(musician and former
Eagles band leader)

APRIL 1992

April is the cruelest month.

The Waste Land
—T.S. Eliot

CHAPTER 1

My father always said I was a fuckup, that the only reason we get along is 'cause he keeps his mouth shut. Maybe he's right: I fucked up high school.

Fucked up college.

Fucked up my marriage.

Fucked up my life by leaving the service.

And now I've fucked up a case.

Fucked it up real bad.

Teddie Matson was different. She had a golden life, until her path had the misfortune of crossing mine. I sat staring out the window of my office, k.d. lang playing in the background. It was a while till the sun would set, that *golden* hour when everything takes on a gilded glow.

Golden hour is the time when the light hits just right in the early morning or late afternoon. The time when movie cinematographers most like to shoot. The light is tawny and warm. Gentle. It makes the stars shine brighter.

Golden hour is the time when Teddie Matson was killed.

◈ ◈ ◈

"Duke Rogers?"

"What can I do for you?"

The Weasel shifted back and forth. Left foot to right. Right to left. Nervous. Fidgety. Blue eyes so pale they almost lacked color darted back and forth across the room.

"I, I want you to find a friend of mine," he said, voice cracking. He slapped a snapshot on the desk, a sleek chrome and smoked-glass job that I'd picked up at auction. A greasy lock of hair dropped over his eye. He shooed it away.

She was a beautiful girl. Woman? No. Hardly more than a girl. Smile was warm and inviting. Dark almond shaped eyes. Long dark tresses curling around her neck. They looked like they were ready to strangle her.

"Who is she?"

"W'we went to school together. I heard she was in town and I–" He sucked in his already-sunken cheeks.

Who was I to argue with him? Just because he looked ten years older than her. Maybe he'd had a rough life. Just because she was black and he was white? That didn't mean they couldn't have gone to school together.

"How much is your fee?" he said. Lit a cigarette. I pointed to the universal "No Smoking" sign over my desk. I needed the gig, but I didn't need it that bad. He grunted. Stubbed it out on the linoleum floor.

"Two-fifty. Sounds simple enough." The words came out by rote. My mind was somewhere else. At the moment, thinking about redecorating the office. Getting rid of the orange crate art, replacing it with Hopper prints, *Rooms by the Sea* and *Chop Suey.* They seemed to go with the building. A little more classic. But I knew I could use the cash for an overdue plumbing bill. Redecorating would have to wait.

The Weasel pulled out a wad of sweaty bills, peeled off a handful. Sucker. The job would take me all of an hour, if that. He was also a dweeb. He deserved to be fleeced.

"Here, write down her name, any other information you might have on her, age, height, scars, that kind of thing. Where she was born." I handed him a piece of paper and watched him scribble in an unsteady hand. He shoved the paper back at me. He had scrawled her name: "Teddie/Theodora Matson".

"How long will it take?"

"Couple-a days. What's your phone number?"

"I'll come by on Thursday."

"Around ten."

He headed for the door.

"Hey, what's your name?"

"Jim, Jim Talbot."

"See ya Thursday, Jim."

He left. I opened the window wider to let in some fresh air. I inhaled deeply, taking in the whiff of orange and lemon blossoms outside the window.

◈ ◈ ◈

I wondered how the dweeb would spend the time between Monday and Thursday at ten a.m. Didn't look like he had many friends. Maybe not any. If he was from out of town he might go to Disneyland. Nah. Not a place you go to by yourself. He might go down to the Santa Monica pier and throw a line off. Sure, the beach. That's where they all go. Isn't that why people come to Southern California anyway? So the beach would be one place for sure. He might take in a museum, but dweeby as he was, he didn't look the museum type. Might go on the Universal Studio Tour. Sure. He could see all the papier-mâché and phony fronts that make Hollywood what it is. Yeah, that was his kind of place all right. Maybe he'd check out Griffith Park or the Observatory or Farmers' Market. He had to eat. Well, what did I care how he spent those days in between?

I called Lou Waters at the DMV. We'd been friends since we went to Fairfax High together a decade or two ago. Seemed more like a century. I'd aged. She hadn't. She was one of those people who actually looked better the older she got – aging like a fine wine, she'd say.

"What's on today, Duke?" she asked.

"Can you run a name for me?"

"You know I'm not supposed to."

"Never stopped you before."

"And it won't stop me this time."

"Why do we always have to play this game, Lou?"

"It brightens my day."

"I thought the sound of my voice alone did that."

"You're not the fair-haired boy anymore."

I never was. But if being a second rate P.I. is success, I guess I've succeeded beyond my wildest dreams. But in the land of Beamers and Benzes, I'm just a Camry.

I gave Lou the info the dweeb had given me. I could hear the clicking of her computer keys over the phone. She had an address for me in a few seconds.

"Thanks, Lou. I owe you one."

"You owe me a ton."

"I'm good for it."

"Yeah, sure." She hung up. I knew she was smiling. We'd dated briefly in our sophomore year of high school. She'd left me for an older, more sophisticated guy – a junior, with a car.

I had to figure out what I'd do between now and the time the dweeb came back. I had a couple other scut cases I was working. Might as well check out some leads on them.

Later that day, while I was trying to decipher a new software program for billing my clients, new business walked in the door.

"Marion Rogers?"

"Yes." She was attractive in a plain sort of way. An all-American way. Open face, cute smile. Natural blond hair. She didn't have the sultry appeal of Teddie Matson, that's for sure.

"You don't look like a Marion."

"Maybe that's why my friends call me Duke."

She introduced herself as Laurie Hoffman, sat down and crossed her legs. I could tell she wanted to get to the point. And she did.

"Someone's following me. I went out with him once and now he won't leave me alone."

"Get a restraining order."

"I have. It doesn't do any good. And by the time the police arrive he's gone."

"Has he threatened you?"

"Not in so many words. He just tells me how much he wants me, things like that."

"I'm not really sure what I could do for you. Surveil him maybe, but–"

"I think he's dangerous."

"He hasn't done anything."

"Yet."

"Problem is I don't really have the time right now. I'm a one man office and I've got more than I can handle already."

"You don't need the money?"

"It's not that. But I honestly don't think I'd be able to devote the necessary time and that wouldn't be good for either of us." I wrote Harvey Zenobia's name and number on a piece of paper. Handed it to her. "This is a colleague of mine. Give him a call. Maybe he can help."

Truth is, I did need the money. I had a second mortgage on the house my dad left me and I could barely make the payments. What I didn't need was another short term shit job that was more trouble than it was worth. Domestic cases, stalking cases are hell. I landed in jail on one once when I tried to intervene between a husband and wife. I got between them when he was coming after her, slugged him, hard. He filed assault charges and I got three days in jail. The fact that he had a knife in his hand didn't seem to matter to the judge.

She stood to leave, looking defiant. Angry. But too proud to say anything.

"I'm sorry," I said as she disappeared through the door.

◈ ◈ ◈

The dweeb showed up at ten on the nose. I knew he would. You can tell these things about a person.

"Didja get it?" He was almost breathless. A bubble formed at his lips when he talked.

I handed him a slip of paper. He looked down at it. His mouth didn't move. But his eyes smiled. He stared at the paper an awfully long time. He was wearing a good suit. English cut. Expensive. Then I noticed his shoes: old. Scuffy. Didn't quite fit.

He turned and left. Didn't say a word. He had paid so I didn't care. He was a happy man. And I was happy to have him out of my life. I'd wish later that I'd never met the lousy dweeb.

CHAPTER 2

I'd gone out of town for about a week on a case. My buddy Jack had collected the mail and taken care of my dog, Baron. I came home, greeted by Baron in his usual overzealous manner. There was a message from Lou on the answering machine. She didn't say what she wanted and I couldn't reach her. Everything else was in order. I went to the office, was sitting in my chair, listening to k.d. lang, catching up on a week's worth of newspapers and taking my lunch break of gin-laced lemonade. I'd cut down on the alcohol. Cut down, not out. I could handle it in small doses. The article I was reading said that a verdict in the Rodney King beating case was expected any day now. But it was another headline that slammed me in the gut.

Another photo.

Made me want to vomit.

Through force of will, I was able to control it.

I crumpled the paper.

Tossed it in the can.

Kicked the can with such force that the metal sides caved in.

Fucked up a case.

Fucked it up real bad.

"Promising Actress Shot by Rabid Fan" the headline read. "Teddie Matson, the 26 year old second lead of such Hollywood sitcom hits as *Day Timers* and *Holier Than Thou* was on her way to becoming one of Hollywood's lights. The, some say naive, young actress answered the door to her apartment building yesterday afternoon expecting a script delivery from the studio. Instead an unknown assailant delivered a .32 slug to her abdomen. Police surmise that it was a berserk fan who fired the gun, but don't have a clue as to who he is."

I knew it was my client. It was a Weasel named Jim Talbot, if that was really his name. But it was how I knew that made me want to split a gut. And it had taken only a few minutes' work, still I had charged Talbot a full day's fee. Talbot didn't mind. He was happy to pay. He had walked out of my office with the biggest shit-eating grin on his face that I'd seen since I left the service.

I didn't know what to do, if there was anything I could do? Should do. I bottomed another glass of the saucy lemonade. Before I could get toasted the phone rang.

"Hello, Duke. Lou."

"Hey, Lou. Sorry I didn't get back to you sooner. I was out of town for a few days." Did she know? We talked a couple times a month, so maybe this was just a friendly call. At any rate, neither one of us brought up Teddie right now.

"Listen," she said, "how 'bout we have dinner tonight?"

"Okay. Usual place." The roar of a Harley chewed up the street below as she affirmed the usual place at seven. She must have known because we normally had dinner about once a year and we'd already met our quota this year. I was about to dive back into the lemonade, when the door opened and Jack Riggs walked in, looking like a Hell's Angel in heat. Tossed his kit bag on my desk and sat down like he owned the place.

I'd known Jack since we went through boot camp together. We'd split up or been split up after that, but we both ended up in the Teams. There was definitely a bond there – after he got over the fact that my name was Marion – though I couldn't say what it was exactly. I had to join the Teams to counter a name like Marion. That's where I got the nickname Duke. Who would name a boy Marion, especially in this day and age? My parents, that's who. They both loved John Wayne and his real name was Marion Michael Morrison. And his nickname was Duke. If it was good enough for him it was good enough for me, on both counts. Only right now I felt more like a knave than a duke.

The first words out of his mouth were, "What's that shit you're playing?"

"k.d. lang. I like it."

"Hell, man, don't'cha know she's lez?"

"I'd heard something about it," I said, "but I don't see how it matters."

Jack poured himself a lacy lemonade. He knew what was in it. "When you listen to a song, a love song, don't you sit there an' think they're singin' t' you? Or if it's a man, that it's you singin' to a girl? But how can you get into that fantasy when you know she's AC-DC, so t' speak?"

I didn't know what to say. I never knew what to say to Jack when he came on like this. How could I argue with that logic? Besides, no matter what I said, he wouldn't buy it. So I said, "I don't know, Jack. It's just a song."

"Man, it's no song. It's a political statement. It's–"

I wanted to shut him up, or off, or something, so I flipped the switch from CD to radio. Eric Clapton was on singing the MTV *Unplugged* version of *Layla*. Tell you the truth, I liked it better than the harder, faster version. But I didn't say that to Jack. It would have brought another lecture in pretzelogic.

He saw the newspaper sitting on the desk. "This Rodney King thing's gonna blow wide open. Whole town's gonna go up in smoke."

"You're crazy," I said, but somewhere inside me I thought maybe he was right. I didn't want to admit it. Not to him. Not to myself. I'm a multi-generation native of Los Angeles, which makes me a rare bird. And I love my home town, not so much as it is, but as it was when I was a kid. I grew up in a real *Leave it to Beaver* neighborhood. No one locked their doors. No one worried about getting shot on the freeways. Of course, my relationship with my dad was no Beaver and Ward thing, but I survived, after a fashion.

He looked down at the paper, saw the headline about Teddie Matson. "She was hot. I wouldn'ta minded havin' a hormone fix with her."

"She was black."

"I make exceptions on occasion. I would've made one for her."

"How *white* of you." I don't know if he caught the sarcasm. If he did he didn't say anything. I was just as glad. 'Cause a mad Jack was crazier than a mad dog. I'd bet on him against five pro boxers at the same time, when he was mad, three when he wasn't. His washboard stomach rippled under the t-shirt that was always at least one size too small. Even if it wasn't, his arms were too big for the sleeves. Had to have his shirts custom made to accommodate them. He'd stayed in shape. I hadn't.

On the other hand I'm not very large to begin with. But wiry and determined.

"Hey, I'm not as bad as you think," he said. "'Sides, I just say what everyone else is thinkin'."

"Not everyone."

"Hell, almost everyone. Especially the damn limousine liberals that wanna baby everyone, make 'em victims. Make 'em dependent on 'em and on ol' Uncle Sam. That's their power base. Hell, the liberals and the–"

"Cut it out, Jack. Segue." It was a command. An order. I didn't want to talk about that shit anymore. Jack stopped. Looked at me. Hurt. He loved to expound. We had a deal. Segue was the end of it. Change of subject. Worked either way, for me or him. We tried not to exercise it too frequently.

"Hell, I'm only saying out loud what you're too afraid to even think. What everyone's afraid to think. 'Cept the niggers. It's okay for them to think it about us. Change history."

I told him to shut up again. But I didn't kick him out. The problem is that Jack's too open. Doesn't even try to hide his prejudices. No veneer of civilization there. Makes me face my own prejudices and fears. Makes me see what I could be and helps me to avoid it. Sometimes I'm successful. Sometimes not. But it's also one of the things I like about him. You know where he's at. So you know where you're at with him.

Jack and I go back a long way and I do like him. But I don't like all of him.

◈ ◈ ◈

The lobby was crowded. Lou's strawberry hair glinted in the lights, accenting a still-perfect complexion. Her Anne Taylor dress highlighted her figure, flaring at the waist. Stunning, as usual. =

She knew. Her eyes said it. The corners of her mouth said it. And her weak handshake instead of a hug said it. She knew.

El Coyote was an old restaurant from the old neighborhood, a few blocks west of La Brea on Beverly Boulevard. It attracted an eclectic clientele. Tonight was no different. Teens in hip-hop drag mixed with elderly couples and homosexual couples and young hetero couples on dates. All inside a restaurant that had been here since before the war – the Big War. Lou particularly liked the decor, paintings made out of seashells. "Interesting," she always said, as if that was enough. And she loved the food. So did I. But I knew a lot of people who didn't. You either loved it or hated it, there was no in between. That's the kind of place it was. I liked their margaritas. They weren't those slushy crushed ice new fangled things you find in most restaurants. They were just tequila, triple sec, lime juice and salt around the rim. Damn good.

"Interesting," Lou said looking at a shell painting, after we were seated. I nodded. There was an awkward feeling between us, a gulf of turbulent air that we were trying to negotiate. There was nothing for me to say in response. This wasn't a social call. She leaned forward, talking quietly. "You know why I wanted to have dinner, don't you?"

I nodded.

"I didn't want to leave any specifics on the answering machine or call a bunch of times."

"In case the cops were on us already."

She nodded. "I shouldn't have run it for you. I didn't know who Teddie Matson was. I don't watch television, especially sitcoms. How was I to know you were asking me to look up a TV star?"

Lou did watch television. Lots of it. She watched old movies. What she meant was she didn't watch sitcoms or dramatic series. Made for TV junk.

"I don't watch sitcoms either," I said. "I had no idea who she was. The headline hit me like a hurricane." What did Lou want from me?

"You know I run these things for you 'cause you're an old friend. But I shouldn't. I could catch hell."

"Does anyone know you did it?"

"I don't think so. There's no record. But you're an accessory. So am I." She looked into my eyes. A searing, guilt-edged gaze that tore into me. She looked away. "Who'd you get the information for?"

"I don't know." My face flushed red. It hadn't done that in years. I was embarrassed. I had fucked up – bad, just like my father always said: *"You're as dumb as the Mexicans at the plant." "Why dad? Because I wasn't a carbon copy of you."* "He paid in cash, up front. I'm sure the name he gave me's a phony."

"You've got to find him."

"I know. I will."

"I should go to the police. They should know everything. It would help them solve it."

"Don't, at least not yet. Give me a few days."

She said she would. Neither of us ordered food. We left a good tip and split.

CHAPTER 3

The light was mellow, soft. It grazed across the row of Spanish style stucco duplexes and apartments, reflected off leaded picture windows and prismed onto the street. Each had a driveway to one side or the other. Gardeners worked the neatly manicured greenery of every other building. It was a nice old neighborhood in the Fairfax district, one of the better parts of town. My old stomping grounds.

The same time of day Teddie Matson had been murdered. I planned it that way, hoping the same people would be around that might have been around that day.

I walked up the street, my eyes darting back and forth, up and down, aware of everything around me – radar eyes – looking at the addresses on the buildings. The number was emblazoned in my brain. I could see it before my eyes, but it was only a phantom. I passed a gardener at 627, coming to a halt at 625. I stared at the building.

A typical stucco fourplex from the '20s. Even though I hadn't been inside yet I knew the layout – I'd seen enough of them. Two units upstairs, two down. A main front door that would lead to a small, probably tiled hall, with an apartment on either side and a stairway heading to the two upstairs apartments. I walked up the tiled walk, stuck my hands through the remnants of yellow crime scene tape, tried to open the front door. Locked. I rang the bell. No response. I felt as if I was being watched. Still no one answered the buzzer.

A silver 1970s era Buick pulled into the driveway, slowing. A gray haired man with wrinkled skin leaned out the window.

"Who are you? What do you want?" There wasn't even the slightest hint of friendliness in his voice.

I started to approach his car. The electric window shot up. He held up a cellular car phone, finger poised over the 9 of, I assumed, 9-1-1. I backed off, holding my hands out in front of me so he could see them. He wasn't dialing 9-1-1 – yet.

"I'm here about Teddie Matson." I had to shout so he could hear me through the rolled up window. I'm sure the gardener next door could also hear.

"You the police?"

"I'm a private detective, looking for her murderer."

"How do I know?" It was hard to tell, but it sounded like he had a trace of an accent. Today, the Fairfax area is home to a lot of people from Eastern Europe.

Gingerly, I pulled my I.D. from my pocket. Held it up for him. He squinted trying to read it, motioning me closer, until I was almost pressed up against the glass. The window zoomed down to the halfway mark. Progress.

He took the card from me and spent three full minutes glaring at it, before giving it back.

"We already talked to the police," he said. "What can you do that they can't?"

"I can help them."

"Who're you working for?"

"That's confidential information." I could hardly tell him I was working for myself, that I'd given the killer the address.

He gunned the engine and the car lurched past me, down the driveway into one of the four garages at the end. I stayed at the front of the building. It looked like he was going to go in the back door, then he walked toward me.

"What do you want? We've been questioned so many times already, the police, the news people. Even her family. It's bad enough to go through something like this, but to have to relive it every day is torture. My wife hasn't slept since the, the–"

"I'm sorry. We're all just trying to help. Just a few questions?"

He nodded warily.

"Was anyone else home when it happened?"

"My wife. She's always home. She's an invalid. But she didn't see nuthin'."

"Might she have heard something?" Was she the person who I felt watching me as I had rung the doorbell.

He shrugged. I asked to see the entry hall of the building where it happened. He was reluctant to show me, but gave in. From the info Lou had given me and looking at the doors in the downstairs entry hall I knew Teddie's apartment had to be upstairs.

Tiled red floor. A large antiqued mirror. Walls a dirty plaster that had once been white. A black wrought iron chandelier hung overhead, showering a dull yellow light on the ashen walls.

"This is where she fell." He pointed to the stairs leading to the second floor. "Her apartment was up there. Number four. We think she came down to answer the door for–"

"Why would she open the door to a stranger?"

"If you'll just let me finish, the intercom was broken and she was expecting a script delivery from the studio. Must've thought it was them."

A heavily carved wooden door off the hall opened a crack. It was to unit number two.

"That's really about all we know."

"You didn't see him?"

He shook his head.

"Or your wife?"

Before he could answer the door swung open and a tiny blue-haired woman stood engulfed in its frame. Blue and white polka dots blurted from her dress. Her hair was neatly done. She hardly looked like an invalid. Her husband, who still hadn't told me his name, looked miffed that she'd come out.

"It was unseasonably hot that day," she said in a strong, grandmotherly voice. "Teddie was a–"

"You don't even know who you're talking to," her husband barked.

"You're talking to him. And I seen him show his card to you outside."

"He's not a policeman. He's a private detective."

"Like Jim Rockford," she smiled. I nodded. Her smile grew. "He's so handsome. I watch him every day in the reruns." She looked me up and down, appraising whether or not I met Rockford or James Garner's good looks. The smile remained, but since it didn't grow I figured I lost to the actor.

"It was terrible," she said, the smile falling off her face.

"Tell me about it."

The old man's mouth turned down. He wanted no part of this. But his wife was in her element, repelled by the horror and drawn to it. Reveling in it.

"Terrible," she said. "He knocked, quietly at first, as if he was afraid of disturbing someone. When no one answered he knocked louder. Then he walked out to the sidewalk."

"You saw him?"

"Only through the curtains. He came back and rang her buzzer. I heard the door lock open on her apartment upstairs and Teddie coming down the stairs. She asked if he was here to deliver the script. He mumbled something. She opened the front door. We always keep the front entry door locked these days. And she asked what he wanted. She was frightened. Then he approached her–"

"You saw this through the crack in the door?"

"No, no. I could hear it. I heard it."

She didn't seem nervous, but I felt that she was holding something back. Looking at her husband I figured she didn't want to deal with him later. He had enjoyed telling me what he knew, even though he would never admit it. But now he wasn't the star anymore. The spotlight was on her and he didn't like that. I pictured him lambasting her after I left. She went on:

"She was scared. I could hear it in her voice. She usually talked smooth and quiet. But her voice was shrill, loud. He kept moving towards her, and finally, finally–"

"Enough," the old man said, cradling her in his arms. "Get out of here." He motioned toward the door with his hand. I thanked them and left, butterflies, no moths, churning in my gut.

"Mrs. Perlman," she shouted behind me.

Yellow streaks of sun pierced the stucco and glass buildings, melting everything in a golden hour glow.

"Hey."

I looked around. The Salvador Dali-mustached gardener next door motioned me with his hose. Was he gonna spray me? It was hot. Not that hot.

"You a cop?" he said.

"Private."

"Didn't think you were the L.A.P.D. type." He took a swig from the gushing hose, then sprayed a flower bed. "I seen 'im. He walked right past me."

"Who?"

"Don't play this shit with me."

"Okay, what'd you see?"

"You gettin' paid?"

I couldn't tell him the truth so I told him I was. I put a twenty in his hand. Disappointment shattered his placid face. I gave him another twenty and a ten. That was more to his liking.

"Brown hair, dark brown. And blue eyes. Pale. Man, they didn't have no passion behind 'em. Nothin'. Steely. Spooky. He didn't look like he belonged in this neighborhood. Kind of seedy looking, white trashy, but tryin', you know, to dress up or look like he was better 'an he was."

The Weasel.

"Did you see him get into a car?"

"No, man. No car. He come from up there, diddy-boppin' along the sidewalk. He stops here and there, checkin' addresses I guess. Then he goes up to that place," he pointed to Teddie's building. I noticed Mrs. Perlman parting the curtains. If only Moses had had her talents. "Guess I don't give you much to go on." He pulled one of the twenties, thrust it back at me. I couldn't tell him I had also seen the Weasel. I shoved it back in his hand, headed to my car.

When the gardener used the term diddy-boppin' I recognized him as a Viet Nam vet. I thought about saying something, brother-to-brother, Desert Storm vet to Viet Nam vet, and all that and normally I would have, but I didn't want to get sidetracked. I was on a mission – the most important of my life, find Teddie's killer – and I didn't want to waste even one second on small talk. I went over to the studio where Teddie's series was filmed. Couldn't get past the guard at the gate. On the way home, I stopped at a payphone and tried to make an appointment to see the producers of her show. They're in mourning, I was told. They just didn't want to talk, for whatever reasons.

The sun was beginning to set. Another Golden Hour – dead.

I pulled up to the house, a Spanish-Colonial built in the twenties. The driveway ran alongside the house back to the garage, which like a lot of people in L.A. I never used as a garage, even though I had a classic Firebird. The stucco was beige, though it might have been lighter at one time. A small courtyard in front was fenced off from the street with a wooden gate. At the back of the courtyard was the front door. I pulled about halfway down the driveway to where the back door was, parked. Baron, my tan and black German Shepherd was waiting for me with a green tennis ball in his mouth. We played catch. He loved running after tennis balls. Seeing him, playing with him, gave me a feeling of normalcy again. Made me forget about things for just a moment. After half an hour it was time to cool off:

Most L.A. pools are small and kidney shaped. Of course some are shaped like guitars or cars or whatever ego trip the ego tripper building them was involved in. And most aren't built for swimming. One of the good things my dad did was build a pool that was lean and mean, long and skinny. Built for swimming, not just skinny dipping. It was wide enough to play around in, but long enough to get a good workout. Problem was, he'd get mad when I'd use it: *"Why aren't you doing something constructive? You never do anything around here. Can't even change a light bulb."* Of course, I changed more light bulbs than you could count, but he never saw it.

Screw the workout.

I floated on a raft, staring up at the afternoon sun, watching a dragonfly dip down toward the water, then retreat. Over and over. Dip and run. Fascinating.

Then he got too much water on his wings. The weight pulled him down. Under. He drowned. I thought it was a dream, or I would have tried to save him. I was too late.

It wasn't the first time:

I was too late in high school when I finally decided to buckle down and study. If I had I might have been able to get into a good college.

I was too late in college to graduate, took too much time getting through the required course work. Spent too much time drinking and fooling around. And I quit early to join the service. At least I'd learned enough in school to allow me to pass the math and diving physics for the Teams. That was saying something.

I was too late to get a real job instead of working for my dad or being a second-rate P.I.

I was too late in my marriage to notice my wife drifting away from me. Slowly. Surely. Anyone would have seen it. Anyone but me.

I was too late in realizing that I should have stayed in the service instead of listening to my dad. I felt at home there. Doing my twenty would have been easy. Life on the outside was hard. I went into my dad's wholesale meat business but it didn't last. We couldn't get along.

It wasn't that I wasn't smart. I was too smart – for my own good. It's okay to fuck yourself, but when you fuck with someone else's life you have to pay. I'm paying now.

◈ ◈ ◈

He walks up the street.

One hand thrust into pockets filled with lint and grime.

Sweaty coins.

The other clutching a crumpled piece of paper.

With an address from a detective scribbled on it.

Passes 625 North.

Turns around.

Heads back.

Gardener at 627 looks up.

Smiles.

He doesn't return it.

He steps onto the walk leading up to the door of 625.

Tries the door.

Locked.

Looks at the names next to the buzzer.

Knocks tentatively.

Louder.

No one comes.

Retreats down the sidewalk.

A whirlpool of thoughts buzz his head.

Can't pick any one out.

A fingerpainting swirl:

Green here.

Yellow there.

Purple

Orange.

Blue.

Red and golden.

Especially red.

Everywhere.

If he doesn't do it now, he never will.

Turns around, heads back to 625.

Walks up to the door, buzzes number four.

Waits.

And waits.

Sun sliver hits the back of his neck.
Speckles of sweat form.
Running down his back.
Shivers.
In the middle of a hot day:
Shivering.
Thinking of it makes him chuckle.
What does the gardener think seeing this man standing here, laughing out loud?
Thinks he's crazy.
But he's not crazy.
Just smitten.

He knows she's the one.
Knew it from the first time he saw her.
Meant to be.
The only one.
There could be no one else.
She has the look:
The smile in her eyes,
as well as on her lips.
The curly dark hair.
Turned up nose.
Skin as smooth as cream.
Cafe au lait.
When she talks, she talks to him.
There's no one else for her to talk to.
She asked him to come out to the Coast – to see her.
So why does he feel funny standing here?
Why should he worry about what the gardener next door thinks?
Why should he worry about what she'll think?

The door opens.
It's her.
Looks just like she does on TV.

The smile.
The hair.
The eyes.

"Yes," she says.
She's speaking to him. Really speaking to him.
"Are you dropping off the script from the studio?"
He doesn't know what to say. Stutters. Nothing comes out.
"Look," she says, "if you're selling something—"
"I, I'm not selling anything. I c'came t'to see y'you."
"I'm sorry, but you'll have to go."
The door drives toward him, an implacable force, meeting an unmovable object – his foot. The smile's gone from her face. She isn't dissin' him anymore. She respects him. His strength. His power.

He walks her back into the entry hall, closing the door behind them. The slightly parted curtains in the nearby window also close.

Light beams in through the leaded glass door. Yet it's dark. The red tile floor swallows the light like a black hole. She backs towards the stairs.
"I'm not going to hurt you."
"What do you want?"
"I, I just want to be f'friends."
"Listen, I'd like to be your friend—"
"Really?"
"Yes, but, but I have a boyfriend."
"But you asked me to come out here."
"I did?" Her eyes open wide. Anyone else would see the terror in them. He sees only love.
"Yes."
"Have we met before?"
She's playing coy.

"You asked me to come out. F'from the TV, you were looking right at me."

"From the TV?" She tries to remember what she'd been told to do in a situation like this. Stars are always being hounded by admirers. Most of them are harmless. There's always a few who aren't. What was he?

She backs into an apartment door on the ground floor. Discreetly putting her left hand behind her back, she tries the knob. Locked. Her heart flutters. He moves closer.

"I, I just want to talk. Be friends."

There's a faraway look in his eyes. He isn't looking at her. Through her. What does he see? If she knew she might be able to talk him out of here. But she doesn't.

"Sure, we can be friends."

His eyes draw narrower. Even in the dark light, the pupils close down.

"You don't mean it. I can tell. You don't want m'me here."

"But I do. I invited you, didn't I?"

"Fuck you. I thought you were different. But you're not. You're just like all the rest."

He balls his hand into a fist. Slams it into his head. She jumps back.

"Why?"

"Why what?"

"Why are you backing away from me? You think I'm crazy. You think I'm going to hurt you? You think—"

"No, of course not." She tries to still her trembling voice. She backs up the stairs. If only she could dash for her apartment. The door is thick. These old buildings were built solid. She could hide behind it and call the police. Damn, why hadn't the intercom been fixed yet? Why did she have to be home when he showed up? How did he get her address anyway? From a Movie Stars'

Home Map? The DMV? How? Her mind races. That's not important. The only thing now is to get away.

She turns and runs up the stairs. If only she can make it to the first landing and around the corner she might have a chance. She hopes he doesn't have a gun.

The crack of the pistol shot reverberates in the tiled hall. Bouncing off the walls, ricocheting. Like being stuck in a metal drum when a construction ball hits. Her scream is swallowed by the shot's report echoing through the black hole. Everything is swallowed by the black hole, light, sound, sight. Only the black is left.

And the red. Red everywhere. Blood.

Her blood.

He looks at her crumpled on the stairs, brushes his hand across her hair. Sounds come from upstairs. People. He runs toward the door. Sees a face in the antique mirror. Disfigured. Grisly. Melting in front of him. Fading away. He runs out the door. The gardener looks at him. Fuck the gardener. He runs down the street. It's Golden Hour. He's heard of it. He's conscious of it. He doesn't care. He remembers the face in the mirror. The face of Duke Rogers.

◈ ◈ ◈

I woke up, my hand dragging in the water next to the raft, splashed water on my face. It'd been a long time since I'd dreamt. I missed it. Now I wasn't so sure about that. It was only a dream – a nightmare. One that I had caused. How much of it was true? The gist of it, if not the details.

I swam to the edge of the pool, climbed out, toweled off and went into the house, Baron trailing behind me. I grabbed a phone book from a kitchen cabinet, found the Perlmans' number. Mrs. Perlman answered. I told her who I was.

"I can talk for a minute only, my husband's in the bathroom," she whispered.

"Is there anything you forgot to tell me? Anything you couldn't–"

"I probably shouldn't tell you this, but you seem like a nice young man–"

Yeah, right lady. A fuckup. A major fuckup, just like my dad said: *"Marion, if we get divorced, it'll be your fault." They argue. They fight. He's mad at the world, but if they get divorced it'll be my fault.*

"I didn't tell the police. They're so, well you know. Anyway, I picked up a piece of paper from the hall. I didn't give it to them. I know I should have. Will you give it to them for me?"

CHAPTER 4

I dressed – short sleeved shirt, jeans, windbreaker – and outta there before hanging up the receiver. When I got to the Perlman's, I wasn't the only one there. Several people were packing Teddie's things up, loading them into a beatup blue van. The usual stuff, posters from movies she'd had bit roles in, stuffed animals, clothes.

Mrs. Perlman waved from the porch. No hiding behind curtains now. The paper curled in her scrawny hand. I made my way up the walk.

Cold eyes turned on me. He was smaller than me, but those eyes spoke of death. Teddie's? Mine? I didn't know.

"What'chu want?" he said. He was wearing blue jeans and a Public Enemy T-shirt. His face was dark. Round. Short hair in a fade. He was a little man. Lean and mean as a pit bull. And I didn't have to talk to him to see the wells of anger behind his tombstone eyes. Didn't have to get close to feel that anger shooting out at me. Where did he keep it all? How did he live with it?

Discretion is the better part of valor. Small as he was he looked tough. Wiry, like me. I could probably take him, but if he was one of Teddie's friends or family I didn't want to antagonize him. Might need him. Hell, he might even need me.

Ignoring him, I went up to Mrs. Perlman. She held out her arms, greeting me like a long lost son, grabbing my hand with hers, pressing the paper into it. She whispered: "I don't want the *schvartzes* to see." She turned to the short man, beaming with pride:

"This is Mr. Rogers. He's a detective."

The man's eyes widened. "What're you doin' hangin' 'round here?"

I ignored him again. He went back to his work. Two other men came down the stairs, carrying a large oak trunk. Both of them were large, over six feet. Mrs. P. and I had to step back into her apartment to clear a path. I backed into Mrs. Perlman, felt her unsteady hand on my back. Was it due to her age or her fear of these black men, I wondered. Still, she had rented to a black woman. Jack would have advised her not to, regardless of the laws prohibiting discrimination.

Her apartment reminded me of my grandmother's. It had been only a mile or so from here. The Wilshire District, east of Fairfax. Doilies on the arms of the couches. Little porcelain knickknacks everywhere. Crystal bowls filled with candies – I left a business card in one. Hardly a sign of Mr. P.'s input or existence.

Mrs. P. and I went out to the lawn. Watched the men loading the van. The short one came up to me. Stood four inches from my nose; stared into my eyes. "I don't know what'chure hangin' 'round here for, but you stay outta my sister's life. Get it?"

He expected me to back off. I didn't. He expected me to dis him. I didn't. I didn't do anything. Just stared back.

"C'mon Warren. Why you wastin' your time an' energy on that shit?" the larger of the other two men said. "Ain't gonna bring her back."

Warren ignored him, still staring at me: "Who hired you? What'chu nosin' 'round here for?" He inched closer. I held my ground. "Don't need no honky motherfuckers nosin'–"

The larger of the other two men walked over. Put his arm on Warren's shoulder, pulled him back a step. Warren's feet were still planted a foot closer to me; the upper part of his body jerked back, followed by his feet. He looked humiliated.

"They call me Tiny," the larger man said more to Mrs. P. than to me. "Don't mind Warren. His mind's not in the right place. You know, Teddie an' all. I'm sorry." He pulled Warren back to the van. I thought about following them, but figured Warren'd be watching for that. I wrote down the license, thinking I'd have Lou run it for me.

"Who were they?"

"The little one is Teddie's brother. Never saw the other two before. Maybe his friends. Maybe other brothers."

"They don't look like family."

"You know how it is with *these* people. None of them have the same father."

There was nothing to say to that, though I knew what Jack would say. He'd probably slap Mrs. P. on the back and compliment her on her astuteness. Tensions were high in the city. A verdict in the Rodney King beating trial was due any day now. Maybe even today. The mayor was blaming the chief of police. Blacks were blaming whites. Whites were blaming blacks. Koreans were blaming blacks. Blacks were blaming Mexicans. The town was ready to explode. Everyone knew it, but everyone was in one degree of denial or another. The biggest problem: no one was talking about the issue that really mattered – race.

My family goes back several generations in L.A. and it's not the same town I grew up in. It used to be a large small town. Now it's a big city, with all the problems of a big city. Some parts of town are hell. You take your life in your hands just by walking down the streets.

People shouldn't have to live like that. Too many rats in a maze.

I don't have the answers for this city, but I try to stay out of trouble. Jack looks for it. I used to get pissed at people in cars, flip 'em off. I hold my tongue today. Today they don't yell back. They shoot. I wondered what would happen if Jack and Warren ever met on a dark street. I wouldn't want to be there.

I thanked Mrs. P. for the paper. Asked her if there was anything else she could tell me. No. I asked for Teddie's family's address and phone number. She gave me the index card and application that Teddie had filled out. Both had been kept in the same folder and both were illegible. Something had spilled on the folder causing the ink to run and blur. I didn't even take them with me.

In the car, I checked out the paper. Thought it would be the sheet I handed the Weasel in my office. It wasn't. It had the address scribbled on it in his hand, not mine. And the name of a motel printed at the top – The William Tell Motel in West Hollywood. The motel where he had stayed?

Orange trim around the windows and dumpy cheap stucco from the '60s defined the William Tell Motel. Real classy. Perfect for the Weasel. Desk clerk's hair was razor cut, short, except for one long strand on the right side of her head. Cute. She didn't look up when I entered. Didn't smile when I rang the bell. Didn't seem to give a damn if I wanted a room or a rape. Just watched Geraldo on the tube.

"Yeah," she said finally getting off her ass and plodding over to the counter. "Can I help you?"

When I didn't smile, when I gave her my hostile face, she tried a smile. I didn't break the corners of my mouth. Hell, if she wanted to play tough mama, I'd play tough too. The customer's always right.

"Wanna room?" she said, softening her voice. Worried that maybe she was scaring a customer away.

"Information."

"Dial 4-1-1."

"Cute."

"This ain't information central."

"Where're you from?"

"That's the information you want?"

"Just trying to make small talk."

"It ain't gonna work."

"I'd say Arkansas. Maybe Alabama or Louisiana."

She couldn't keep her lips from curling into a slight smile. She tried though. "How'd you know. I thought I'd lost my accent."

"I know a lotta people from down that way. Got some former in-laws from around Selma. I hear them in your voice."

"I dunno if that's a compliment or not."

"Neutral." She looked at me funny. "It's neutral."

"You the heat?"

"I'm looking for a friend."

"Yeah, right."

"Squirrelly kinda guy. Nervous. Pale blue eyes you can almost see through. Dart back and forth a lot. Dark brown hair."

"You gotta name on him, your friend?"

"Jim Talbot."

"'s almost as bad as John Smith, ain't it?"

I grinned. She looked through a box of cards behind the counter. No computers for William Tell. Crossbows?

"No Jim Talbot. When did he stay here?"

"A few days ago, within the last week."

"Guy was here a few days ago, might be him." She riffled through the cards. "Here he is. Talbot Sparks."

She handed me the card. I wrote Sparks' vitals down in my notebook. If Jim Talbot was a phony name, Talbot Sparks might be too. So could his address and all. What the hell. A lead's a lead. 'Sides, a lotta these guys do a turn on their real name, so even if Jim Talbot or Talbot Sparks weren't his real name, the overlapping Talbot might be a clue. Of course, he might also be smart enough to play the alias game and not get caught.

"Did he give you a credit card?"

"Paid cash." She pointed to a spot on the card. Gave us a hundred dollar deposit for a few nights. Then split without paying the last night's rent. I had to pay it outta my paycheck since I signed him in."

"Tough."

"Yeah, man. Tough shit." She turned back to Geraldo and transsexuals who were about to have an operation to make them what they were in the first place: "Women Who Used to be Men Who Want to be Men Again" was the subject. Then a promo for the news. The King verdict might come in today. Stay tuned.

She tossed me the keys to a room. "Check it out."

The room was bleak. Motel cheapo. I tossed it. Nothing. Besides, how many other people were in here since he left? It hadn't been that long, but in this kind of place– I returned the keys to the clerk. I dropped a twenty on the counter.

"What's that for?"

"What do you think?"

"I ain't no prostie."

"Get yourself a new barber."

"Why don't you get yourself a life?"

She meant it to hurt. And it did. "Will it cover Sparks' room?"

"More than. But I–"

"You provided a service. Information. I'm giving you a fee for that service. That's how the world works. Capitalism, you know. Don't make a big thing out of it."

"Hey, he said somethin' about he was only stayin' here till his apartment was ready."

"In L.A.?"

"Yeah, maybe, I dunno for sure." She talked to me, but I could tell her heart was with Geraldo. "Maybe I shouldn'ta talked to you. Maybe–"

I let her ramble on as I hit the street and my car. Two men walked by arm in arm. One had a goatee and short, close-cropped hair. The other a moustache and long straight hair almost to his shoulders. They stopped at the corner waiting for the light to change – French kissing. Jack would've blown them away. Hell, he wouldn't even listen to k.d. lang.

CHAPTER 5

Next morning, I phoned the number Sparks-Talbot had left on his room card. 415 area code – San Francisco. A nice old lady answered. Said she'd had that number for several years. Never heard of Sparks or Talbot. I figured the address was a phony, punched it and the phone number into the computer and threw out my spiral notebook page. The guy was a Weasel, but Weasels are smart. Cagey. My respect for him began to grow. Not much. A little.

Where'd that leave me? Dead in the water – like the dragonfly. I called Lou.

"You're outta your fucking mind," she said in a loud whisper after I told her what I wanted. "Look what happened the last time I ran someone for you."

"I know, Lou. But this is the yang of that yin. I'm trying to right the situation."

"When are you going to the police? Your few days are running out."

"I need some more time. It's only been a couple days. Give me a week."

"So the trail'll grow cold."

"No, damn it. So I can clean up my own mess. Run the damn plate for me."

She finally agreed. I gave her the tag number on the blue van. The address was on Florence, near downtown, close to the area known as South Central.

My car is a '69 Pontiac Firebird. Orange paint. Black vinyl top. Black interior. Man, she flies. State of the art sound system. Four on the floor. They don't make 'em like that anymore. They don't guzzle gas like this baby anymore either, but you gotta make some sacrifices. I hit the CD button. My indulgences were my car and my stereos, home and for the car. When times were good that's where my money went. My player scrambled among six CDs loaded in a cartridge in the trunk. Time-Life '60s series. *Get Together* by the Youngbloods blasted out.

I hit a Taco Bell on La Cienega. I was sitting in the driveway, waiting to get into the street when some slime-muffin cut across two lanes of traffic to pull into the driveway. The way he cut across, his car almost nosed into mine. He pulled up alongside me:

"Hey, fuck you," he said.

I smiled at him. Hell, I was in the right place. He was the lunatic. That's the problem today. City's filled with 'em. I could've pulled the Firestar 9mm that was nudged under my right thigh. Normally I wouldn't have a gun under my thigh, after all it is illegal, and I didn't really expect the worst, but it never hurts to be prepared. The verdict in the Rodney King cop trial was due any day now. And he might have had a gun, might not have. But who needed the fucking paperwork? I might have gotten off, might have gone to jail. Hell, it wasn't worth the trouble. He pulled into the driveway, barely missing my car. I let it go, pulled out and headed towards Florence. A comfortable April L.A. day.

The address for the van was a truck rental facility on Florence near Normandie. The building looked as if it had been there since the '40s or before, but had gone through a lot of different uses. This week it rented blue vans to friends and family of Teddie Matson.

Strange looks intercepted me as I debarked the Bird. Locked the door with the electronic lock I'd had installed. Set the alarm. I was out of my territory, on foreign soil – Indian country. The only white face on the street. A few might be driving by; none on the pavement. The Firestar was tucked inside my in-the-belt conceal-carry holster. Hollow points in the mag, an extra mag tucked in next to the holster. Several sets of eyes followed me into the office. Is this what it feels like for blacks in a white neighborhood? Knowing everyone's wondering what the hell you're doing there. Are you going to rob them? Are you a cop? A junkie? What the hell's going on? Eerie.

I walked into the office like I didn't notice any of it, but my eyes and ears were fine tuned, radar and sonar. SEAL training. I didn't like to think of myself as being like Jack. Maybe I was more like him than I cared to admit. Maybe some of these folks were also more like him than they cared to admit, but coming from the yang side instead of the yin.

The man behind the counter was large, black: unsmiling. I could almost see the chip on his shoulder. A small TV was on in the corner behind him. The news gurus were still waiting for a verdict in the King case.

"You lose yo' way?"

"I don't think so. I'm pretty good with directions." I thought I'd try to lighten things up.

"A comedian."

Two other men came in from the lot. "Don't look like no Richard Pryor. Not even Eddie Murphy."

"M'be he Slappy White."

"Sho' is white."

"Mus' be all that white milk his mama feed him. We like chocolate, don' we?"

They laughed. I didn't. They obviously didn't think I was a cop, or didn't care.

"Okay, you've had your fun, can we get down to business now?"

"*Yussah, massah.* What'chu be wantin' me a do fer you, White Boss Man?" one of the men who'd followed me in said in his best Stepin Fetchit dialect. If I didn't know better, I would have thought he was committing a hate crime against me. He sounded like Jack. And I was sounding more and more like him too. Spooky. I found myself thinking of jokes I could say back. Of course the odds were against me. And The Powers That Be probably *would* prosecute me for a hate crime. Instead, I stood my ground. Didn't say anything. They kept on for a couple minutes until the guy behind the counter finally spoke:

"Awright. You ain't lost, so what'chu want?"

Someone was moving around in the small room behind the counter. Might have been a petite little accountant or receptionist, but I didn't think so. I moved to the side of the doorway. Some might consider that a racist action. I considered it a move to possibly save my life.

"I'm looking for some people who rented one of your vans."

"An' why should I help you?"

"So maybe I can help them?"

"Big White Brothah gonna help us y'all," one of the men behind me said. It didn't seem like the situation was easing up at all. I was nervous, fingering my belt near the concealment holster.

"Okay, never mind." I backed toward the door. The man behind the counter called out.

"Why you wanna be helpin' them?"

"Forget it."

The two men behind me moved in closer. "Brother asked you a question honky."

"Don'tchu mean Mistah Honky?"

"Massah Honky."

The two behind me kept at it. They hadn't touched me yet. But I was waiting for it. Hell, I hadn't done anything to them. I was a symbol. And I didn't like it. Not one fucking bit. I pivoted on my heel and backed into a corner that didn't have any windows or doors. They were in front of me now, not behind. I might have been backed into a corner, but no one could come at me from behind now. I could see them. And if I could see them, I might be able to get away. I was well trained. I doubted they were. I didn't want to use the gun. That was a last resort. Put my hands in front of me in a defensive position.

"All right. Let's cut the crap. You want me, come get me. You don't want me, leave me the fuck alone."

"Big talk, white boy," said the man nearer me. "He think he Mohammed Ali dancin' like that. You ain't no butterfly, boy. An' I'm sure you don' sting like no bee."

"Queen bee, mehbe."

"Ye-eeeeeh."

I'd thought maybe his partner in crime had given up, but I was wrong. The guy behind the counter just stood there, watching me, the TV. Back and forth. I was still aware of someone in the back room. Were they toying with me for fun, or were they toying with me before moving in for the kill? I didn't know. I didn't really care either. I wanted things to come to a head. This game playing was bullshit. There was no point in trying to reason with them. They were pissed off at white people. Didn't matter who you were. And I was on their turf. They might not have been planning to harm me, but they sure as hell wanted to let me know that I was in the wrong part of town. Didn't matter what I was there for. Get the hell out and don't come back. That was their message.

I didn't care anymore about finding out who rented the van and where they lived. I was happy to get out with my pride, as long as the rest of me was in one piece. If that meant fighting my way out, so be it.

I jabbed at the dude closest to me. He feinted. Good move. Crack. A baseball bat slammed into the counter. The man behind the counter had slammed the bat into the Formica top, splintering it. All three of us on the other side jumped, looked at him.

"Cut the shit," he said to all of us. "Go on. Get out."

His word was boss around there. The other two parted to let me pass. I walked carefully, checking all sides. Making sure no one was waiting for me on the outside. Looked clear.

Before I got out the door, the guy behind the counter turned up the volume on the TV. The four cops who were caught on home video beating Rodney King had been acquitted. I knew I had to get the hell out of there pronto. People were already filling the streets.

CHAPTER 6

What I didn't know when I stepped out into the abyss that day was that the night before Laurie Hoffman's unwanted admirer had called her again:

The phone rang at eight p.m. sharp. She knew who it was. He'd called the last three nights in a row – at eight sharp. The same guy she'd told me about. Last night she didn't answer the phone. She let the answering machine pick up. Her incoming message tape could take sixty minutes of messages. That was his first call.

"Laurie, I know we only went out once, but I know we're right for each other. It's meant to be. Does that sound corny? Jeez, that's not me. That's what you do to me."

After that message, she turned off the machine and unplugged the phone. When she plugged it back in an hour later, it was still ringing off the hook. She unplugged it for the rest of the night.

She pulled all the shades down, closed the curtains and hunkered on the floor of her living room, all-night *Gilligan's Island* reruns on Nick at Nite in the background for company. She didn't know who to call. There was no way to prove it was him after the first call. The restraining order only specified he couldn't get within a hundred feet of her. So unless he came in through the window, there was nothing the police could do.

Their first date had been rather ordinary. He had responded to her ad in the back of a magazine:

Looking for love in all the right places. Feminine lady, fun and frolicsome, looking for a fairytale love. Candlelight dinners, sunset walks on beach. Let others romance the stone, I'll romance the man. 5'7" tall, 120 pounds. Curly blonde hair. Cute smile. Non-smoker. UB2. Looking for intelligent, humorous, caring man for serious, long-term relationship. SASE and photo to Laurie, P.O. Box 986321, Los Angeles, Calif.

◈ ◈ ◈

"Hello, is this Laurie?" the man's voice smooth and cool. Confident.

"Yes."

"This is Gary Craylock. You sent me your phone number, in response to my answering your ad."

"Yes, I remember. How are you, Gary?"

"Now that I've met you, so to speak, fine, just fine. I don't want you to think I'm just a physical kind of guy, but, wow, judging from your photo, you are truly gorgeous."

"Thank you. You're very kind."

"And you make me blush."

Laurie laughed. She liked a sensitive man, even if he was only joking.

◈ ◈ ◈

Kate's was one of those trendy places, here today, gone tomorrow. Today it was the hottest place in town. Laurie had never been there. She doubted she'd ever go again, unless she and Gary hit it off. She'd called in sick to work. Spent most of the day primping and preening. She looked as good as she would ever look, blond hair glinting in the light. Jade eyes clean and clear.

She didn't want to appear star struck on their first date, but the fact that Patrick Swayze was at the next table was hard to avoid. She'd never considered herself impressed by the surface glitz that movie stars possessed, but being so close one could really feel it.

"I don't normally answer personal ads," Gary said after ordering Courvoisier for both of them. "But yours sounded so genuine that I couldn't resist."

"Thank you," she said, hoping she wasn't blushing. Her face grew hot.

"It's so hard to meet people these days. I guess the in place is the gym."

"Or laundromat."

"Yes, I've heard that. But what kind of people are you going to meet there? And I don't have time to take classes where you might have a better chance of meeting, um, a higher class of people."

She laughed at his pun; he smiled. In her grandfather's words it was a "million dollar smile." Who was this knight in shining armor and could he really be as good as his first impression? She hoped so.

Their drinks came and he toasted their relationship. He could have toasted her health, others had. He could have toasted her future or her looks. But he had toasted their relationship. She liked that.

He had picked her up in his BMW. She normally wouldn't give a stranger her address on the phone, would have met him at the restaurant. But he had sounded warm and sincere and, truth be told, she was feeling a little desperate after a string of frogs. The drive to the restaurant was smooth and filled with small talk: what music do you like, which movies, do you go to art galleries? Pleasant enough. Non-threatening.

He had opened the car door and the door to the restaurant for her. Did all the right things. That was rare today. Some men were afraid women would think they were wusses. Some women wanted doors opened for them. And some women didn't. So some men stopped doing it. Laurie didn't care one way or the other. That's not how she judged men, or anyone else. Still, when he did it, it felt good.

All the way to the restaurant, she had fondled the single long-stemmed rose he had brought her. Other men had done the same or similar things. With him it was different. More elegant. More exciting. He was dashing in a way the others hadn't been.

"In this age of AIDS you've really got to be careful," he said, sipping his drink. "That's one of the reasons I don't date very often. Besides, there's not very many good women out there." He winked at her.

"Or men." She winked back.

They hadn't planned on dinner, only a drink or two to see if they were "companionable." Then Gary had asked her if she'd like to eat.

"Of course," she said.

They ordered steak and blackened red snapper. The conversation continued genially. Mostly small talk and small jokes. Entertainment Light. He was a psychologist. Made good money. Had good looks, almost movie star looks. Could this be love at first sight? She thought Gary felt the same about her.

"What is this?" Gary blared when the waiter brought their order, interrupting Laurie from her reverie. "I ordered the two inch steak, medium rare. This is overcooked shoe leather."

People at other tables turned to look. The waiter took the plate away. Laurie put her hand on Gary's to calm him. He looked at her, realized what he was doing and cooled off.

"I'm sorry. I guess it doesn't make a good impression on the first date, but I'm very particular.

When I pay a lot of money for something, I expect to get what I ordered."

"I don't blame you." She squeezed his hand.

❖ ❖ ❖

A chill breeze sliced through Laurie and Gary as they walked to her front door.

"I didn't know it would be so cold tonight."

"It's that time of year. Warm days, cool nights."

They stood at the door while she fumbled in her purse for her keys.

"Thank you, I had a lovely evening."

"Aren't you going to invite me in?"

"There'll be plenty of time for that."

"What's the matter? Don't you like me?" An edge in his voice.

"It's our first date. I like to get to know someone a little better."

"I'm not saying we have to, you know. But maybe just a cup of coffee and some good conversation. Besides, let's talk about our plans. Friday, I have tickets for the Dodgers. Then Saturday I've got two tickets to the Music Center, but I didn't know who I'd go with. Now I do. And Sunday I thought we could drive up to Santa Barbara. I know this great place for brunch and–"

"Listen, Gary, I like you. But it's late and I have to go to work tomorrow."

"You're sure you're not just making excuses."

"I'm sure."

She gave him a peck on the cheek. He tried to move around to her lips. She slid away and in through the door. He trudged back down the walk. What did he have to be so incensed about, she thought as she bolted the front door.

The next morning, he was waiting for her, bouquet in hand, as she came out to her car. Wanted to take her to breakfast. When she declined, he followed her to work. Up to her office. The receptionist thought he was cute. Laurie thought he was scary.

The pattern continued. A few days later she came to see me for the first time.

◈ ◈ ◈

The morning after he had let the phone ring all night, she woke up to find a stuffed teddy bear on her front porch, a small heart shaped necklace clutched in the bear's hand. The note from Gary quoted lines from *And I Love Her*, an old Beatles' song. She called me and left a message on my machine. I was already on my way to South Central. She said she wanted to talk to me again. She'd heard I was a good detective – I should've told her my dad's opinion of me. Should've told her about Teddie Matson. She wanted to try again with me before looking for another private dick. Besides, Harv was out of town on a case and wouldn't be back for several weeks.

CHAPTER 7

*S un shoots streaks of blinding light into my
eyes.*
      I squint.
Put on my shades.
Head for the Firebird.
People running down the street.
Suspicious looks shoot my way.
Already they've got armloads of loot.
TVs. Stereos.
A huge mattress.
Some have smaller things, more practical things:
Food. Diapers. Baby formula.
Running.
Jostling.
Accosting people in their way.
Not everyone loots.
Some have just come out to watch the show.
Several gang bangers heading my way.
I have a gun.
I can protect myself.
But this isn't the time.
I duck behind a low wall.
One of the bangers sees my car.
Rushes to it.
He breaks the driver's window.
Glass shatters.

The cacophony of shattering glass fused with blaring
sirens, droning chopper blades. People shouting.

When he couldn't hot wire the car, he started smashing all the windows. His friends joined in, slashing the seats and tires. Great, how was I going to get out of there? I thought about using the gun to scare them off. What was the point? The damage was done. Besides, they were probably better armed than me.

The smoke from fires hadn't blotted out the sun and sky yet. A large shadow hovered over me from behind. I turned around to see a huge barrel-chested black man standing over me. My hand was already on the gun. He looked familiar. Tiny, the man helping to move Teddie Matson's things out of her apartment. I had to assess the situation quickly. Go for his knees? Groin? I was crouching. Even if I were standing, he'd have a great height advantage over me. I felt confident. Not that confident. Not when I was so outnumbered.

He stuck a hand out. I didn't take it. Got up on my own.

"Relax," he said.

Sure. I fingered the trigger with my other hand.

The bangers saw us. Headed our way. Caught between a gang and a Tiny. I almost saw my life passing before me. I wasn't a big guy. Sort of compact like a mortar shell – powerful like one, I hoped. And if the body was a Volkswagen, under the hood was a Porsche engine. I had the training and a gun, but what good would it do if it was twenty against one? This wasn't a Hollywood movie, after all.

"This yo' car?" the leader said. He wore a red bandana on his head. Bloods.

"Yeah."

"We customized it fo' yo'."

"Thanks. I was getting tired of it always looking the same."

"Ha ha. Very funny."

They moved closer. Tiny didn't move. Neither did I. I figured if it was over it was over. But I wouldn't go down without a fight.

The leader lifted his shirt, revealing a semi-auto pistol underneath. Another banger pulled an Uzi from under a jacket.

"Now we gonna customize you." He took a step closer. Tiny didn't move.

He put his hand on my shoulder, gripped tight. I was about to make an evasive move when he shoved me aside. He stepped between the bangers and me. "Why you wanna do this shit?"

"Fo' Rodney, man."

"Yeah, fo' Rodney."

"This boy ain't done nothin' to Rodney. Not to you either," Tiny said in a deep baritone.

I didn't want to be protected. I thought I could take care of myself. But, as they say, discretion is the better part of valor. I held off. This was probably the better way.

"His people done it to Rodney."

"Yeah, man, white people."

"Aw go on," Tiny said. "You boys wanna loot, get a free TV, go on. Hurtin' on someone's different."

"Who gonna stop us? You?"

"Yeah, man. Me."

"There's six a us. One a you. An' him, if he can even fight fo' himself."

"Yeah, whyn't you let him speak fo' hisself?"

"He's my friend. Now you done wrecked his car. Go on. Party. Get outta here."

The bangers stood there a moment. Anything could have happened. I was still standing behind Tiny. I moved next to him. The leader turned to me.

"What'chu think about this verdict?"

"Don't answer, man," Tiny said. "These guys don't know 'bout Rodney. Don't give a fuck 'bout Rodney. They're just lookin' for an excuse to party."

"We don' need no excuses. We gonna take this city down." He turned, followed by his comrades. Headed out to the street.

"Thanks."

"I don't want no killings on my head. Not on my property either."

"This is your company? That was you walking around, looking out from the backroom?"

"Yeah. Maybe I shouldn't have let my employees get on you like that. C'mon." He led me into the back door, to the back office. It was cluttered with papers, folders, notebooks. Girly calendars. The desk was old, wooden, stained brown. He sat behind it. I moved a stack of papers, sat on a spotted couch. He gave me a cup of coffee. "This city's going to burn." He leaned back, let out a huge sigh. Sipped his coffee. His voice softened, his manner relaxed. He didn't have to put it on for the bangers anymore. "Not a smart move coming down here today."

"I didn't know the verdict would be coming in. Probably wouldn't have made a difference anyway. I've got a job to do." I drank the coffee. It was cold. Bitter.

"And what is that?"

"I need to find Teddie Matson's family?"

"Seems her brother didn't want to talk to you."

"Look, what is this resistance? I'm trying to help find her killer."

"Nobody trusts you."

"'Cause I'm white. Jesus, what difference does it make?"

"To me it doesn't. To Warren it obviously does."

"Hell, Teddie didn't live down here. She lived in a white neighborhood. I don't see–"

"Maybe that's one of the reasons Warren's so pissed. Maybe he didn't like her living uptown, so to speak. Maybe he felt she had some success, then abandoned her own. Maybe–"

It wasn't a maybe for him. He knew what he was talking about.

"Will you tell me where her family lives?"

He leaned back so far in his chair it looked like he was going to fall over. It looked like the chair could hardly hold his bulk. But it did. He leaned back farther, till the back of the chair hit the wood paneled wall. The panels were dark with grease stains. It was like that in just about all the automotive businesses I'd ever been in. Grime everywhere.

"You can't drive home in your car. I'll loan you a truck. No charge. Well, I have to charge you a buck just to make it legal."

"I appreciate that. But I don't want to go home. I want to find her family."

"Man, you're the end. Like my mother used to say, you're a persistent little cuss. Why do you have such a bug up your ass? And don't tell me it's your job. You can come tomorrow or the next day, when things quiet down."

"The longer I wait, the colder the trail gets. I'm already down here."

"Your white face is gonna act like a trouble-magnet."

"I'll take that risk."

"Are you stupid or gutsy?"

"A little of both, I guess."

"Man, I just don't get it. What is this, some kind of white guilt?"

It was guilt, but not the way he was thinking of it. Not white man's guilt. I felt guilty about Teddie. More than guilty. Sick. I couldn't bring her back, but I could do what I could to help bring her killer to justice. Noble thoughts? Lofty? Maybe. I couldn't help it. I wanted the Weasel. I wanted to kill him. Maybe that's why I didn't pull the gun on the bangers. I was saving my bullets. But a quick gunshot death would be too easy for him. Maybe I'd tear him apart with my hands. Maybe I'd slice the layers of his skin off one at a time with the razor sharp Gerber dagger I always carried strapped to my boot. Yeah, a gun was too quick. Let the bastard suffer.

I didn't like myself much for thinking like that. It seemed so primitive. But what the hell. The son-of-a-bitch deserved it, and it hardly looked like a civilized society anymore. Not just the day of the riot, but for a long time before.

"Not guilt. Duty."

"But you're not going to tell me who you're working for or why this person is so concerned about finding Teddie's killer." Before I could speak, he put his hand up. "Don't give me that crap about client confidentiality either. Let me see your investigator's license."

He took it from me, perused it for a couple minutes. I guess it passed inspection. He got up, tossing what was left of his coffee cup in the wastebasket.

"Let's go."

He locked the back door. Went to the front turned off the lights, took the cash from the register, stuffed it in his pants. He grabbed a .38 revolver from behind the counter, put it in his belt and covered it with his shirt.

"Help me with this."

We pulled a large, hand painted sign from behind the counter. It was awkward. Bulky. We taped it across the front window. In two foot high red letters it read "Black Owned and Operated."

CHAPTER 8

We stepped outside, squinting into the sun. People were running by, in both directions. Police cars, sirens wailing, sped by. No one stopped to help a man laying in the street. Tiny looked around, surveying the situation: "The good life is just a dream a way," he said.

He went to the cab of one of his trucks, started the engine. Motioned for me to get in as I was about to head for the man bleeding at the curb. I went to the downed man. He was Asian. Korean? A gash was leaking blood over his right eye.

"You all right?" I started to reach for him.

"Lemme 'lone," he said, pushing himself up off the curb. He staggered away. I started to go after him when Tiny called out.

"Let's go, man."

I jogged back to Tiny's van, got in. He eased it toward the street. A rock cracked the windshield. Thrown by a boy who couldn't have been more than nine or ten. Tiny didn't make any attempt to chase him down. He killed the engine.

"This is shit," he said, surveying the street up and down. "We better walk." He looked at me. Studying my face. No emotion in his eyes. "You're gonna stick out like a sore thumb. At least in the van you couldda ridden in back."

"Got some shoe polish? I can go in blackface."

"Not funny."

But he didn't seem to take offense. I wasn't trying to be racist or offend, only to make light of a bad situation. The humor may have been in bad taste, but that's how I deal with tense situations. Bad jokes.

Tiny and I closed the wrought iron gate that led to his lot, locking it with the biggest padlock I'd ever seen. The rusty chain that he triple wrapped around the two sections of fence had to be almost an inch thick.

"Hell, this won't keep 'em out," he said, clasping the lock shut. Tugging on it. "Nothing will." He spun the cylinder of his revolver, snapping it back in place. "Let's go. No use keeping the vultures waiting."

We started off down the street. The acrid smell of smoke blanched my nostrils. He pulled out a green kerchief and held it over his nose. Not red or blue. No identifying with Bloods or Crips. A neutral green. But hell, that was probably somebody's colors. Somebody's signal to go to war too. I coughed. Tiny ripped his kerchief in half, handing me a ragged end. I flashed him the OK sign. I wanted to say thanks, couldn't talk. The green cloth made a fair smoke screen. But hey, fireman, how 'bout one of those oxygen bottles you've got on your back? That's something I'd be tempted to loot for.

Running, jostling bodies sprinted up and down the street, loaded with booty. VCRs. TVs. Even mattresses. It was as if there was a giant sign hanging over L.A., being pulled along by the Goodyear blimp, that said: "Free Shopping Day."

A police car pulled up in front of a stereo store. The window had been bashed in, the door pulled from its hinges. People were running in and out, taking anything they could carry. Going back for seconds. Thirds. The cops jumped out of their car, pounding batons on a low wall. People zipped off. The cops headed back for their car. Three young men came out, loaded for bear. They started chanting: "Rodney King. Rodney King. Rodney

King." It lasted about five seconds. They laughed self-consciously. Gave up the chant. Ran off with their loot. The cops didn't give chase.

"This isn't about race anymore," Tiny said. "Got nothing to do with Rodney King."

A mob of kids ran toward us. We ducked into the doorway of a book store. No looting there. It didn't seem to interest them as they kept running. If I had been at home, I'd probably be shouting at the TV for the police to "shoot the looters," like Jack was, no doubt, doing now. But down there on the streets, it was different. They were just people. Maybe doing things they shouldn't. But still people. Still Americans. At least most of them. There were, we learned later, a lot of illegal aliens taking part in the Big Party.

And it was a party. Giddiness run rampant. These people acted as if they didn't have a care in the world. Most of them grabbed stereos. The brand didn't matter. They'd keep the ones they liked best. Sell the rest. Some of their situations were a little sadder, though the people were just as giddy. They were taking cartons of Frosted Flakes, diapers and Tide. Whole families participating together. Real family values.

Tiny and I bolted from the doorway, ran down the street, ducking for cover by low walls, doorways, shrubs all along the way. We weren't out to party. We were on a mission. He was taking me to Warren, to Teddie's family. I didn't know why, but I was curious about it. Warren obviously wanted nothing to do with me. Yet here was Tiny taking me to him. What was this all about? Was it a setup? Were they going to beat some confession out of me when we hooked up with Warren? Was I being paranoid? Were my own prejudices coloring my thoughts? Was I scared shitless to be one of the few white faces down there when the fires of hell were breaking out all over? I didn't know. I didn't care. I just wanted to find Teddie's family.

Maybe I should have gone home. Watched the whole conflagration on the tube with a gun in one hand, a beer in the other. Hell, we could've had a party. Like a Super Bowl party, only this would have been a Hellfire party. Everything's burning. Get out the violins and fiddle while the city turns to dust.

But my car was trashed. And though Tiny would have let me borrow a van, something told me not to go. Maybe it was the same crazy something that had made me join the Navy. Maybe it was the same something that had made me fuck up my marriage? My life? Maybe my dad was right. Maybe I was a fuckup. Maybe I'd fuck myself for good down here – *Marion you're always going out of your way to hurt yourself. Mixing where you don't belong.* – in the middle of this inferno?

Maybe that's what I wanted.

A group of men came out of a trashed beauty shop with armloads of blow dryers. What were they gonna do with all those?

We came to Florence and Normandie. Half a block away the cops were regrouping. Or retreating. Or hiding out. It was hard to tell. There was a swarm of them, but they weren't doing much of anything. People were looting, throwing rocks, bottles and the like right under their noses. As we left the intersection, I glanced back. A large semi was pulling into the intersection. We continued away from the intersection. Later I learned that this was where Reginald Denny, the driver of the semi, was pulled from the truck. Beaten within an inch of his life. We were gone before it happened. But I still have pangs of guilt for having been so close and having done so little. Now I know how lucky we were.

In a sense it was a *quid pro quo* situation. Tiny's black face was my passport among his people. My white face was his insurance that the cops might just leave him alone – if they knew he was with me. That might have been why he wanted to help me out. Protection. But it wasn't an uneasy truce. I felt comfortable with him. Like we'd known each other all our lives. Maybe we had. The last thirty minutes had been a lifetime.

We crouched behind a low wall at a service station, surveying the situation. He watched two sides. I watched the other two, covering each other's backs. We were both armed; neither of us wanted to use our guns.

Noise barked from every direction. Sirens. Shouts. Choppers hovering. Shots. Too many shots. It all blended into a cacophony of confusion. The din was ear shattering and lifeless, inert, all at the same time.

"Why're you helping me?" I asked Tiny as we scoped the street out. He never answered my question, though I asked several more times.

There was an explosion in the distance, then the shock wave. A new column of black smoke appeared every few minutes. Slow-motion funnel clouds.

"Man, don't they know they're tearing down their own goddamn neighborhoods," he said, scanning the horizon. "Where're they gonna get food and clothes when all this burns to the ground?"

We were on the move again, ducking in and out of doorways. We ducked into a mom and pop grocery. The owner came at us with a thirteen round semi-auto pistol. He was Korean. He wasn't shouting at me when, in pidgin, he said: "Get out. Get out now. Don't come back. Don't never come back. I don't need your business. Animal. Animals. You peoples are all animals."

The Korean racked the slide of his pistol. Tiny and I split, two jackrabbits in a hunter's sights. Tiny never said a word about the Korean. About the animosity between blacks and Koreans. It was hard to tell if he didn't care. If he'd made peace with it in his own mind. Or if he was storing up a reserve of rage that would explode sooner or later.

For the moment, Teddie had become lost under a pile of ashes – the ashes of Los Angeles, my home town. I wasn't concerned about her now. I was worried about getting out alive. Part of me wondered if I didn't want to make it out at all. The rest of me would have done anything to survive.

We turned down a sidestreet. It was quieter than the main drags had been. A pretty young woman was sitting on the porch steps of an old California bungalow. She held a large black cat in a cardboard carton, soothing its eyes with a damp cloth. There were tears in her eyes. In ours. The smoke stung. Our nostrils were dry, our throats raw.

"He saved my life," she said. "One night three men were coming over the fence in our backyard. He woke us up before the men got inside." She tore a fresh piece of cloth from a large strip, dipped it in a bowl of water and put it on the cat's eyes. She offered us each a strip. We declined. We hadn't said anything to her. Hadn't asked what she was doing with the cat. She had just started talking to us. She needed someone to talk to. We all did.

"Will you be okay?" I asked.

"I think so. The fun's up that way," she said, pointing to the main drag.

I wanted to offer her something. Anything. I had nothing to offer. Except a gun and a knife. If she didn't know how to use them they would be useless. We wished her the best and headed off, eventually making our way back to Normandie.

People were still running every which way, carrying home the desserts of their shopping spree. The cops continued to do next to nothing. A security gate at Wherehouse Records was breached. A black man turned to a young white kid and invited him to join the celebration. He did.

Two other men stood outside talking.

"I don't steal," one said, palming his hands upwards, almost embarrassed.

"Neither do I," said the other, "but–" He showed a large canvas bag he'd brought to haul stuff way. "This is different. Society's rules don't apply no more. There is no society here. No civilization. Not today. Anarchy is king."

A black and white pulled up, wailed its siren. Throngs of looters dispersed. The cops drove off. The looters were back within seconds, picking up the goodies they had set down on the street. Two women argued over an electric piano someone had put down when the cops came. One snapped out a switchblade. Slashed the other. She fell, bleeding. A melee ensued. No one knew anymore what started it. Everyone just piled on for the fun. The Big Party.

We asked some people if they knew if there was a curfew on the city? No, they told us. The mayor hadn't done anything yet. We moved out. In the crowd. Swirling. Sucking us in. Down. Under. We moved along with the flow. My hand kept checking my gun. Was it there? Would it be there when I needed it? I didn't take my hand off it.

The crowd surged toward another small grocery/liquor store. We were caught in it. No escape. The store owner, shotgun in hand, hard-charged someone who'd broken off from the crowd. He waved the gun wildly, maybe at the man who'd broken from the crowd. But we were all in his kill zone. Through the smoke it was hard to tell if he was Mexican, Korean, Armenian – didn't matter anyway. He was shouting. I couldn't understand what he was saying. Neither could anyone else it appeared. It wasn't English, and the din was too loud to figure out what it was. No one was listening anyway. He jacked the slide of his twelve gauge. People hit the deck, dispersed, fell all over each other. A blast rang out. A young woman fell. I rushed to her, tearing my belt off, making a tourniquet on her arm that was bleeding profusely. Tiny pulled me off.

"It's no use. We got business. Leave her be."

"Somebody's got to."

"She's dead," Tiny said. Get it? She's dead. Doesn't matter what you do."

I didn't move. He lifted her head. The side that had been facing away from me was a mess of bloody hamburger. How could I not have seen it? Maybe I didn't want to.

He pulled me away. I let him.

We dashed across a gas station where two men were lighting a Molotov cocktail. Behind us the sound of shattering glass. I slid beneath a car on the street. Tiny hugged a wall. The gas station went up in an overwhelming fireball of light and heat. White heat. And it seemed as if the Post Modern Age had gone up with it.

Welcome to the Apocalypse.

CHAPTER 9

People on the sidestreets were mostly hunkered behind closed doors or heading for the main boulevards. Not many people sitting around shooting the breeze. Gang graffiti littered walls and sidewalks. Some cars. Broken glass everywhere. I noticed a couple bullet holes – at least that's what I thought they were – in one of the houses. I thought I stood out like a Dodger fan at a Reds game on their home turf. But no one seemed to pay us much mind. A short, small boned very black man whacked a teenager across the cheek. The boy lurched back. He was twice the man's size, three times his weight. The boy looked frightened. He dropped the 25" TV he was holding.

"You don't steal," the man said.

"It ain't stealin'. They's Ko-reans."

"Don't matter. Stealin's wrong."

"Ev'erbody's doin' it."

Whack. The man slapped the boy again. He looked at the TV. "If that TV's broken, you gonna pay for it."

"Fuck that shit." The boy spun on his heel, walked off – toward the main drag. The man stood watching. Trembling.

The boy strutted towards us. Tiny and I took up the whole sidewalk. The boy didn't care. He headed straight for us. He wasn't about to step off the sidewalk either. He barged into us. Right into Tiny's uplifted forearm. A forearm that looked like it was reinforced with steel.

"Honky pig," he said to me as he pitched backwards from Tiny's arm. I didn't mind a good fight now and then, but down here the odds just didn't seem to favor it. I was about to say something when Tiny spoke:

"Seems this boy's colorblind. Boy, the arm that hit you is black. Black as the night sky. Ain't white." Tiny was back into his tough-guy mode.

The boy stood up. Glared at Tiny. At me. "Why you bringin' a cracker fuck down here, Tiny."

"Listen, Maurice, why you gotta dis yo' daddy?"

"I ain't dissin' no one. I thought he'd be proud havin' a big TV like that."

"He would be proud. But he be proud if you earn it for him. Not if you steal it."

"Ever'one's doin' it."

"Don't make it right."

Maurice fixed his gaze on me. His eyes were narrow slits, his pupils tiny bullets – aimed at me.

"'s his fault. All this shit's his fault."

"What'chu talkin' 'bout?"

"What'chu doin' bringin' the man down here?" Maurice turned to me again: "What'chu doin' here, white man? Come to see all the bad niggers? See why they shoulda never let us off the plantation?" He spit at my feet. "I ain't no slave no more."

"None of us are. That was over 'hundred years ago."

"He keeps us down. He–"

"He don' do shit. You keep yo'self down. Nobody does it to you but you."

"She-it." Maurice went around us, heading for the boulevard.

Tiny turned to me, "Used to be a good kid. Got in with the gangs. He doesn't dis me though."

"You in a gang?" I said.

"Used to. I got out. I'm a lucky one." Tiny resumed the march up the street. "Hey, man, what's your name?"

"Everyone calls me Duke."

"Like in Duke Wayne?"

"Exactly."

"Well, everyone calls me Tiny. My real name's Tee-won. Sounds Ko-rean, doesn't it?" We laughed. "It doesn't mean anything. I guess my mama and daddy just thought it sounded good. That was before we had all these problems with the Koreans. I guess they wouldn't have known it sounded anything, one way or the other." He coughed. The smoke was heading our way. "Duke your given name?"

"No." It blurted out. I didn't like talking about my real name. And down here I thought it would only make things worse. I was waiting. It came:

"What is? Your real name that is."

I would have given anything for a gang fight at that moment. We were the only people on the street now so there was no one to rescue me. I tried to ignore him, pretend I didn't hear the question. It was no use.

"Must be a pretty bad one," he said. "Can't be as bad as Tee-won though."

"Marion. It's Marion."

His eyes sparkled and a big grin rode across his wide face. "I was wrong. That's pretty bad."

An explosion in the distance. A plume of smoke hit the sky.

"They don't realize that they're only wrecking their own backyard. One of the first things my daddy taught me was never to piss in the wind and don't shit in your own backyard. Problem is, too many of 'em just don't have daddies," he said wistfully. He stopped, turned up a walk. "Here we are, Teddie's family's house."

The house was a Craftsman bungalow. It had a low-pitched roof, a stone fireplace that was also seen from the outside, exposed struts and a wide porch. It wasn't big. It wasn't small either. Comfortable might have been the word. It looked almost rural with its magnolia trees, shrubs and wood and stone exterior. Looked like a nice place to grow up. In fact, the whole street was clean and well tended except for the graffiti and broken glass. I assumed the broken glass was from that day. I hoped it was.

We walked up the walk. Someone moved about inside. The door opened. A woman in her fifties stood behind a screen door. She wore a flowered house dress and slippers. Her hair was in a bun. Her eyes were splotchy, red. She'd been crying.

"Hello, Tiny." She forced a smile. We walked up the steps to the porch. Her face was striking, very angular, high cheekbones, smooth caramel-colored skin. The housedress was on the frumpy side. Under it was a slender figure that still looked pretty good. "Won't you come in? I'd ask you to sit on the porch – I used to love to sit on the porch and swing – but the smoke is so thick I think it's better inside."

We followed her in, past the swinging love seat. We sat on a well used but comfortable sofa. The room was dark. The shades drawn down to within half an inch of the window sill. The floors were hardwood. Highly polished. Throw rugs were scattered about. The mantle was filled with photographs, Teddie, Warren, other children, teens and adults I didn't recognize. An antique coffee table was in front of the sofa. Mrs. Matson poured us all iced tea. It had an odd taste. A good odd taste. As if there were raspberries mixed in with it. It went down easy on my parched throat.

"Mrs. Matson, this is my friend Duke."

"Pleased to meet you."

"Same here, Mrs. Matson." We shook hands. Her grip was firm.

"Forgive the way I look. I haven't been feeling too well lately. Just sort of staying home and keeping to myself so I don't get much dressed up."

Of course she was staying home mourning because her daughter had been killed – murdered. And I fired the bullet. If not in reality, real enough for me. I wasn't about to tell her or Tiny that reality. I was the fuckup.

"Isn't it terrible what's happening outside?"

"Yes, ma'am." Tiny said. He seemed deferential towards her.

She talked about the riot, the kids rushing back and forth earlier, empty-handed one way, full of goodies coming back.

"This isn't such a bad neighborhood. We got nice homes and yards. Can even afford a new TV every once in a while. I don't see why they got to go crazy. The Rodney King verdict isn't no excuse to be crazy. If they only knew what things were like before. Thirty years ago. If they only knew how far we come. Maybe we ain't there yet, ain't where we wanna be, but nothing happens overnight."

"They'd call you an Uncle Tom, Auntie Tom for talking like that."

"My own son thinks I'm a Tom. Makes me cry." She sniffled, wiped her nose with a tissue. "I'm sorry. What brings you two gentlemen here today?"

"Duke's been wanting to meet you. He got stuck at my place, waylaid is more like it. Car annihilated. But he was looking for you. I didn't know if I should bring him, but I figured for all his trouble, maybe I should."

"Yes."

"It's about your daughter, Mrs. Matson."

She stifled a cry.

"I'm terribly sorry about what happened to her." More sorry than she would ever know. "I'm a private detective. I've been hired to help track down her killer."

I waited a moment while Mrs. Matson gathered herself together. It was painful to watch. Watching any mother mourn the loss of a child would have been painful. This was a lance through my gut. If I could have traded places with Teddie, I would have. Gladly. I would have done anything. I was doing what I could.

"Who are you working for?"

The guillotine blade was dropping. "I'd like to tell you, Mrs. Matson. But I can't. I know it sounds corny as all get out, you've seen it on TV over and over, but it's client privilege. All I can say is it's someone close to her."

"From the studio?"

"It's someone she worked with."

"Then they do care. I thought the studio wasn't going to do anything. She gave so much to them, and I know she was paid for it, but it seemed like after the funeral, after the flowers and all that they didn't care anymore." Her smile brightened the entire dark room. What I'd told her was a lie. As far as I knew the studio didn't give a shit. It made her feel better though and that was enough. Now I'd never tell her the truth. "What can I do for you, Mr. Duke?" It wasn't worth correcting her.

I proffered my I.D. wallet. Showed her that I was truly a licensed private detective. "We believe the man was a fan, a deranged fan. I thought maybe if you have any fan letters that I could look at. Other correspondence. It might give me a lead."

The tears welled up in her eyes again. "The police were here. They also asked about the fan letters. They're so busy though. It's just another case to them. To you too?"

"No ma'am. It's the only case I'm working right now. I can give it my full time."

She got up, went to an ornately carved chest. "I gave the police all her letters I had here and they took what was in her apartment. But I got my lawyer to have them photocopy all the letters so I could keep the originals. The police already checked them for fingerprints." She opened the chest. It was filled with letters, from top to bottom, side to side. "These are all to Teddie."

The pile was intimidating and black here and there with fingerprint powder..

"You can sit at the breakfast table and go through them if you like."

"I'd appreciate that. Before I do though, can you tell me, do you know if she got any calls or if there's someone from her past that might have been more, um, interested in her than she might have realized."

Mrs. Matson thought a moment. "She was always getting calls. She had an unlisted number. Somehow people would find it out. I even took a couple calls for her here."

"Did they leave a name? Phone number."

"No. I wish they would have. Even if they did I would have thrown it out by now."

"Well, thank you. I think I would like to go through these."

She showed me to the breakfast table. It was beautiful. Inlaid wood in lighter and darker shades. Flower pattern. The kind of piece about which you'd say "they don't make 'em like that anymore." There was a faux Tiffany shade on the lamp over the table. The letters were neatly bundled and rubber banded together. I started with the most recent bundle, figuring the Weasel was probably in touch with her right before he came to me. He had to tell her how much he loved her. How he'd sacrifice for her. Do anything for her. And, of course, how much she loved him. How they were meant to be. I lost myself in the piles.

Tiny fell asleep on the couch in the living room. I don't know what happened to Mrs. Matson. I hadn't seen her for at least an hour when the back door swung open. If Maurice had stared bullets in my direction, Warren was staring missiles.

"What're you doin' here?"

I stood up.

"Get outta my mother's house."

"She invited me in."

"You musta deceived her. What she want with you?"

"Listen pal–"

"–I ain't your pal. An' don't be dissin' me."

"Listen Warren, I'm trying to help."

"I want you out of here."

"I'm not leaving. Unless your mother asks me to go."

He looked at the piles of letters sitting on the table. Grabbed one. "This's my sister's stuff. Pers'nal."

"Yeah, real personal. Fan mail."

"Well you got no right to be lookin' at it."

"Listen, man, what's your problem? I haven't done anything to you? Where'd you get that chip on your shoulder?"

He stormed out the kitchen door. I went back to the piles.

A few minutes later, the door burst open again. Two young black men charged in. Low rider pants, prison style. Unlaced tennis shoes, also adapted from prison garb. Backwards Raiders caps. Tats up and down their arms. Bangers from top to bottom. Two angry young black men. Two angry young black men with guns. I had already reached for my gun. It was a standoff. There was noise in the front of the house. Seconds later, Warren and Maurice marched Tiny into the breakfast nook at gunpoint. They'd already relieved him of his revolver. He didn't look any too happy about it either.

They shoved him in a corner, forced him down into a chair. Sweat beaded on his forehead. I took that to mean that he knew these guys would use their guns, especially today.

Where the hell was Mrs. Matson? I still had my gun in my hand. Maurice put a short-barreled Uzi to Tiny's throbbing temple.

"Gimme the gun," Warren said to me, "or Maurice'll blow this niggah's fat head off."

"Don't do it," Tiny said. "Don't give in to these hardhead punks."

I took a step back. Eyeing down the barrel of the Firestar.

"You boys should—"

"Don' lecture me. I don't need no lectures from Mr. White-man."

Maurice jacked the bolt on the Uzi. Short barreled Uzis were illegal, even before the ban on certain semi-auto rifles. I guess these guys didn't know the law. Maurice jammed the gun into Tiny's temple. The raw metal bit his skin, blood trickled down. Maurice smiled. There was a bit of the sadist in him. I put my pistol on the table. One of the others snatched it – slapped it across my cheek. Blood dribbled from me. I didn't fall though. Held my ground.

Warren approached.

"What's your name, boy?"

"Duke."

"Got a last name?"

"Rogers."

"Duke Rogers. Man, we got royalty in this house to-day."

CHAPTER 10

Warren shoved me into the corner, knocking several clusters of envelopes to the floor, started rifling my pockets. Didn't come up with much. My wallet. Extra pistol mag. Spiral pad and pen. Some change. He looked disappointed. He opened the wallet, checked my I.D. Both my driver's license and P.I. license are in the proper name Marion, not Duke. If he noticed he didn't say anything. He forgot to frisk me, missed my boot knife.

With my training in hand-to-hand combat and martial arts, I thought I might be able to fight my way out of there. Might get hurt in the process, but hell, I might have gotten hurt anyway. Problem was, I didn't want to endanger Tiny. He was big and he looked tough, but looks can be deceiving. Some of the toughest guys I know are some of the smallest. And vice versa. He had, of course, clotheslined Maurice, so he might be okay in a fight.

Warren grabbed my gun from his buddy, buried its nose in my ribs. Jammed it in. Twisting and turning it.

"Why'n't we prone him out?" his buddy said.

Maurice grinned. "Why don't we prone out this mother-fuckah white niggah? Shit, he can't help bein' white," he waved the Uzi in my direction, turned back to Tiny: "this niggah can." The muzzle of the Uzi whipped across Tiny's face leaving a trail of blood. The big man didn't make a sound. Hardly flinched. He didn't need to say anything. His eyes said it all, burning with contempt. Indignation. Maurice saw the anger in Tiny's eyes. Shoved the barrel of the Uzi in Tiny's mouth. He gagged. Maurice liked that. He drove the Uzi in deeper, down Tiny's throat. Blood oozed out the corner's of his mouth.

Warren had me backed into the corner, my own pistol tickling my ribs. I was biding time. Waiting for the right moment. Time was running out. Maurice was ready to play. Chomping to get out of the starting gate.

"Now tell me who you workin' for?" Warren said. "Tell me now, tell it all, tell it clean or I'll let my friend there rip into yo' friend Tiny. An' when that Jew-zi's done with him, he'll be like his name, *tiny* strips-a flesh hangin' out to dry." Warren and his cuzzes laughed.

"Different sense of humor down here," I said.

"Different sense of everything. Now tell me."

"In your mother's house. You'd—"

"Don't lecture me, white boy. I've had enough lectures to fill a lifetime."

There was no point arguing with him. Tiny must have done that in the past to no avail. He was into his speech, into an almost trance-like state of mind, ready to reel off all the indignities that had been done him by the white man. Ready to make me pay.

I was ready to kill him.

Warren was left handed. I'm a righty. I was primed to thrash him in the neck with my left, seize the pistol with my right. Failing that, I'd reach for my knife. As he prattled on, Maurice smirked, gouging the Uzi deeper into Tiny's throat. Tiny kept gagging. Blood and saliva foamed around his mouth. The other two watched. A voice broke into the room like an ice breaker smashing through the Arctic. Everyone stopped. Turned.

Standing at the back door, hands on her hips, was Mrs. Matson. "I can't believe what I'm seeing. I just can't believe it."

Warren let the gun drop to the floor. Maurice eased off of Tiny. The other two boys lowered their heads. Mrs. Matson took two steps deeper into the room. She glared at each of them in turn. She walked to Maurice. He didn't move. She put a weathered brown hand on top of the Uzi, stepped between Maurice and Tiny. Removed Maurice's hand from the gun. He stepped back. Tiny reached up to take the weapon. She gently pulled it from his mouth. She held onto it; he dropped his hands. Raised them again to wipe his mouth. His breath was short and raspy.

"This thing loaded?" she said, grasping the Uzi. "I'm sure it is. You boys don't play with toy guns no more."

"Listen, mother–"

"No, you listen to me, these men are my guests and this is my house. You got a problem with that? 'Cause if you do you can find your own place to live. And the rest of you. I know all your mothers. Do you think they'd be proud of you? Do you think this is what they want for you? Do you think–"

"This dude's got no business here."

"If I say he got business here, he got business here. I don't want to have to say it again."

"First Teddie, now you," Warren said.

"What'chu talkin' 'bout, boy."

"Sellin' your soul to the white man. Sellin' your soul to be white."

Slap. The sound reverberated in the small kitchen and breakfast nook. Must've stung Warren pretty bad. He winced. Tried not to show it. It showed.

"I'm black and I'm proud. I'm also proud to be an American. Maybe there's problems, but you got a nice house. You never wanted for anything, you–"

"My people want."

"My people. My people. What do you know about your people? What have you struggled? What have you–"

Before she finished, Warren was out the door. His three *cuzzes* followed. Mrs. Matson did not give up the Uzi. She laid the gun on the breakfast table, went over to Tiny to see how he was doing. I dropped the magazine from the Uzi, and ejected the shell from the chamber. Put my pistol back in my belt holster.

"I'm sorry," she was saying to Tiny. He couldn't talk. Was still gagging. Spitting blood. I was about to try to help him when the back door opened again. I spun 'round on my heels, reaching for the Firestar. The safety was off. It was aiming at the back door when she walked through.

For a split second, I thought maybe Warren had done more to me than I'd realized. Maybe I was dead, dreaming. The young woman in the doorway was stunning. A stunning beauty and a stunning twin for Teddie Matson. Same eyes. Same smile and glowing caramel skin.

Tiny spit up blood, said with almost a smile: "Looks like you seen a ghost."

It might have been in bad taste any other time. Now it was a good tension breaker. Mrs. Matson laughed, then Tiny. Then me. Only the vision in the doorway didn't laugh. She was late to the party. Didn't know what was going on. We laughed for over a minute, that uncontrollable laughter where you've forgotten why you're laughing in the first place, but the laughing is self-contagious. And self-perpetuating. You're laughing because you're laughing.

"What's going on? I just saw Warren, Maurice and a couple others charge out of here like they're on their way to a–"

"–riot." Tiny finished the sentence for her, laughing even harder. Spitting up more blood and sucking down air with a wheeze. He stood up, wobbly.

"We need to get you to the hospital."

"I'm okay." He waved us off with his hands.

The woman in the door still wasn't laughing, but the other three of us began all over again. The young woman saw the Uzi on the table. The gun in my hand. The blood at Tiny's mouth. What must she have been thinking? All of that horror and there we were, laughing like naughty kids at the back of the classroom.

"This is my daughter LaRita Matson. I'm sorry, I've forgotten your name in all the excitement."

"Duke. Duke Rogers."

"People just call me Rita."

"Rita." We shook hands. Hers was soft and smooth. The opposite of her mother's hard, crisp hands. She was Teddie's older sister – twenty-nine. Teddie had been twenty-six. I had never seen Teddie in person, but from her pictures, I figured they were both about the same size, petite, same coloring, same soft hair. She had full lips and perfect teeth. She could've been a star too. I wondered what she did.

"What's going on here?" Rita asked, explaining she had been at work when the rioting began and they'd let her go early. She had made her way through the flying bottles, rocks, bullets and flaming cocktails and had gotten to her mother's safely. Mrs. Matson told Rita why Tiny and I were there. Explained that while I was looking at the letters in the kitchen and Tiny was sleeping on the couch, she had seen some neighbors out front and gone to talk with them, then had joined them for coffee in one of their houses.

She left the room. There was an uneasy silence between Tiny, Rita and me. Mrs. Matson returned with a bottle of Listerine, poured some in a glass full strength and asked, no ordered, Tiny to gargle with it to kill the germs from the gun. Tiny did as he was told.

"We better get you to the hospital, just to be sure," Mrs. Matson said.

"I don't need no hospital." He had trouble getting the words out. Each movement of his mouth looked measured. Painful.

"You know you won't win with her," Rita said.

Tiny nodded. His head began to loll. Mrs. Matson and I caught him, eased him back into the chair.

"Rita, if you and Mr. Rogers would be so kind as to drive Tiny to the hospital. Then loan him your car so he can get back to his neighborhood."

Rita didn't seem to like that idea, but she didn't say anything. At least not about that. "Which hospital?"

"MLK."

Having just sat Tiny down, we helped him up. I wanted to ask Mrs. Matson if I could take some of the letters home with me. Read them and return them. It seemed inappropriate with Tiny the way he was. We took him outside and laid him in the backseat of Rita's dark gray Dodge Shadow. It was a small backseat and the car was only a two-door. It was decided that I'd ride up front with the gun in case there was trouble on the way. It was no easy task getting Tiny into the small backseat.

As we pulled down the driveway, Warren slammed a fist into the passenger side of Rita's car. He leaned in, glaring at us. Nothing needed to be said. He knew where we were taking Tiny. He didn't approve. Didn't seem to approve of much of anything. I was sure he didn't like a *honky mothuh-fucker* driving with his sister. Might even be dangerous, if there were others like him about – and there were – by the bushel.

He leaned into my window. "You will never understand. Never."

Rita drove off. I rode shotgun, literally.

CHAPTER 11

The night Rita Matson and I took Tiny to the hospital, Laurie Hoffman came home to find a letter tucked in her front door. Not in her mailbox. Jammed between the door and the molding. One way or another she knew it was junkmail, she told me later. Either some company advertising a product or service she didn't need. Or a man – a man named Gary Craylock – also advertising goods and services she didn't need, didn't want and would have preferred to forget about all together.

She debated whether or not to open it. Whether or not to call me again, or another detective. Or the police. She took it into her living room, set it on the glass-topped coffee table. She turned on the television and watched the riot news. Fires everywhere. Gunshots. The conflict heading north and west, out of South Central, towards Hollywood and West Los Angeles. Even Beverly Hills. Scary. She'd never owned a gun. Never even held one. Didn't know how to use one. She wished she knew now. Wished she had one. Was it for the looters or for Gary Craylock that she wished it? She didn't know. Maybe both, she thought. But guns were out of bounds. Even if she could buy one that night, she'd have to wait two weeks to pick it up. That was no good.

Laurie went to all four windows in the living room, closing them, dropping blinds, closing the slats tightly, hoping no air, let alone light would escape them. She did the same for the rest of the small house. The phone rang. A jagged sound startling her. She was afraid to pick it up. Afraid it was Craylock. She had left the answering machine off when she went to work because the day before Craylock had called several times, filling up the entire sixty minute tape. Some of the messages were short, not sweet: "Just calling to see if you're home." "Just calling to see if you got home safely." "Just calling to see if we might have dinner tonight."

Others were long dissertations on this and that. Mostly on how much he loved her. How the hell could he love me, she asked me later, when he didn't even know me? That's why she was afraid to open the letter. She knew it was from him. There was no return address. No stamp. It was thick. For a minute she almost thought she could see his greasy fingerprints on the envelope. She imagined him sitting in his house, under a small desk lamp throwing off yellowish light, writing feverishly. Making sure every word was perfect, every letter perfectly formed. He was obsessed. She was scared.

The riots didn't help.

Every channel she turned to: fire engines screaming, smoke rising, choppers hovering, people running. She turned off the TV. Sirens still wailed all over the place, choppers crisscrossed the skies. Anne Tyler's *Dinner at the Homesick Restaurant* sat open on the coffee table next to the letter. It was a good book. Not what she wanted to read right now.

The phone continued to ring. It had to be him. She unplugged it. She thought it wasn't a good night to unplug the phone. She didn't feel she had a choice.

The walls seemed to grow closer together. The room was hot with the windows closed. It was funny, the neighbors were probably terrified by the riots, and here she was more terrified by one man than the mass violence going on around her. Should she go outside, see what the neighbors thought, what they were doing to protect themselves? She decided not to. They didn't know each other. Didn't give a damn about each other; as long as your avocado tree wasn't hanging into my yard, no problem. Typical L.A. neighborhood of the '90s.

Laurie checked the kitchen door. Locked. She opened a drawer, stared at the steak knives. Too small. Opened another drawer. The carving knives, butcher knives. More like it. Butterflies raced through her stomach. She placed a hand on the wooden handle of a knife she'd held a thousand times. It felt different. She felt different. She wasn't pulling it out to carve a roast. She didn't want to think about why she felt the need to keep it nearby. A foolish feeling passed through her. She was overreacting. Craylock wouldn't come over. Wouldn't break in. The riots were far enough away. She put the knife back in the drawer.

As long as the electricity didn't go out, she felt she'd be okay. She had a flashlight in her earthquake kit and was pretty sure she'd kept updating the batteries for it. She pulled the kit out of the hall closet. Set it near the coffee table in the living room. Stared at the letter again. What harm could a letter do? It wasn't a letter bomb, she hoped. She thought she was being paranoid. Crazy. It wasn't like her. She was a down to earth, logical person. She picked up the letter. Hefted it in her left hand. Then the right. She tore open the end and pulled out the contents.

The top sheet was a letter that began: "I dreamt about you last night. All night long. Ever since we met, you are the only vision in my dreams. A vision of beauty. Of loveliness. Sincerity and hope. And I do sincerely hope that we'll be together for the longest time. The longest time is eternity."

That frightened her. She stopped reading. Her hand trembled slightly. She let the top two pages fall to the floor. Below them were pen and ink drawings. He wasn't a bad artist. She saw herself in the woman's face in the various pictures. His in the man's. That made it even more frightening. One was of a wedding cake. The bride and groom on top – you guessed it. Another was of Gary and Laurie in bed. Fully clothed. Staring amorously into each other's eyes. There was one of them on the beach, another in front of a Vegas style wedding chapel. They made her gag. She crumpled the wad and threw it to the floor.

There was a noise outside. Sounded like footsteps. Was she being paranoid? Was it one of the neighbors checking things out? The rioting and looting hadn't spread to her neighborhood yet. Was it now? She went back to the kitchen for the butcher knife. Picked out the one with the largest blade. Made sure it was sharp. It was. She was good about those things. She plugged in the kitchen phone. It wasn't ringing. Helicopters and sirens wailed in the distance. People hunkered behind their doors. And she was alone. All alone.

She picked up the receiver, relieved to hear a dial tone. She dialed her mother. The line was busy. Who could she call? She called my office. Left a message on the answering machine. Asked me to call as soon as possible. I was incommunicado at the moment, making sure Tiny would get some kind of care in the damn hospital. She started to call a couple of friends. Put the phone down when she heard another noise outside.

From previous experience, she knew the blinds weren't light-tight. They gave her a certain amount of privacy. Still, if the lights inside were on, people outside could tell. The living room was quiet and she hoped her shadow couldn't be seen moving around from the outside. She sat on the floor in the center of the room.

There was a knock on the door. She jumped, letting out a little gasp. Her hand shot to her mouth in an automatic response to stifle herself. She clutched the knife and shifted to a prone position on the floor.

The knocking continued. Louder. Persistent. It had to be him. Looters don't knock. It might have been a neighbor, checking on her. The neighbors didn't care. No. It had to be him.

Her heart fluttered, racing along. Beads of sweat broke out on her forehead, her back. She ran her finger across the blade of the knife. She almost cut herself.

She chided herself for worrying too much. He hadn't actually done anything to her. Hadn't threatened her. The pictures were hardly obscene. He was just obsessed with her. Her mother thought she should be happy. She thought her mother was crazy. Her best friend, Sue, thought she was making too big a deal out of it when she had told her about the earlier incidents. What would Sue think now? Where was Sue now? Was she okay? No time for that. She had to worry about herself.

"Laurie, are you in there?" Him. Her hands shook as she flattened herself as flush with the floor as she possibly could.

"Laurie, it's Gary. With all this rioting going on I wanted to see if you were okay. Your car's at the end of the driveway, but maybe you're with friends or neighbors. Are you in there? Let me know. I'm worried. I care about you."

She didn't know what to do. He seemed genuinely concerned. He was also crazy. She decided to stay flat on the floor. She wanted to turn the lights off. That would have been a giveaway. She hoped he'd leave soon.

He went around to the kitchen door. Knocked again. It sounded like he was trying the windows. God please. No! It was impossible to meld with the floor any further. That didn't stop her from trying.

"Laurie, if you're in there, open the door. I want to protect you. I love you. Don't be scared. It's only me."

He sounded like they'd known each other for ages, instead of having only been on one date together. He sounded like she'd reciprocated his feelings. She never had. That date had been okay, barely. There was no need to see him again. How did he get this idea that he loved her – and that she loved him back? It was crazy. He was crazy.

She crawled to the still-unplugged living room phone. Plugged it back in, dialed 9-1-1. The line was busy. She hit the redial button. Still busy. What good was a restraining order? She couldn't get through to the police. Even if she could have gotten through that night, they probably had other things to do.

"Laurie, I don't know if you're in there. I'll sit in my car for a while to make sure nothing happens."

Footsteps padded away. She crawled to the window, peeked under the blinds. He got in his car, rested his head against the headrest. She crawled back to the center of the room, lay on her back, staring at the ceiling. Wide eyed, for hours.

At 5:30 the next morning, the footsteps came back to the front door. "Laurie, I have to go home and shower for work. You didn't come home. Maybe you're in there, maybe not. I have to go. I'll call you later. Things shouldn't be so bad in the daylight." He started to walk off. Walked back. "I love you."

The footsteps receded again. She crawled to the window and looked out under the blinds. Watched him drive off. Her heart finally began to return to its normal rate. She was tired, but wired on adrenalin. She waited a few minutes. When he didn't return she went out the front door to get the morning paper. There was an audio cassette on the mat. A red rose was attached to it. She picked it up, looked at it, a compilation Beatles album: *Love Songs*.

CHAPTER 12

The streets were on fire. If I was a user – drug user – this would have been the worst bad trip of my life. It was anyway. We raced through Dante's inferno. Demons appearing on all sides of us. My pistol was in my lap, ready. Was I? That was the real question.

Geysers of flame shot up on all sides of Martin Luther King Hospital. It was almost pretty. Almost. It wasn't almost hot – it was blistering. We were all coughing. Rita and I started to pull Tiny from the backseat. It wasn't easy. We had to roll him this way and that to get him out of the car. He tried to help as best he could. He wasn't doing well, having trouble breathing, not from the smoke but from the damage the Uzi jammed down his throat did. We finally got him out, standing between us, and walked him into the emergency room. You'd have thought the Dodgers and Giants were in the playoffs. We had to take a ticket. A nurse practitioner went around triaging the incoming patients. She looked down Tiny's throat, took his pulse. He was stuck somewhere in the middle, after the gunshot, knife and burn victims, before the broken fingers. He signaled us to leave. We didn't want to.

"It's best if you do leave. He'll be all right," the nurse said. Her arm swept across the no-longer sterile hospital hall. Now it was a mass of bloody brown, black and white bodies.

"What do you want to do?" Rita said.

"Let's stay."

Tiny looked up, forced a smile, still having trouble breathing.

"You really must go," said the nurse. "We don't have room for any extraneous people."

Tiny tried to talk, squeaked out: "Go on. I'll be okay. I'm feelin' better now." His voice was weak. He looked around, scanning the hall. Was he checking to see if Maurice was there? "All these people–" He put his hand out for me to shake. I did. But we didn't go. Until he had seen the doctor and been assigned a bed.

"We'll check up on you," I said as he was being wheeled down the hall.

"Take care of yourselves. It's murder out there." This time he wrote instead of trying to talk. He leaned his head back against the pillow.

Rita and I walked a gauntlet of crying mothers, screaming babies, hurting men and boys, out of the hospital to her car. Her car wasn't dark gray anymore. A thin mist of light gray ash covered it. She opened the trunk, took a spray bottle with blue liquid in it and a roll of paper towels and cleaned the front and rear windows. Even in this mess, she didn't litter, throwing the used paper towels in a small plastic bag in the back seat.

Traffic moved slowly along Compton Avenue. There weren't many cars out. Everyone drove cautiously. No one wanted to antagonize another driver and get blown away for no good reason. Hell, why should this night be different from any other in the Big Orange? City of Angels. City of Dreams. And like most dreams this one was going up in smoke.

We were silent. The tension wasn't between us. It was outside, a steady stream of ash and smoke, sirens and thudding choppers. Bangers banging, people running. Looters looting. Anarchy. I think neither of us knew just what to say. Rita started to laugh.

"I don't even know where I'm heading. I'm taking you home, right?"

"You don't have to."

"Mama said I should loan you my car. If you don't mind, I'd rather just drive you there so I can have access to it."

"I don't mind. But if you just get me out of this area, I can make my way home."

"Am I heading in the right direction?"

She was heading north. I nodded.

"Of course. North and west."

The better L.A. neighborhoods were north and west of South Central. I didn't know if she was being snide or just stating a fact. White people – most of them – lived north and west. Plain and simple.

"How do you know Tiny?" I said, trying to change the subject.

"He's a friend of the family, grew up in the same neighborhood."

People ran in front of us, causing Rita to slam on the brakes more than once. And more than once they were carrying TVs, VCRs, anything they could get their hands on. One couple had a six foot tall refrigerator they were moving across the street in starts and stops.

I looked across to Rita, a face of calm silhouetted by flame and smoke. It was hard to think about Teddie during the fracas in the house with Warren, Maurice and their cuzzes. Hard to think about her while we were taking Tiny to the hospital, hard to now, with the ruckus outside the Shadow – I wished it was a shadow, slipping silently and unnoticed along the street. Looking at Rita reminded me of Teddie, of why I'd been in South Central in the first place. Teddie was cute. Rita was beautiful. She definitely had it over her sister in the looks department. Why wasn't she a star?

"What do you do?"

"Huh?" She looked at me, then turned back to the road. "Oh, yeah. I'm a draftsman."

"Architect?"

"No, draftsman. The architect designs. I draw lines. Only today I do it on a computer. Some day I might go back to school, become a full-fledged Frank Lloyd Rita."

"I like that, Frank Lloyd Rita. I'll just call you Frank from now on."

"And I'll call you Johnnie."

I looked at her quizzically. She saw from the corner of her eye. "Frankie and Johnnie," she said.

It felt like flirting. I wasn't sure. In the middle of a riot that had to do largely with race, two of the major protagonists of color, black and white, were flirting. It was more surreal than the motion picture flashing by outside the car's windows.

"Should be a lot of work for you when this is over, Frankie."

"Unfortunately. This makes me very sad."

Lucy's, the taco stand at La Brea and Pico was still standing. The fires hadn't gotten that far – yet. And we were closer to home, my home. Not much traffic on the streets. Not many people about up there either.

"Are you hungry?"

"A little. But I don't think we should stop out here," she said. I gave her directions to my place from there. Keep heading north on La Brea. Turn left at Beverly Boulevard. Then it's only a few blocks and a right.

We pulled into my driveway. Everything was quiet in the immediate vicinity, except for Baron's anxious barking. There was the now ever-present sound of sirens and choppers in the distance. The smell of smoke. But my little piece of heaven seemed just fine.

The light from my security lights hit her just right through the car window. She was half in silhouette, half in the dusky light. She could have been a model. Should have.

"Would you like to come in?"

She thought about it. "I'd like to call my mother, tell her I'm okay."

"No problem, assuming the phones are working. I'll even fix you up something to eat, if I have anything to fix."

Baron greeted us, jumping on me to say hello, then on Rita, checking her out. I pulled him off.

"It's okay, I love dogs. What's his name?"

"Baron."

"Good boy. He looks like a handful to take care of."

"Hell, he takes care of me."

Her mother's line was busy, or out of order. I fixed a healthy high cholesterol meal of eggs and bacon. The pistol sat on the table next to us while we ate in silence. I wanted to talk to her. Didn't know what to say. I didn't want to talk about Warren, Teddie, Maurice or her mother. Not about her job, or mine either. I wanted to talk about us. Was it because she reminded me of Teddie? I hardly knew Rita well enough to fall for her so strongly, even if she was beautiful. I didn't know anything about Teddie either. Maybe it was just the fuckup part of me looking for trouble. I didn't know. Didn't care. What I did know was that I wanted her.

I put on the little TV in my breakfast room. Every channel had the riots. I'd figured they would. Hell was breaking out all over L.A. Maybe Rita would see it and not want to drive home. But where would she stay? No point staying in a motel. Why spend the money? Why chance driving on the streets anymore? I had a spare bedroom.

I hated myself for being so insidious. Not enough to stop:

"Pretty bad out there," I said.

"It's terrible, really terrible."

"Still can't get through to your mother?"

"No." She looked bleak. "And Warren's probably out doing who knows what?"

She dialed the phone again. It was a few minutes after 11:00 p.m. Her mother picked up. "Mama, I was worried about you. You're line's been busy." She waited while her mother talked. "Yes, I'm okay. I'm at Duke's house. Tiny's being taken care of at MLK. Yes, there were a lot of people out. Lots of fires....I'm sorry, I thought I should keep my car and drop him off home....No, we made it here in one piece, no trouble....His neighborhood's kind of quiet. At least right around us....Mama, I hardly know him....Okay." She turned to me. "She wonders if it will be safe to drive home this late."

"You're welcome to stay here." More than welcome. I had nothing nasty on my mind. I wouldn't force anything. If it happened, I wouldn't fight it either. If it didn't happen, we could stay up watching the City Fireworks Show or an old movie.

"Yes, yes, mama, that's what he said." Mrs. Matson had obviously heard my invitation.

"I have a spare bedroom. It'd be no problem."

Mama heard that too. It was settled. Rita was staying. She was worried about what she'd wear to work the next day. That was quickly gotten over.

Baron followed us as I showed her the spare bedroom. It was in the middle of the house, halfway between the front and rear. A good size. The walls were eggshell white. Levelor blinds covered the windows. A never-used desk sat in one corner. A double bed across from it. One wall was lined with bookshelves, filled with books. My library. Two windows that didn't get much light since they were on the north side of the house. Rita approved. It was comfortable enough.

She headed back, out of the room. I was blocking the doorway. She stopped, three feet in front of me. I didn't move. It was awkward. She looked at me. Didn't avoid my eyes. I looked into hers. It lasted only a fraction of a second. I backed out. She walked through. We ended up in the den, at opposite ends of the couch. The TV droned in the background. I thought about offering her one of my special lacey lemonades. Thought better of it.

It didn't feel right to make a move. She had just lost her sister. Her brother was walking around with a chip on his shoulder that someone was bound to knock off and shove in his mouth sooner or later – might even be me – and here she was in a strange man's house – a white man's house – in the middle of a major riot. I wanted to talk to her, if nothing else. Didn't know what to say.

"I'll give you some pajamas or a T-shirt to sleep in. You can also have my robe."

"I'm not sleepy."

"Who would be tonight? I don't think anyone's going to sleep well." I shifted to face her better. "I can put a tape in, comedy or something. Maybe that'll help."

"No thanks. I think I'd like to leave the news on."

"Afraid of seeing Warren?" I knew I shouldn't have said it as soon as it sprung from my mouth. I thought she'd be pissed. She wasn't.

"I do worry about him. He's so angry."

"How come you're not?"

"How do you know I'm not?"

"You don't seem to be."

"There are things that upset me, sure. Some of the same that upset Warren. But why go around being mad all the time? You just got to pick yourself up and go about your life. You can do it if you want to. I have a good job. There are still some problems, but when I hear my mother talk about how it was when she was my age, or my grandmother. I don't expect things to change overnight."

"You know what I think, I think life's hard for everybody. Doesn't matter what color."

"It is. But it's still harder for black folks."

"Maybe. Maybe not. People do make it."

"It's a struggle."

"For all of us."

"At least you're honest. The one thing that does make me mad are these white liberals who don't speak the truth about their own prejudices. They patronize. They're hypocrites. What I'd like to know is what schools do they send their kids to, public or private? I'd rather know a bigot and know where he stands for real than some of these phonies who smile to your face, then stick a knife in your back."

"You'd love my friend Jack. He says what he thinks and means what he says. Sometimes he's not such a nice guy, but he's loyal."

"Like a dog? I guess we all have a friend Jack. They're mean and nasty, but they tell the truth."

"He speaks his mind, that's for sure."

She got up. "I think I'll wash up now. Maybe try and get some sleep."

I showed her to the guest bathroom, gave her a new toothbrush, my robe and an old pair of pajamas. I hadn't slept in anything but the buff in years. "If you need anything just let me know. If not, I'll see you in the morning."

I went to my own bathroom, washed, put on a pair of old pajama bottoms. I walked through the house, turning off lights, locking doors and windows. Walking down the hall, I came to Rita's room. The door was half open. The light on. She was sitting at the desk looking through musty notebooks of my butterfly collection. I hadn't collected since I was a kid. Hadn't looked at the books since I went into the service. She saw me in the doorway. Looked up. The smile that crossed her lips was a slight one. Barely a smile at all. It was beautiful.

"Did you collect these?" she said.

I took a step inside the room. "When I was younger. I haven't looked at them in years."

"I know," she said, brushing dust off the cover. "It's hard to imagine you collecting butterflies."

"It was a phase." I was embarrassed.

"Don't be embarrassed. I used to collect them myself."

"Really?"

"What made you start?" she said.

"One of the first memories I had as a child was being in my grandmother's yard, seeing a Monarch butterfly. It flitted about. It was beautiful. I didn't know what it was. My grandmother told me."

"In L.A.? Did your grandmother live in L.A.?"

"On Fuller, near Beverly. Not too far from here."

"I haven't collected in a long time either. Maybe we can compare collections some time."

"I'd like that."

◈ ◈ ◈

It wasn't planned on either of our parts. We'd both been thinking about it. Somehow we ended up in the guest bed together. Her naked body was sleek and taut. Perfectly proportioned. It didn't seem like a one night stand to me. I wondered if that's what it was to her. Two people coming together in the midst of crisis, letting off some pent up emotion. I hoped not.

We fell asleep wrapped up in each other, a tangle of limbs. My dreams were nightmares. Back to the Inferno. I woke up in the middle of the night, sweating.

The light from the hall fell across her body in a chiaroscuro of light and dark. She woke up.

"Is anything wrong?" she said.

"Nothing, just a bad dream."

CHAPTER 13

Sun streaked the windows. It bled through the blinds casting *film noir* shadows across our naked bodies. Rita lay soft and warm next to me, taking long, quiet breaths. Baron was on the floor next to the bed, laying on his back, feet in the air. The sirens and chopper blades had died down somewhat. We had made love again, long and hot. Didn't take any precautions. In the heat of passion, you don't always do what's right. At least I don't. We didn't talk much. What was there to say?

We had the same thing for breakfast that we'd had for dinner the night before.

"Lots of variety around here."

"Heinz 57. Fifty-seven ways to cook eggs, as long as they're not runny. I do have a variation on the bacon routine. I can heat up some tortillas. You put on some mustard or hot sauce, wrap the bacon in the tortillas. And–"

"Hmm hmm good." The expression on her face didn't believe it. Hey, I'm a bachelor. We're inventive. It was better than eating Doritos all the time – or tofu. "I better shower and get out of here."

"Going where?"

"To work."

The TV droned on in the background. The city was still on fire. It didn't seem like a good day for going to work, or anywhere else for that matter.

"I think it's a good day for taking off."

She wanted to smile. Wouldn't let it show. "I still have to call them. And I want to call my mother."

While she made her calls, I showered. Got dressed. She was still on the phone with her mother when I came out. She hung up.

"How's your mother?"

"She's fine. Their street's okay. Next street over a house caught on fire."

"Molotov cocktail?"

"They think it was from flying embers."

"What about work?"

She turned away from me. I thought she was trying to hide another smile. "I have to go in."

Wrong. "Where are they, your offices?"

"On La Cienega, down near Pico."

"That's pretty close to the–"

"I know."

I turned to the TV. The sun was still ascending. The all night party was never-ending. "Don't they ever sleep?" I said.

"I suppose not." She burst out laughing.

"What is it?"

Uncontrollable laughter. She couldn't stop and she couldn't tell me what was so funny. So I started laughing too. We were almost rolling on the floor.

She fell into my arms, looked me in the eyes. Her eyes were a deep shade of chestnut. Large and clear. She may have known pain; it didn't show in her eyes. Not now. She was still laughing.

"What is it?" I said, finally, hoarse from all the gaiety.

"I don't have to go to work. I was just kidding."

I looked at her. "That's what was so funny?"

"I guess it really isn't. But it sure felt good to laugh."

That it did.

It also felt good to kiss her again. Until the back door opened. She jerked back, out of my arms. I didn't blame her for being scared. With all the shit flying, people bustin' other people, the door bursting open would make anyone jump. The man in it: slitty, squinting eyes. Stringy long blond hair. Three days unshaven beard. Six foot two of solid muscle in dirty jeans and workshirt. Jungle boots. Looked like a white trash nightmare. I almost jumped myself, except that I recognized the beast as Jack. I'd heard the roar of his Harley. Felt the house vibrate. Didn't want to break the mood with Rita, so I hadn't said anything. Baron greeted him with a sloppy kiss on his cheek. Jack wasn't a dog lover, but he liked Baron.

He had a key to my place; came and went when he felt like it. He had fierce eyes, of a color I can't describe. They were almost black in a certain light. He stood in the doorway staring. We had never talked about it, but I was sure he didn't approve of interracial romance. Unless it was a one-night stand. I wondered if it was.

I introduced Rita and Jack. They shook hands tentatively. He tossed his kit bag on the table. He carried it with him all the time. I guess he thought he had to be prepared for Armageddon. I guess he was right.

We sat at the breakfast table, the TV still droning. I was worried about what Jack would say. He had definite opinions about the riot, I was sure. He had them about everything else.

He pierced the set with his eyes. Watching intently. Then it came:

"This is all crazy. Damn looters should be shot on sight. No questions. No second chances. No chances to cry how oppressed they are. Hell, next thing you know they'll be inviting gang bangers to the White House."

He looked at Rita. What was he thinking? I would have given the proverbial anything to know.

What was she thinking?

He looked at her. At me. Back to her. She squirmed. I was uncomfortable. He was never uncomfortable.

"Hey, don't get me wrong. It's not a race thing. Don't matter if they're white. Looters should be shot."

That didn't help.

"But you know what I just don't get. The system worked. The four cops were tried, by a jury of their peers. They got justice. I mean, what do these people want? A jury of junkies and homos? Bangers. That ain't a jury of their peers. We don't know all what went on in the trial. We don't know. And King, man, he was stoned on something. A stone-ass criminal to boot. And if you watch the entire tape, he got up. He charged the cops. I know what I wouldda done in their situation. And ol' Rodney King Cole wouldn't be here to talk about it today. Someone charges me. One of us dies. Doesn't matter which one. But one of us eats the cheese. They got justice. What else do they want?"

Rita didn't say anything. She didn't avert her eyes. Didn't shift position. But she didn't respond. I thought the beating had gone too far, but I agreed with Jack in part. If King had come toward me, what would I have done in the heat of the moment? I might have gone crazy and killed him. The cops didn't do that.

Jack and Warren were opposite sides of the same coin. I was in the middle, I hoped. But it was a hard balancing act. I wondered where Rita fit. She loved Warren, even with his positions and attitude. And I loved Jack.

"I guess you guys don't have opinions," he said. It was a challenge. He was looking for a fight. Rita knew it too.

"Oh we got 'em, least I do," she said. He glared at her, challenging. "What's going on out on the streets is wrong. What happened to King is wrong. Cops do treat blacks differently. I wonder what would have happened if he was white."

"I'll tell you what would've happened if I was the cop. I wouldda killed him. Color don't matter. He's not special 'cause he's black. Another guy wouldn't be special 'cause he's white. Someone comes after me, I–"

"You really think he went after the cops."

"Hell, he was tased twice. Didn't go down. All he had to do was lie down on the ground."

"He should have. I'll admit that. Still, the cops went too far."

"Maybe," Jack said. That was victory enough for Rita.

He turned to me: "Hey, buddy, I only came to see if the house was still here. I called last night, but no one answered, no answering machine. Nothing."

"Yeah, I forgot to turn it on. Must've slept like a log."

Jack panned from me to Rita. His look said, "Yeah, right. Slept."

I had purposely left the machine off, turned the bells on the phones off. I wanted privacy.

A sly grin formed at the corners of Jack's mouth. "Hey, he play k.d. lang for you?"

I had.

"I think so. I think it was her."

Jack snorted a laugh. "Well, I hope it's not contagious." He got up, headed for the door. "Don't forget, don't you dare capitalize her initials or name. It ain't PC."

"Where're you going?"

"You know what they say, two's company, three don't fit with family values. Besides, some of us have to work."

Work, I thought. Jack worked about every third day. He was an antiques refinisher. Could have made a good living at it if he put more effort into it. It was more important for him to be able to ride his Harley up and down the coast. Come and go as he pleased. On leaving the Navy, he promised himself he'd never work a nine to five job. He never did.

"Today?"

"Yup."

He grabbed his kit bag and was gone.

"Don't let him bother you," I said to Rita as we cleared the breakfast plates. "He'd give his life for you."

"For you. I'm not so sure about me."

"He'd give it for you too. I'd bet my own life on it. But he has a certain way of looking at the world."

"We all do. I have a friend just like him. If he knew I'd slept with a white man last night he'd slit my throat."

"What would he do to me?"

"Nothing."

"Nothing?"

"You're not a black woman."

After breakfast, we didn't know what to do with ourselves. It wasn't a great day for doing the touristy spots. We went back to bed.

◈ ◈ ◈

We lay in bed, wrapped in each other's arms. No TV. k.d. lang spilling from the five disc CD player, which had speaker outlets in almost every room.

"Why doesn't Jack like her?"

"She's a lesbian."

"I bet he'd give his life for her," she said with a mocking smile. Was she baiting me?

"I believe he would." I really did. "But that doesn't mean he has to support her lifestyle."

"Oh, he's one of those 'I-may-not-agree-with-you-but-I'll-fight-to-the-death-for-your-right-to-say-anything' guys."

"You got it." I sat up.

"What's wrong?"

"I think I'm feeling guilty."

"Guilty – for sleeping with a black woman?" There was a hint of seriousness under her joking demeanor.

"Guilty that I should be pursuing Teddie's case."

"Today?"

"Yeah, even today."

"Can you tell me who you're working for?"

Was that the only reason she'd slept with me? There were so many things to consider. So many layers. So many possible ulterior motives. For both of us.

"I can't. You know that." And I couldn't tell her where the guilt really came from. "You wanna go down to my office with me? I want to make sure it hasn't been broken into, check the mail. Then we can go to lunch."

"How far away is it?"

"Not far. Over on Beverly."

She agreed to go. I fed Baron on the way out. We talked about Teddie on the way there. She had been a normal little girl. Closer in age to Warren. Had helped to bring him up. Liked dolls and baseball as a kid. Outgrew the dolls, not the baseball. She decided to become an actress when an Englishman had brought a rag tag group of actors to her junior high school and put on a play of Shakespeare's. Then he did workshops with the students, where they did Romeo and Juliet. Instead of the Montagues and Capulets, the warring *families* were the Crips and Bloods. That was Teddie's introduction to acting. She had a small part in the play, but longed to be Juliet.

I told Rita about going to Teddie's after the murder, seeing Warren. His attitude, which she knew quite well. About heading down to Tiny's, reading Teddie's letters, which, I informed her, I still wanted to do. I told her I had come across a possible suspect I was calling the Weasel – I didn't tell her how. I described the Weasel to her. She didn't have much to add about who he might have been. Rita and Teddie hadn't been close since they were kids because of the age difference. While Rita had been away at college Teddie and Warren had gotten closer. He'd be the one who might know something.

There wasn't much traffic on the streets. Some looters along La Brea. Police were out now. No sign of the National Guard. Not in this area. Not yet.

No problem finding a parking place in front of the office. I didn't bother putting a quarter in the meter. It was an older two story building. Stunning red brick, with leaded glass windows. At golden hour, when the light falls just right, it looks like something out of Edward Hopper.

My office was on the second floor. The mail hadn't come yet. There was an urgent message from Laurie Hoffman on the answering machine. She wasn't home when I called her back. We called the hospital. The nurse said Tiny was in good condition but his throat was swollen from having the gun stuck in it. She wanted to know who'd done it. Tiny wouldn't tell and neither would we. He wouldn't be allowed to talk for a couple of days she told us. They were keeping him there for observation. She'd relay our message.

We started to leave the office to go and get some lunch. As we were leaving, we ran into Laurie on the stairs. There were dark circles under her eyes. She was fidgety. We went back to the office.

CHAPTER 14

Back in the office, I introduced Laurie and Rita.

"Are you Mr. Rogers' secretary?" Laurie asked innocently. Rita chose to ignore her. I intervened, escorting Laurie into the private office, while Rita waited out front. I closed the door.

"I need your help, Mr. Rogers."

I gazed out the window. Smoke and ash rose from all points south. The symphony of sirens and choppers continued from all directions. The city was on fire. I felt like Nero. It's not that I didn't care about Laurie Hoffman's problems. I cared more about finding Teddie's killer. I owed her and her family that much. I also cared about what was happening to my home town. And had no idea what I could do about it. Yet here was this woman in need. She looked like she hadn't slept in days, and I didn't really want to help her. More important things on my mind.

I suggested she call Kevin Tracy, another good private detective. I started to write his name on a piece of paper.

"Please, Mr. Rogers. I can't go calling every detective in the book. I know you're busy, but can't you just check into it for me."

"I'm not sure what there is to check into. I can take a photo of your stalker coming within a hundred feet of your house so you can possibly have a judge throw the guy in jail."

She looked like she had something to say. She didn't want to say it. What was she afraid of? She finally spoke: "Maybe you could, uh, talk to him." She said *talk* to him; she didn't mean with my mouth. She might have meant with fists or a club. I didn't think she meant I should let my trigger finger do the walking or talking. "I'll pay you double your rate. Just go and talk to him one time, let him know that I'm not in this alone."

One silky leg crossed the other. Was she really uncomfortable or was she shifting to give me a better view? To entice me? Or was I being totally sexist by even thinking it? It didn't matter. I decided to talk to the guy for her. If I could help her that might be a little payback for Teddie too.

"I'll talk to him, one time. At my normal rate. I charge by the day, one day minimum."

"Agreed." A wave of relief washed over her face. The muscles around her eyes and mouth unknotted. A hint of a sparkle flashed across her hazel green eyes. She was pretty. I guessed her age to be mid-thirties, a very attractive mid-thirties. She'd lost ten years in ten minutes.

She handed me a piece of paper with Gary Craylock's name, address and phone number already written on it. She had come prepared. I smiled at her, trying to let her know that it would be all right. It wasn't easy. It didn't come immediately. She smiled back. I felt good knowing that I might be able to help her.

"I have to be honest with you," I said, feeling good to be honest with someone, "but I don't know how the riot will affect things. I'll try to get to him today or tomorrow. I don't make any promises. This mess throws everything out of kilter. If he harasses you, call me." I handed her my card. "If I'm not in, I'll get back to you as soon as possible. Also fill out this contract and make sure both your work and home addresses are correct. Also in the 'other' section at the bottom, put down your normal home, work and other activity hours. I know it seems like prying–"

"Hardly. I'll be happy for someone to know my whereabouts. Someone besides him. All my friends think I'm crazy, making too much out of nothing. Some even think I should be flattered." She looked me in the eyes. "I was at first. It wore off quickly."

"I imagine it would."

◈ ◈ ◈

It dawned on me after she left that I didn't have a car to get around in. We had come to the office in Rita's car. I hardly knew her well enough to ask to borrow it. She took me to a car rental place. I rented the cheapest car they had available, a fire engine red Toyota Corolla, and hoped that it wouldn't get damaged in the riot. Normally, I wouldn't have bought the extra insurance the rental companies offer. I did that day.

Some places were closed, others open. It was real hit and miss. El Coyote was open. Rita and I met there for lunch after she took me to get the car. It wasn't very crowded.

"This way, senor," the hostess said. She wore a multicolored dress of green, white and red. The skirt billowed out for miles in every direction. We were seated in the No Smoking section. Chips and salsa were brought. We dipped in. I could tell the salsa was too hot for Rita. I liked it that way.

Awkward. Neither of us knew what to say to the other. We'd spent a night of heat and passion in the middle of a night of heat and passion in the larger city. She was black. I was white. Blacks were pulling whites out of cars and beating on them for no reason other than that they were white. If certain of her friends or family knew, they might have beat on me. If one friend of mine in particular knew, he might look at me differently from then on. And he knew. If people saw us driving together, they might pull us both out of the car and put a brick, or worse, through our heads. It was the best of times, it was the shittiest of times.

Was it the heat of the moment that brought us together intimately and lustfully, just as the heat of the moment had led to our initial meeting at Rita's mom's house? Or was there more? I wanted to know. Was afraid to ask. I wondered what she was thinking. What the people in the restaurant around us thought of this *zebra-striped* couple. Did they notice? I was sure they did, especially today. Did they care? I didn't know.

"What're you thinking?" she said, not looking at me.

"Will the city still be here tomorrow?"

"The question is, will the National Guard be here tomorrow?" she said. It was a good question. The Guard had been delayed. The police didn't have enough manpower and seemed to lack a plan. It was a damned good question. But it wasn't what I was thinking about.

"What will you do the rest of the day?"

"Guess I'll try and work the case."

"Did that woman we met on the stairs hire you?"

"Yeah, but it's a quick job. Some dude's stalking her. Just gotta put the fear of God – or someone – in him."

"I imagine you could do that quite well."

I wasn't sure if it was a compliment or not. "What about you? What'll you do?" I was hoping she'd say she wanted to stay with me. Of course, I hadn't said that I wanted to spend the afternoon with her, so it was probably asking too much. Maybe we were both scared.

"I need to check on my mom. See if she's all right. Then I want to check on my apartment."

"I'd like to come by your mom's again, look at those letters."

"I don't think today's a good day."

"No, you're probably right." I had fucked myself, for a change. I didn't know if I'd ever see her again. At least socially. I knew I might run into her at her mother's. We never did order food.

◈ ◈ ◈

Craylock's house was in Rancho Park, on Tennessee, a block west of the Twentieth Century-Fox studios. It was an expensive one story Spanish job, not unlike my own house. A new jet black BMW sat in the driveway. Pickup car, I thought. She hadn't mentioned what he did for a living; it must have been something where he could charge people more than he was worth, Hollywood. A doctor. Plumber maybe.

The riots hadn't stretched this far west, yet. It was a good neighborhood, if there was still such a thing in L.A. I used to live only a couple blocks from Craylock's before I moved back into my folks' house. The first street north of Pico. The Olympic Marathon runners had run down Pico just across the alley behind my apartment. I watched from my breakfast area window. It was a different L.A. then. It wasn't that long ago.

I walked to Craylock's front door. Rang the bell. A pretty-boy handsome man in his late thirties or early forties answered. His dark hair was slicked back, the way Tyrone Power used to wear his. I guess the fashion had returned. He wore a polo shirt with an alligator, naturally. Dockers pants and Gucci loafers. Dressed to kill. I perished the thought.

"Gary Craylock?"

"Yes."

"Laurie Hoffman asked me to come see you."

His eyes lit up at her name, but he still blocked the doorway. I didn't want to go inside anyway. I thought it best to keep things formal and let him know I wasn't his pal. I stood my ground.

"Ms. Hoffman–"

"–Ms. Hoffman. Laurie."

"Ms. Hoffman asked me to ask you to leave her alone." The lighthouse in his eyes began to flicker. "She doesn't want you coming by her house, leaving her notes, calling her. She doesn't want you showing up at her work or any other place she might be." The beacon died. He did a tactical retreat in his head. I could almost see the wheels spinning.

"You can't mean Laurie. My Laurie."

"Listen, pal, she isn't your Laurie. She doesn't want to be. Lay off. Stay away. I can't make it any plainer."

"Or what? Maybe I should call the police. You're threatening me."

I was threatening him.

"Go ahead. But I think they might have better things to do today."

He knew they did. Besides, he didn't need the police on his tail. I'd tell them about Laurie. About the restraining order. He may have been a pest. He didn't appear to be an idiot.

"There's already a restraining order in place. You could be in a lot of trouble."

"Don't threaten me. I don't like being threatened." His voice quivered. He was nervous. He knew he didn't have a leg to stand on. Had to save face. It was a pretty face, too. One I'd just as soon have punched in the nose as looked at. I didn't know the S.O.B. Didn't need to. I knew the type. God's gift to women. Hell, God's gift to the world. Everyone should like him. Especially if he liked them. And get out of the way if they didn't return it.

It wasn't that he really thought he was so wonderful. It was that he doubted it. Doubting yourself can make you crazy. Make you look for love and reassurance and respect in every quarter. When you don't get it, you get pissed. Maybe punch someone out. Maybe yell at strangers on the freeway. Maybe yell at the people closest to you and push them away. Maybe if you're crazy enough you go into a McDonald's or a schoolroom and open fire with a semi-auto rifle.

I knew all about wanting respect from every quarter.

CHAPTER 15

I left Craylock standing in his doorway. He had the forlorn look of a lost puppy. I went home. Tried calling my insurance company about the Firebird. Constant busy signal. Played catch with Baron a while. I threw a tennis ball across the yard, Baron fetched it. When he was tired of the game, he gnawed on the ball. He went through five or six balls a week. Maybe one a day. I crashed on the raft in the pool. Baron crashed next to the pool, after a short swim. Sun glared down at me through the smoky haze. Ugly. Angry. Squinting. Me. It.

The water was cool. The raft cut through a layer of gray ash on the water's surface. No dragonflies. Dead? Scared off by the smoke? Siren bleat. Music. L.A. in the '90s. Wasn't the town I grew up in. Wasn't the town anyone grew up in.

Get on with it. I had a case to solve. A client to please. The worst client in the world – me. Where to turn? I needed to see those letters again. Timing wasn't right to go to South Central. I didn't know if I could get down there with the National Guard arriving and the police staking out turf. The roads might have been closed. Wanted to see Rita again. Warren was another story. I didn't think he could hurt me. I didn't want to hurt him. If it came to it, I knew I would. Thought of Tiny. Call him when I get out of the pool.

Stainless steel jabbed into the raft's cupholder. Better than mountain spring water on a brisk L.A.

spring day like today. Seven rounds in the mag. One in the chamber. Wet and wild. California funtime. Will a gun work after it's been in the water? Ask the SEALs.

Leads. None. Nothing. *Nada* – there's a '90s L.A. word for you. Hip. Flip. Hip Hop.

Where to turn? Letters. The William Tell Motel. Weasel. Grinning. Like he's about to drool spit. Paid me cash. Paid the motel cash.

Why the William Tell? Did he know it? Did he like the overture? Like the Lone Ranger? Chance? Significance? Nothing came to mind.

The Perlmans. Maybe the old lady would remember something else. Maybe she wasn't telling all to begin with.

Damn riot. Cramps my style. Already too much time lost on Teddie's case. Trail getting colder with each passing day. Nothing like a riot to make a Weasel's day. Drool dribbling, must be laughing to himself.

Black chicks? That his gig? Black movie stars? TV stars? Check into it. See if any other good looking black actresses got harassed. Scary letters. Calls. Followed. If that doesn't work spread the search wide.

Go back to Mama Matson's. Those letters. The only tangible piece of anything so far; hardly enough to warrant calling it evidence.

Sun glaring. Squinting.

Drive by shooters laughing at silly boys and girls playing in the street.

How stupid of them.

Crack.

It wasn't meant for you.

For your older brother.

Bang.

You're dead.

My little girl was killed–

My sister raped.

Mother shot.
Father strongarmed, robbed.
Son murdered.
Spanish.
Korean.
Chinese. How many dialects?
Japanese.
Tagalog.
Polish.
Yiddish.
Street jive. A language to itself. Only for the initiated.
English?
Tears streaming.
Hate burning.
Getting a hamburger is an exercise in survival.
Driving – forget it.
Armed. Better be.
Fear.
Anxiety.
Alarm.
Panic.
Terror.
Frenzy.
Hysteria.
Rampage.
Riot.

Riot.

Chaos.
Confusion.
Commotion.
Pandemonium.
Mayhem.
Anarchy.

Riot.

Never Never Land: Kids who'll never grow up. Lost to a bullet. Lost to a gang. Lost to themselves.

Scared?
Scared shitless. Scared to death–
L.A. for the '90s. La La Land.
California dreamin'.

◈ ◈ ◈

"Murder City U.S.A.," Jack said after I told him about my dream. "Animals. They're all fuckin' animals. I don't care what the fucking bleeding hearts say. These people are responsible for themselves. Hell, half of 'em don't even belong here. Goddamn illegal aliens."

The dream: a kaleidoscope of images. Flashes. Light. Dark. Brown. Yellow. White. Black. Missing blue. Heart pounding, sweating dream. Shouldn't have told Jack. Had to tell someone. He popped by. Harley lullaby charging down the driveway, waking me not so gently. Do not go gently into that good night. I promised myself I wouldn't.

"Segue." I wasn't in the mood. Teddie filled my waking dreams, if not the sleeping ones.

I told Jack about my lack of leads while I got dressed.

"Brown babes. Don't forget the brown babes. They're not a subgenre of black. They're separate entities. Coconuts. Not Oreos."

"Shut up."

"These fucks are burning your hometown down. Don't you care?"

"I care about finding this girl's killer."

"Hey, bud, if you're so damn sensitive you better get it right. She ain't a girl. She's a woman. Don't wanna be politically incorrect."

"Sometimes you give me a pain in the—"

"Sometimes I save your ass blind."

Touché. I had no comeback for that. Sometimes he did.

We had roast beef sandwiches for lunch. The meat was deli-cut thin, the bagels onion, a couple days old. I thought about asking him how come he ate bagels. What was the point? Mustard oozed out the sides of his bagel.

"I heard 'bout this Mex actress." Nothing else came. He chomped on his sandwich.

"Yeah, so."

"So lemme eat, will ya?" He spooned more mustard on the edge of the sandwich. A bright yellow moustache instantly grew on his upper lip. A Chia moustache. Just add water. "I heard 'bout this Mex bitch, or to be politically correct, *puta*. Got her ass whupped good."

"I don't remember hearing about anything like that."

"Was hushed up. I don't remember why."

"What show was she in?"

"Don't remember."

"You're a big help."

"Hey, man, I don't need the sarcasm. I'm tryin' to help you. Mighta been a small story on some back page of the Times. About a year or two ago. Check it out. All I remember is she wanted some part, it was going to a Caucasian. She protested, along with a bunch-a her sisters. I mean, hell, acting's acting right? So any actress should be able to play the part. But no, they gotta make a stink."

"Get to the point."

"She got beat one night after the protest. That's all I remember. 'Bout a year ago. Maybe longer."

A few minutes later, a plume of gunmetal gray smoke belched out of the Harley lullaby machine, wafting skyward, joining the ever-present smog and riot smoke.

Would the libraries be open? A phone call would have sufficed. I was itchy. Had to get outta there. Hopped in the car and went to the John C. Freemont branch. Open. I searched the L.A. Times on microfilm. What a pain. Checked all of '91. Nothing. Should I go back as far as '90? What else did I have to do?

The library was closing early. I had about an hour left. I didn't have that much patience. I had started with December of '91, working my way backwards. I was at July. About to give up. Something caught my eye.

A photo. An actress. Kind of cute. Dark skinned. Originally from Mexico City. A fan had tried to get close to her. Too close. He was in love with her. He thought she was in love with him.

Coincidence?

How'd he find her? Found her family. Told them he was an old friend?

Sound familiar?

Coincidence?

Probably an M.O. used by a lot of Weasels. Could it be my Weasel?

Another article a month or so later, which I'd missed the first time around, said she'd split town. No trace. No trace of the suspect either. A white male. No firm description. But about my Weasel's age?

Coincidence?

CHAPTER 16

The girl's family wasn't hard to trace. East L.A. I could hit El Tepeyac on the way home. By the time I got there I figured there wouldn't be a line half way around the block. I drove across the Macy Street bridge, over the L.A. River. It was like going to another country. Thinking like that made me think of Jack. I didn't want to think like him. Sometimes I couldn't help it. Signs were in Spanish and English, some not even in English. Street vendors sold tacos, not hot dogs, Jalisco, not Good Humor ice cream. All that's not what got me. The streets were filthy. Trash everywhere. Empty garbage cans. Trash piled up under bus stop benches, solid. Graffiti on the walls, dirt and litter, everywhere.

It didn't matter then though. What did matter was getting through roadblocks and not getting my rental car or myself smashed. It wasn't as hard as I'd figured. The National Guard still wasn't fully deployed. Most of the rioting was happening farther south and farther west.

I pulled up in front of a ticky-tacky house on Folsom Street. Parked. A couple punks eyeballed me. I glanced their way, went about my business. Headed to the door. Small white frame house. Paint peeling in places. Overall in pretty good shape. New Honda Accord in the driveway. Knock-knock.

A small man opened the door. Henna colored skin, sagging at the edges. Small white moustache. Zinc gray hair. Half moons under his eyes you could drop a penny into and it wouldn't fall. Baggy brown pants, cuffs. Yellow, viscous eyes. Huaraches. Looked like he was just off the farm. Looked old. Tired.

"Yes," he said. No trace of accent. I felt foolish for thinking he looked like a recent arrival.

"My name's Duke Rogers. I want to talk to Pilar Cruz's family."

"Who are you?" Teary eyes. Because of the smoke and smog? Because of what I asked?

"I'm a private detective. I'm looking–" I handed him my card.

"–For Pilar's attacker?"

"No, I'm sorry."

"For Pilar herself? Someone has hired you to find her."

"No. She's only peripherally involved."

He peered around me. "Your car?"

I nodded.

"Be careful. Damn *pachucos*'ll take everything but the car alarm if you're not careful," he said using the argot of his day.

"Why don't they just take the whole car?"

"They'll do that too. Pull it into my driveway."

After I did, he invited me into the house. He had just fixed lunch. Invited me to join him. We sat in the kitchen, eating chorizo and beans. Fresh salsa with cilantro. Homemade. I wouldn't be stopping at El Tepeyac on the way home.

"Eat. *Mas*?"

He reminded me of my grandmother. He reminded me of all grandmothers.

"Pilar was my daughter. I am Ben Cruz."

I stopped chewing. He saw.

"You are thinking I look old. How does this old man have such a lovely young daughter? I am not that old, *senor*. I am older than my years. Losing my daughter, losing my wife, that will do it to you."

I didn't know what to say. I had some feeling for his loss. Not much. I didn't know him. Didn't know his wife or daughter. What do you say in a situation like this? "I'm sorry."

"The police don't care. She's Mexican. They put her case in some file cabinet or computer somewhere. Low priority. They don't care. You're the first person's come around here asking me about her in over a year. At first there were a few fans. They came by – I don't know how they knew where to find me – or they sent cards. She could have made it big."

Teddie Matson had made it big and was on the road to making it bigger. It was no protection for her. It might have been her downfall, along with me.

"I'm trying to find the man who killed Teddie Matson."

"A terrible thing. Similar to the attack on Pilar."

"That's what I was thinking. I was wondering if there was anything you could tell me. Anything at all that might help me in my search. You said that some fans came by after she left."

"Yes. There was a handful."

"Who were they?"

"Some were from a Latina actress group. They wanted to find her. Help her. I couldn't help them. I didn't know where she went myself. They didn't believe me. After a couple of visits they gave up."

"Anyone else?"

"There were a couple of young men that came by. Maybe three or four. It is hard to remember."

"You've got to try. Tell me about them. Were any of them white?"

"Two were Mexicans. I think the other two were white."

I asked him to describe the white ones to me. One of them sounded like he might fit the Weasel's description. "Do you have any idea how to find them? Did they leave anything?"

"I will give you everything. She was not a very big star. Not a star at all. She had a couple of bit parts on TV and did a couple plays. She was known in the Hispanic community more than the general community."

He led me to her bedroom. A Mexican flag hung over the bed, Mexican pottery and a brightly colored shawl decorated the dresser. He pulled a small box, little bigger than a shoebox, from under the bed. Put it in my hands.

"Take it."

I hesitated.

"You wonder, how I can trust you? I don't know you. Maybe you are the one who attacked her. Maybe you had cards printed saying you are private detective."

I didn't say anything. I was too busy thinking that, while I had nothing to do with Pilar's attack, I might just as well have been the one who attacked and killed Teddie.

"You have an open, honest face. But that is not why I am willing to trust you with these things. I do not think you are the attacker. He would be nervous. You are not. Maybe you are a very good actor. I don't think so. So maybe you will find Teddie Matson's killer. And maybe along the way you will look for and find my Pilar. I have some money I can give you." He reached for his wallet.

"Later." I would look. I wouldn't take his money. I didn't tell him then. I would if I found anything.

"And you tell her to come home. It is not me she is hiding from. I will protect her." He sat on the edge of the bed. Didn't care if I saw him weeping openly.

"Do you have any idea where she might be? An old girlfriend she might have gone to stay with. Anything?"

He kept weeping as he pulled another box from under the bed. This one was bigger. Stuffed to the gills with letters and cards. "These are her personal mails, from friends, not fans. Maybe there is something in there. I read through everything after she left but couldn't come up with anything. I called her friends. They didn't know anything or wouldn't tell." He went to her desk, opened the center drawer, pulled out a small address book. Handed it to me. "These are her friends. Her best friend Anna Martinez."

"Boyfriend?"

"No good punk. *Se llama* Ramon Martinez."

"Related to Anna?"

"*Si, her brother.*"

I left Cruz in Pilar's bedroom. Found my own way out. The punks were waiting for me in Cruz's driveway.

"Get lost, *amigo?*" One of them grinned, a gold frame sparkling around one tooth.

"You need a sunburn to be in this neighborhood."

"Who writes your dialogue? You need a rewrite man."

"Very funny. Very funny."

Tom Bond, my buddy in the L.A. Sheriff's, had more occasion than I to come down to this part of town. He said these kids would just as soon kill you as look at you. These two didn't have weapons showing. I thought I saw a bulge in one of their waistbands. That's what flashed my brain at that moment.

"What'chu doin' here, man? Lookin' for some dark meat?" They laughed.

"Don' white boys like white meat?" Gold frame leaned on my car.

"Get off my car. Get outta my way."

"Tough guy."

"It ain't no time to be doin' your thing here, man. You're outnumbered. Might be only two of us here, but everywhere you turn you gonna see people look like us."

"I don't give a shit what you look like. Get off my car." I stepped toward the driver's door. Gold frame didn't budge. I pushed him aside. His *amigo* dove for my knees. I was ready, lurching out of the way. My own leg came up kneeing the diver in the nose. He careened back into the car, sliding to the pavement. Blood spilled from his nose. Pivoting on my heel, I heard the unmistakable racking of an automatic slide. Turned to face down a blue steel 9mm semi auto.

"What now, *gringo*? Might be your country, but it's my street. My gun." He was only a couple feet away from me and he was in love with his tough talk. While he savored the words, I swung my foot high. High enough to broadside his face – hard. It shook him up. He didn't drop the gun, until I rammed my finger into his eye. That did the trick. I stuck the gun in my belt. I'd get rid of it later, where no one would ever find it.

"Tell the ACLU you were just an innocent victim." I got in the car. Drove off. I wondered if he'd slap me with a suit. I thought I was sounding more like Jack than ever.

◇ ◇ ◇

Drove by Craylock's on the way home. Not sure why. It wasn't on the way. A thought zapped me, Craylock a stalker. I wondered if the Weasel was a stalker, not just a celebrity stalker, but a plain-old-brown-paper-bag-vanilla-flavored stalker. Thought I might call Tom Bond, check out stalkers.

Knocked on Craylock's door. Not happy to see me.

"Get the fuck outta here. I'll get a restraining order on you."

I strongarmed him into the foyer of his house. I hadn't seen the inside before. Crummy art on the wall. Streaks of paint, mostly black, white, gray – how politically incorrect, where's brown, black, red, yellow? – that didn't make any sense. Ponderous. Someone like Craylock figures he doesn't understand it, it must, therefore, be meaningful.

"Whadda you want?"

"I want to talk."

"About what?"

"Stalking."

CHAPTER 17

I started through the entry hall toward the living room or den. He cut me off, steering me toward the kitchen. Expensive tastes. Real hard wood cabinets. None of that paste on stuff. Newly tiled counters it looked like. Hazy sun streaks shot in through a window box filled with green stuff. A mini herb and vegetable garden right there in the kitchen. He motioned for me to sit at the counter that divided the kitchen from the breakfast room. I chose to stand. So did he. A siren whizzed by outside. The first one I'd heard in a long time, say about five minutes.

He offered me orange juice. He started: "I'm not a stalker."

"Some people have other opinions."

"Some people lead people on. I may be in love, but I'm no stalker. I'm just a romantic guy, like to make my woman feel special." He smiled a slight smile, trying to be friendly. Trying to disarm me. I wasn't about to be disarmed. "Laurie and I are friends."

Yeah, right. Friends.

"If you're friends, why don't you leave her alone when she wants to be left alone?"

"She doesn't want to be left alone."

"That's not the way I hear it."

"She's playing hard to get."

I was trying to figure out how to get direct answers to questions about stalking. But it was impossible. He was smitten. In his mind, she was playing hard to get. He wouldn't take no for an answer.

"We're friends."

"You think that by giving her gifts you can win her?"

"I would never buy a woman's love, or interest. I give them to her to show my affection."

Affection? Affectation.

"How'd you meet her?" I knew the answer. I wanted his version.

"I answered her personal ad in the back of Los Angeles Magazine."

I never could understand people placing those ads. Every man is an intellectual hunk with a good sense of humor. Hung, no doubt. Every woman is into long walks on the beach, reading, and gorgeous. Hung up, no doubt. There should be truth in advertising laws about personal ads.

Was he dangerous? The kitchen didn't seem to have anything unusual about it. Carving knife set. Everybody has one. I started through the breakfast room to the dining room, hoping to get to the rest of the house. He cut me off again. It wasn't the time to push it.

"I should call the cops on you. But I'm fascinated."

"Guess I'm not the usual stiff you hang with."

"Definitely not. Much more unpolished. More real."

"Thanks. I wouldn't wanna hang with the automatons you hang with."

"Oh, I don't hang with anyone in particular. I'm a self-starter."

"Loner."

"Not a word I prefer."

But a good word to describe you. And maybe the Weasel. That limited the possibilities.

"Besides, why do I need friends when I have Laurie?"

Fantasy Island. Goof's living in a parallel universe.

There was a glint in his eyes. A tiny speck of light, sparkling at the inside corners. Hard to tell if it was coming from the sun or somewhere inside him. Made him look demoniac. Possessed. Which I was sure he was, if not by the Devil then by devils within himself.

He started toward me. I wheeled aside, ready. He went past me to the sink. Rinsed his glass.

"Are you done psychoanalyzing me now?"

"Sure, I'll bill you."

He didn't laugh. Didn't crack a smile. The glint in his eyes grew steely. "I'm not used to being a guinea pig."

You smell like one. I didn't tell him. I wanted to see the rest of his crib. Figured I'd do it when he wasn't there. Might be of some interest. Tell me more about the Weasel. I could've strongarmed the goof. Probably wouldn't have helped me get anymore info from him. Would've helped me vent some bile though.

I was about to leave, turned back: "Did it ever occur to you that Laurie may not be playing a game with you? That maybe she really doesn't want you."

"You just don't understand, do you?"

What could I say to that? It was the second time in as many days that someone had said something like that to me. But he was right. I didn't understand.

◈ ◈ ◈

I cut down to Pico, heading east. Things were pretty calm down here in Rancho Park. By about Fairfax, people were running wild in the street. Party Time! *Sales* in almost every store.

Turned north on Fairfax. Traffic commotion, tie up, near Wilshire. Cars blocking the intersection. Others going around them. No one paying attention to lights.

Crash. Plate glass shattering.

Get whitey.
Get whitey.
Screams.
People rushing.
Angry black faces.
Shouting.
Mad brown faces.
Shrieks of terror.
Scared white faces
Dodging.
No cops in sight.
Squeal of brakes.
Mine.
Stop now or hit the damn car in front of me.
Nowhere to turn.
No way to get around.
Nissan 300-ZX mid intersection.
Lights change.
No one moves. Cars anyway.
People scrambling.
Woman screaming.
Dragged from car.
Help. Someone help me.
Power kick to the belly.
Grab her purse.
Rifle it.
Out of my car.
Running.
Hand on Firestar.
Two men and a woman on her.
People here and there on the sidewalk.
Looking.
Gaping.
Gawking.
No one helping.
Some cheering muggers on.

Stomp to the face.
Blood.
Glasses broken.
Moaning.
Blood.
Safety off.
No words.
Why bother.

Blam.

Blam.

Blam.

I could have shot them.
I fired over their heads.
Crowds scatter.
No cops in sight.
Three rounds off. Four to go.
Gun in right hand.
Woman in left.
Grab her license, credit cards. Keys.
Drag her back to my car.
Jam in reverse.
Bumper kiss car behind me.
Driver's startled.
Too scared to get out of his car.
Pushing him back. My tires slipping on the asphalt.
He jams it into reverse. Hits car behind him.
Everyone's trying to backup. Not a lot of room. Finally
enough for me to back up, ease car to make U turn.
Cars on other side of road. But not as bad as my
side.
Make the turn.
Got a ticket for pulling a U-ey once.

No ticket this time.
Woman coughs blood.
Rented seat. Rented rug of rented car. Bloody.
Jam it down Fairfax. Back the way I came.
Double park across street from Westside Hospital.
Pistol in belt.
Take woman with both hands.
Dodge traffic across Fairfax.
Honking at me. At my parked car.
Pull her inside hospital.
Nobody helps.
"We don't have an emergency doctor on duty. No emergency room," bitch at front desk says.
"This woman's dying."
Set her down on lobby couch.
Melodramatic. Only way to get action.
Still no response.
"Does she have insurance?"
Gun flies from belt.
Smells recently fired.
Bitch notices.
Safety still off.
Barrel jammed on receptionist's forehead.
"Best insurance in the world."
"I'I'll call a doctor."
Life during wartime.

◈ ◈ ◈

I left the woman at the hospital, a doctor looking at her. At the very least, he said, her nose was busted and she'd have to have her jaw wired. Some fun. Not only free TVs, free-for-all. I didn't hang around to tell them who I was. No need to get tied to the shooting at Fairfax and Wilshire, even if I didn't shoot anyone. Probably would have gotten off. Though you don't know these days. No need to hassle the paperwork. An

Alice In Wonderland World, where the good guys are the bad guys and the bad guys good.

I started thinking about Teddie. I felt numb. Pushed the guilt down inside, in a black hole where the rest of my guilt hid. Where the bile for my father lived. A seething reservoir inside me, waiting to explode.

I pushed down hard on the accelerator, heading farther west. There wasn't much traffic and no sign of cops. I could have gone ninety and gotten away with it.

The office was quiet. No messages. No mail. No nothing. Called Tom Bond at home. His wife said he was on duty. She was worried. I tried to calm her fears. Told her that he'd be all right. That it looked worse on TV.

I lied.

She said she'd have him call me if he called her.

I sat back in my ergonomically correct desk chair, feet on the desk. Which probably defeated the ergonomic design of the chair. Thought about Craylock and the Weasel. Teddie Matson and Pilar Cruz.

What was there to tie them all together? Both women had been in show biz. High profile targets. Even if Pilar hadn't quite made it, she had been seen. I sued someone once. Made it to *People's Court*. My Fifteen Minutes of Fame. Segment lasted all of ten minutes. People recognized me for weeks afterward. If Pilar was on a couple of commercials that aired constantly, she'd be easily recognizable, especially if someone were looking. Teddie was on a hit TV series. Millions of people all over the country would know her.

A thought hit me. What if Pilar's commercials were local? If they weren't national spots, I could narrow down the search geographically. Of course, that still didn't mean that her stalker was the same as Teddie's. It wasn't much. It was all I had.

Pulled the Firestar from my belt. Dropped the magazine and replaced it with a fresh, fully loaded one. I wouldn't have minded shooting those people, but I didn't need the paperwork. I also didn't want to be like Jack in that way. I would have felt justified in killing them, but there's still a part of you that smarts. It's never easy killing someone. Some people get used to it. Some have no conscience. Don't even have to get used to it. It's just another high.

I had brought up the box with Pilar's letters and skimmed through them. Nothing out of the ordinary. Fan mail. Puppy love sentiments. No threats. Nothing bordering on harassment. I was dying to compare notes with Teddie's fan letters. Then I might be able to make some comparisons that would be helpful. That would have to wait. I turned on the Call Forwarding on my phone so my calls would be routed to the house. Hit the stairs. Thinking:

I'd have to talk with Ramon and Anna Martinez. I wasn't looking forward to meeting them. I didn't think they'd appreciate being questioned by a white man. Especially now. But judging from some of Anna's personal correspondence with Pilar, I figured if anyone knew her whereabouts it was Anna. Their letters were deep, introspective. Intimate. Almost sexual. Ramon's notes were scribbled in a near-illegible hand. Talked of love and body parts. Of course, I didn't have Pilar's responses to them. Nor her responses to Anna. But it seemed to me that the real relationship here was not Ramon+Pilar, but Anna+Pilar. It was hard to tell if it had ever been sexually consummated. If it wasn't, I was sure it came close.

I wanted to find Pilar. Find Teddie's killer. Keep Craylock off Laurie's back.

I wanted penance. Needed it.

My first act of penance already completed: I didn't kill those scumbags when I could have and gotten away with it.

◈ ◈ ◈

Except for Baron's raucous greeting, my place was quiet when I got there. Smoke loomed in three directions. The sky was hazy. Gray. Dialed Martin Luther King Hospital. Tiny couldn't talk. The nurse said he was improving. He'd be able to talk in a day or two.

I wasn't home long when the doorbell rang. Who the hell could it be?

Rita was framed by the door. I was glad to see her. More glad than I showed. I invited her in. We collapsed into each other's arms.

CHAPTER 18

We didn't say anything. The sun was still high in the sky when we went to bed. Was it love or tension release? We glided in and out of each other in easy, smooth motions. Practiced motions. A thought shot through my mind: what was she doing here? Why had she come back? In the middle of a riot.

What was I doing here, making love – if that's what it was – to a black woman when blacks and whites were at war with each other? Were we like Teddie in her school play, Romeo and Juliet, Capulet and Montague?

Would we end up like Romeo and Juliet?

I put it out of my mind, concentrating instead on the moment. Her eyes, her lips, her skin.

Her eyes were heavy lidded. Sultry. Heat-simmered brown embers. What was she thinking? It didn't matter. We continued our cruise into the sea of *Terra Incognita*. Black heat. White heat. Until we were both spent.

My fingers gently drifted across her caramel-colored skin. Would I be making love to her if her skin was ebony? Black.

We lay wrapped in each other's arms, cradling each other tight. Holding strong against the storm raging outside. She my protection, me hers. k.d. lang singing her crystal clear voice out on the CD player, helping to muffle the outside world even more.

No riots.

No Teddie.

No Warren.

No Jack.

No Pilar.

No Laurie.

No father.

No black.

No white.

"What're you thinking?"

"I'm wondering what I'm doing here. Why I came back."

"I was wondering that too."

"Maybe it's best not to think about it," she said.

"Maybe it's best not to think about anything." I bit into her neck. She pulled away.

"I don't want to be an ostrich. I hardly know you. Hell is breaking out all over. But do I stay with my mother? Do I go to a friend's? Do I go home? No. I go to the house of a man I hardly know. A white man. Something's missing."

"You're being too analytical. Who was it who said 'don't be too profound in analyzing history, for often the causes are superficial.' Maybe you just like me."

She tried to stifle a laugh. Couldn't. "Maybe I do." This time she didn't pull away. We drew closer together, if that was possible. No kissing. No anything. Just holding each other tight.

"I like your house," she said, finally.

"It's solid."

"It's beautiful. Hardwood floors, real plaster walls. Spanish tile in the hall. Tile in the bathroom. Scrollwork along the ceiling." She knocked on the wall. "Solid? That's all you can say about it?"

"Hell, if it wasn't for my parents, I wouldn't have this house. Might even be living in a cardboard box or under a freeway offramp." I paused, stared at the walls: "This was their house."

She heard the guilt in my voice. "They're gone?"

I didn't respond. Looked away.

"I'm sorry," she said.

"Don't be. You didn't know them."

"Not very nice people, huh?"

I pulled back. Separated now by a sea of blue sheets. She sat up on one elbow, looking into my eyes.

"I guess I shouldn't be talking about that. But my father was no great shakes either. He left when I was fourteen. I was glad to see him go. Used to beat Warren to a pulp just for the fun of it. He was unhappy with his own life, his station in life – couldn't hold a job. Mom worked. Worked hard. But daddy couldn't cut it, so he took it out on poor Warren."

"Maybe that's where some of his anger comes from."

"He doesn't blame daddy."

"He blames whitey."

"Says that if the white man hadn't held us down none of it would've happened."

"Why don't you blame whitey?"

"Maybe I do." She looked at me intensely, the brown coals of her eyes challenging me.

"If you did you wouldn't be here."

There was a long silence, as if she was debating whether or not to come clean, to tell me something. Then: "What's the point of blaming anyone else? We each of us have to live our own lives. Be responsible for ourselves. No one else can be responsible for us. No one else gives a damn. I'm a black woman trying to make it in a white man's world. It's not easy. I've seen prejudice. So what should I do? Holler racist. KKK. Wait for a lynching?"

"What do you do?"

"The best damn job I can. Not because I'm black. Not because I'm trying to prove something. Because I'm me. And I have to do the best I can for me. No more. No less. And you know what?"

"What?"

"I always get by. Still, I suppose it's easier for you."

"Why, 'cause I'm white? You don't know anything about me. Nothing at all."

"Maybe more than you think."

"Nothing."

"Then why don't you tell me."

"You sit here spouting off how you don't care about this and that, about the KKK or racism and all. And then what do you come back with? 'It's easier for you.'"

"I shouldn't have said it. You're right and I'm sorry. I would like to know you better. Tell me something you never told anyone else."

It took me a while to respond. Took me a while to get the courage up, not just to say it, to admit it out loud: "I'm a fuckup," I said. "Excuse my language. No, don't excuse my language. It's what I am. Might as well call a sp–"

She laughed. So did I. We moved a little closer again. Not too close, but closer. Less ocean of blue between us.

"That's what I am, a fuckup. I've fucked up almost everything I've tried in my life."

"I've seen you. You're a hard working private detective."

"Not a very good one." I was thinking of Teddie more than anything. I didn't want to tell her. Couldn't.

"I see you working your cases – hard."

"I try."

"You make the mortgage on the house."

"Barely. Okay, I'm an okay private dick."

"You said 'almost,' you fucked up almost everything in your life."

"I didn't fuck up the Navy. In fact, I was damned good there."

"Why didn't you stay in?"

"My father. He thought I fucked up just by joining the service. Thought I could do better. Like him. Wanted me to be a businessman. But a nine-to-fiver wasn't for me."

"Your heart wasn't in it."

"Damn straight. I did spend some time after college working as an investigator for an insurance company. That's what gave me the background to become a P.I. But then I decided to go into the Navy."

"Why don't you go back to the Navy?"

"Too late now. I've lost the fire. I could never do what I was doing, at least I don't think so."

"And what was that?"

"SEAL Team. You know, join the Navy, see the world."

"Pretty heavy duty stuff. Does it help you in being a detective?"

"There's some crossover stuff and if there is any strongarming that needs getting done, I can do it."

"Before the Navy, did you have a goal?"

"*Razor's Edge*"

"What?"

"*The Razor's Edge*, I wanted to explore the world like Larry Darrell in *The Razor's Edge.*"

"Why didn't you ?"

"My dad thought it was a waste of time. I figured a good compromise was the Navy. Thought he'd think I was finally a man."

"Why'd you care so much about what he thought? Why are you rebelling so hard?"

"Nothing I ever did was right. Everything was my fault. Hell, I couldn't even go to school without a hassle. He wanted me to work for him. When I told him school was my job he beat the shit out of me." I could feel the veins in my neck sticking out, the blood rushing in my head. My tone got angrier. Louder. Couldn't control it. "But hell, he was never there when I needed him. He hated the fact that I collected butterflies."

"Can't go on blaming him forever."

There was a silence. I was thinking about the Navy. Finally said: "I liked the Navy. Did see a lot of the world. Saw a lot of shit too. I shouldda done my twenty."

"You can still see the world."

"It's not so easy. I've got the house now. Gotten used to creature comforts. I'm not twenty-one anymore."

"Who is? Then be the best damned detective you can be."

I didn't say anything. After several minutes of silence, I turned to her: "I'll tell you something I haven't told anyone, not even Jack." Another silence. Then: "My father's not dead. He's in a rest home. Alzheimers. I had to put him there two years ago." I paused, collecting myself. "I never visit him, never call. I just pay the bills."

She took me in her arms, holding me close to her breast, stroking my hair. It was comforting. Baron loped back and forth a couple feet away.

"I always hoped my father would die first. Didn't happen that way. Mom died in a car accident. Always hoped they'd get divorced. I'd lay in my bedroom and listen to them arguing at night. Bitch this and fuck that. Every bad word I knew I learned from him calling it to my mom. I'd pray they'd get divorced. They never did. And he laid the blame for everything that went wrong on me. I was the cause of all their troubles. Never took any responsibility for himself. Never even gave a thought that his temper, his perfectionism, his insecurity, might be the cause of it all. Had to blame someone else. Always. We never got along, my dad and I."

"He made you think you're a fuckup."

"What else could I believe? He was my dad."

"But that was a long time ago." She took my hand in hers. "You're not a fuckup, Duke. I know."

She pulled me closer yet, if that was possible. Didn't say anything, just let me know she was there. I made a promise to myself to be the best damned detective I could be. I made a stronger vow to get Teddie's killer, no matter what it took, including my own life.

CHAPTER 19

Rita didn't stay long. Just long enough. Soon after she left, I heard someone coming up my walk. Gun in belt, I headed outside. It was Sing, the mailman.

"Good morning, Mister Rogers," he said. Baron barked from inside the house, held back by my hand. Sing saw the gun in my waistband. His eyes narrowed, as if he was X-raying it to see if it was loaded.

"I didn't think the mail would be delivered today."

"Through sleet and snow and L.A. riot," he grinned. "Actually in some parts of city if they want mail they have go to post office. No delivery. We dedicated. Not *loco*," he said in Spanish-tinged Korean-pidgin English and laughed out loud.

"Multicultural humor," I said.

He handed me the mail, which had to be sniffed and approved by Baron. It was pretty thin. Not the usual lot of junk mail and other fun stuff. Mostly bills. I flipped through them as he walked to the next house to bring mail and mirth on a pretty mirthless day. There was one item that wasn't a bill. A plain white envelope. No return address. My address was neatly typed on it, correct down to the last zip plus four digits. I sliced it open as soon as I got inside with my downsized Ka-bar look-alike letter opener that Jack had given me. It didn't say much:

"Lay off. I know where you live. Let sleeping dogs lie. Or they will lie. You too."

That's all it said. It could have been from anyone. A former client, not all of whom were quite reputable? Someone I'd found for a client? My first thought was the Weasel. But how would he know where I lived? How would he know I was even after him? It wasn't exactly making the headlines. Next thought was Craylock. They were the two most recent cases. Neither was exactly a goody-two-shoes. I didn't give it much thought other than to tell myself I'd have a *chat* with Craylock one of these days. He hadn't been violent with Laurie yet. I doubted he'd get violent with me. And I just couldn't believe the Weasel could find me. Still, if the Weasel had found Teddie what was to say he couldn't find me?

The phone rang. I jumped half a foot into the air. Was it the riots, the threat letter? The days of rage? I didn't know. What I did know was that my nerves were on edge. A glass of straight Scotch would help that.

"Duke, Duke, Duke, Duke of Earl, Earl, Earl," the tired voice sang over the phone.

"Hey Tom when're you gonna get it right? It's Duke, Duke, Duke, Duke of Rogers, man."

Tommy tried hard to laugh. All that came out was a small choke.

"Having fun?" I said.

"Hey, the ads said the Sheriffs would be an adventure."

"Kinda like Disneyland?"

"For the young at heart. Too bad I ain't so young anymore. Jenny said you called, important."

"Could've waited till Disneyland closed. I'm on a stalker case. Couple of 'em actually. Wanted to see if you could run some stats for me."

"No problem. But you'll have to wait till the South Central Olympics're over. Computers are all tied up now and much as I'd like to help you and take some stalkers off the streets, it's low priority now."

Crack!

"What was that?" I said.

"Gunshot."

"I knew that. What's going on?"

"Gotta go. I'm at a CP, shouldn't even be on the phone. Talk to you in a couple days, if I don't get my ass shot off." He hung up. I lit out. Wasn't really sure where I was headed. Didn't have a plan. I could try to track down the Martinezes. Or I could bring Pilar's letters down to Mrs. Matson's and compare and contrast them. That's what I decided to do. The Martinezes would happen tomorrow. Maybe the riots would cool off by then. I knew the situation at the Matson's: unpleasant. But I could handle it. The Martinezes were an unknown. They would have to wait.

❖ ❖ ❖

Mrs. Matson didn't seem particularly glad to see me. She also wasn't particularly unglad. She sat me at the dining room table this time, with a glass of lemonade, and gave me the boxes of Teddie's correspondence, including the personal stuff. She hadn't seen Warren since the day before. I was just as glad about that. I had hoped that Rita might be there. She wasn't.

The ride down had been uneventful. Still, it seemed like all there was in the city anymore was smoke, sirens and some gunshots, but the police and National Guard were better organized now. It wasn't like it had been the first day of the riots.

I poured over the letters, first Pilar's box – it was smaller. Then Teddie's boxes. Anything that seemed similar to something in one of the letters to Pilar I put aside. After three or four hours, the double check pile was beginning to grow. There were about a dozen letters or cards in it. And I still had three other boxes of Teddie's to go through. My eyes were starting to blur. My temples ached. It was after curfew. I didn't think I'd have much trouble getting home. I'd tell the cops I was stuck somewhere, afraid to come out, and now that I had the chance I was heading home. There were a million things I could make up to tell them. I decided what the hell, I'll just stay the night, if Mrs. Matson would let me. I didn't ask her. I just kept working.

Lots of mash notes. Lots of hearts and flowers and "you're the one for me" stuff, from both men and women. A few gifts: some flowers, long dead, dried and rotted. Brittle to the touch and falling back to the earth, dust to dust style, when I did touch them. Most of the flowers were roses or carnations. But there were two with what looked like orchids, one for each woman. Could they be from the same guy? And was he a big spender? I put those cards aside.

Teddie's said: "Only being with you can put out the fire in my heart. Sparks fly whenever I see you."

Pilar's, attached to a Smokey the Bear teddy bear, said: "You'll need Smokey to put out the fire when the sparks start flying between us."

Close enough for me. The signatures on each were illegible. Neither had a return address or envelope. I had a friend who did forensic work for the city on occasion. I made a note to call her, stuck these two cards and orchids in my coat pocket.

Mrs. Matson, in a flowery robe now, poked her head in: "It's late. Would you like to curl up on the couch, Mr. Rogers?"

"Maybe in a while. I think I'd like to keep working."

"I hope you find something."

"Me too."

She walked off. "Me too." She couldn't know how much. It was my atonement. Atonement for being a lousy detective. For not having my heart in my job. Not doing what I wanted to do. For not living my own life.

A few minutes later the back door flew open. Warren, gritty with sweat and ash, charged in. He looked at me from the corner of his eye as he barged past, off to some other part of the house. Not a word. Not a grunt. No kind of acknowledgement for the white devil in his dining room.

I kept at my work until I fell asleep around 3:00 a.m. I had tried to stay awake as I didn't want Warren sneaking up on me. He didn't. When I awoke again around seven, my gun was still on me. The letters hadn't been touched. It was only four hours' sleep. It felt wonderful.

Mrs. Matson was already in the kitchen. Glorious smells permeated the house. The smells of food that we're not supposed to eat anymore – real food: bacon, eggs, hash browns, nice and greasy. Love is the food that you put on the table. I wondered why it hadn't worked for Warren. She came into the dining room: "Breakfast's almost ready," she said.

I was more than ready. Famished. Couldn't remember the last time I had eaten. She put plates and glasses out on the breakfast room table. I set the silverware. Three places. Mrs. Matson, Warren and me. I squeezed fresh oranges in an electric juicer as she finished up the bacon, eggs and spuds. The bouquet of smells made my stomach growl something fierce. Mrs. Matson smiled at me. I smiled back sheepishly.

Everything was ready and on the table, enough to feed an army of private detectives.

"Come and get it," Mrs. Matson shouted.

Footsteps echoed throughout the house. Warren padded towards us. Mrs. Matson and I were already seated. Waiting for him before we dug in. He bounded into the room, stopping in his tracks. The expression on his face went from satisfaction to malice. His mother looked at him: "Warren, please," imploringly.

He shoved his hand deep in a pocket. Instinctively, I reached for the gun in my belt. Didn't pull it out, just let my hand rest on it. Warren's eyes smoldered with hate. For me. For himself? He charged through the room, out the back door. A thick silence hung in the air. Then:

"I'm sorry, Mrs. Matson. I'll go. He'll come back when he sees me leave." I started to get up. She laid a firm hand on my arm.

"This is not how we treat guests, Mr. Rogers. Especially guests who are trying to help us. Please sit down and enjoy your breakfast. It isn't often that I go to all this trouble. If he wants to eat he'll come back."

We ate in silence except for the sounds of silverware clinking on china plates.

"It's delicious." It was. The best breakfast I'd had in years. Filling and tasty. Not in that order.

"Thank you." It was just something for her to say. I'm sure she meant it, but her mind was in another place. I cleared the table, rinsed the dishes, put them in the dishwasher. Soft sobbing came from the next room. When it subsided, I went in.

"I'll pack everything up now and leave in a few minutes."

"You don't have to." Her eyes said otherwise. She appreciated what I was doing in trying to find her daughter's killer. Of course, she didn't know the whole truth and nothing but. She also would be just as glad to have me out of there and get her son back, if it wasn't too late. Not because of me, but because of where life had taken him.

I wondered about Warren. Where was he coming from? Why all the anger directed at me? Just a symbol of the white man? Or was there more? I hoped to see him on my way out.

Didn't take long to pack up. I took several of Teddie's letters, put everything else back the way I'd found them. Packed up Pilar's letters and took those. Mrs. Matson walked me out to my rental car.

"I won't come back. I held up a handful of Teddie's letters. I'll either mail them back or send them with Rita."

Her eyes smiled. "I thought you and Rita might be seeing each other. She didn't say. But I figured–"

I was almost ready to ask her permission. What was the point? Rita could make her own decisions. So could I.

"I'm sorry for any trouble I've caused."

"Isn't you. He's been goin' bad for a long time. Nothin' I can do about it." She put her arms around me. "If I don't see you again, I thank you from my heart for what you're doing trying to find my daughter's killer."

What could I say? Guilt stabbed at my gut. I felt nauseous. Hoped I could hold breakfast down. As I drove out toward the main drag, I scanned for Warren. No sign. I pulled into an alley and vomited my guts out. It wasn't breakfast. It was my life.

I didn't know what the Weasel had wanted the info for. Didn't even know who Teddie Matson was when he'd come to me. What was I to do? But I was also stupid. Hadn't even made the Weasel fill out the standard contract forms 'cause it seemed like such an easy cash case – no forms, no IRS report, the better to pay the mortgage or the plumber with.

My dad was right. I was a fuckup. Never took things seriously. I was paying for it now. I wasn't the only one. That was the killer.

◈ ◈ ◈

Pockets of rioting flared and exploded on the way home. It wasn't confined to South Central as the Watts riots of '65 had been. These fires engulfed large parts of the city. Ugly. Very ugly.

I waited in a long line of cars at one of the few open gas stations for a fill up. The radio blared riot news. Everyone was blaming everyone else. Mayor Bradley blamed Police Chief Gates, who blamed Bradley. The city council blamed both of them. No one took responsibility.

I was glad to pull into my driveway. Something was wrong. I could sense it. Baron's familiar greeting wasn't there. I threw it in park; jumped out before it stopped moving.

The backyard gate was locked from the inside. I jumped it. No time for the latch. No Baron. No barking. No nothing.

Heart beating double time.
Firestar in hand.
Safety off.
Why am I acting this way?
Paranoid?
Crazy?
Check Baron's favorite spots.
Behind the garage.
Nothing.
Run on the other side of the house.
Nothing.
Smell something funny.
Burnt almonds.
Silence.
Deafening, deadening silence.
Check the trashcans.
There, behind the cans.
A paw.
Bloody.

Jesus!
Baron.
Dead.
Mangled.
Slit across the throat.
Ice cream.
Smells like burnt almonds.
Cyanide.
Must've been one hell of a lot to smell up the yard.
Melted ice cream on Baron's jaw.
Cyanide laced ice cream.
Blood on his paws.
His?
His killer's?
Goddamn it.
Goddamn you God.
Do you exist?
Are you the Devil?
Evil?
Why?
Damn.
Damn.
Damn.
A note stuck into Baron's hide with a nail.

"'Let sleeping dogs lie – who wants to rouse 'em?'
—David Copperfield / C. Dickens."

CHAPTER 20

Checked out the garage first. No sign of the killer. I covered Baron with a tarp from the garage. Gun in hand, I went in the backdoor. Service porch – nothing. Kitchen. No sign he'd been there. Breakfast room, living room, den, bedrooms. Nothing. Bathrooms. *Nada.* Didn't look like he'd come into the house. I was glad of that.

He was toying with me. Teasing me. The question was, who was he? Was it a *he*? Craylock – I wouldn't put it past him. Besides, the Weasel wouldn't know the Dickens quote. Or would he? I'd underestimated him once. Shouldn't do it again.

House secure, I went to talk with the neighbors.

"Didn't see a thing," Mrs. Fraley said. "I wouldn't even be home if not for the *troubles.*" If Mrs. Fraley didn't see anything, I doubted any of the other neighbors would have. She knew everything about everyone in the neighborhood. Probably knew I was shacking up with Rita. It was there in her eyes, if not on her tongue. Even when she wasn't home she had antennae out that gave her the lowdown on everyone's lives. Hers was the first house north of mine. After checking with her, I went to the Timmerman's on the south. They hadn't seen or heard anything either. Neither had anyone else.

Three fourths of the neighborhood were home due to the riots and no one had seen or heard a thing. Maybe it was the Invisible Man.

I picked up the ice cream container with a Kleenex, only touching one small part of the rim and slipped it into a plastic bag. I put it in the outside freezer, careful how I opened the door so all the bottles I was saving on top of it wouldn't topple. Grabbed a shovel from the garage and dug a hole behind it for Baron. Wrapped in the tarp, I laid him in the hole and stood over it for a few moments of silence. My eyes teared – something that didn't happen often. I loved that dog and he loved me, in a way no person ever had. I didn't know if anyone ever would. Now I had two missions: find Teddie's killer, and find Baron's.

Burying him in the yard probably wasn't legal. But I knew the response I'd get from any city authorities – can't come out. The riots. I tried a couple of vets' offices. Closed. The riots. What else could I do? I wasn't about to let him rot behind the garage until sanity returned.

I went back in the house, grabbed the gin-laced lemonade from the fridge. I needed a drink and it was the handiest thing. I picked up the phone. Dialed. It rang and rang. I was just about to hang up. Then:

"Lab."

"Yeah, hello," I said, polishing off a lacey lemonade. "Is Mary Kopeck there?"

"Not in today."

"Is she home?"

"She's out in the field."

"Today?" I didn't mean to sound surprised. It just came out that way.

"She's dedicated."

"Can you tell me where she is? I need to talk to her."

"Who is this? Is this official business?"

"It's Duke Rogers, I'm a–"

"Duke Rogers, yeah, I remember her talking about you. I guess it'd be okay. You know that last major turn before Coldwater turns down into the valley?"

"Yeah."

"There's a little arroyo on the west side of Coldwater. That's where she is."

"Thanks, I know the place."

Grabbed my keys, headed for the door. Near it, on the floor, was a chewed green tennis ball. Baron's favorite chew toy. I was about to pass it by, head out the door. Instead, I bent down. Picked it up. It was still moist from his chewing. I didn't throw it out. Set it on the hall table. I hadn't cried since I was eleven years old – since I stopped collecting butterflies. I bent my head and sobbed for the second time in an hour.

❖ ❖ ❖

Traffic was light. Not a lot of people venturing out. It took me about twenty minutes to get there. Cars were parked up and down Coldwater where cars didn't normally park. People sifted dirt in screened boxes. Others scooped at it with spoons or soft brushes. A uniformed cop stopped me.

"Are you part of the forensic team?"

"I'm here to see Mary Kopeck."

"That doesn't answer my question." He looked nervous. Itchy. Hoping for some action. Hey, the action was somewhere else today. I was the only one he'd get to have fun with. Before I could respond, Mary saw me. Saw my distress. She let me wriggle a moment longer, then came over, half eaten sandwich in hand.

"It's okay, officer. He's got big feet, but I don't think he'll mess anything up." Mary's face was covered with soot and grime, the badge of her profession. Her long brown hair was pulled into a bun on top of her head, a couple wisps dangling on each side, and buried in a funny looking green Robin Hood hat.

"Very funny," I said, as she led me to the site she was working.

"Wood rats built a nest out of twigs, leaves and bits of human bone." She took a bite of her sandwich. Crunched it gleefully. "Looks like the bums, er, excuse me, the homeless individuals that lived here had dinner one night – feasting on one of their own." She dug dirt from her fingernails. They were medium length, black top and bottom. Almost looked in fashion. When I'd first met her I asked her why she didn't keep her nails shorter. "Got to be able to pick up those bone fragments," she had said.

She showed me the charred bones and badly decomposed body of a man, flesh ripped from his arms and thighs. She turned him over for me to get a better view.

"They would have felt at home with the Donner Party."

"Passionate society we're living in. Legacy of the Sixties," she said, taking another bite of her sandwich. "No one's responsible for anything. There are no moral laws. Everything's relative."

She must have seen the look in my eyes.

"I'm sorry. I get on my soapbox every once in a while. I see too much." She sat down, so did I. She offered me a sandwich out of a cooler.

"No thanks. How can you eat with him staring up at you?"

"You get used to it. Hell, I don't even wash my hands."

I supposed if I'd had to I could do it too. But I wasn't out in the bush. Didn't need to. And I wasn't that hungry.

"What brings you out here, Duke? Slumming?"

"Someone killed my dog. Poisoned, I think."

"Baron. No. He was the greatest dog. He–"

"I–"

"I'm sorry. You must be in a lot of pain."

"Enough."

"Remember though that life goes on."

I winced.

"I know it's a corny cliché. But people talk in clichés. Keeps their lives normal." She put the sandwich down, put her arm around me. "You want me to take a look at him."

"I buried him. There was ice cream on his mouth. A half eaten container on the ground near him."

"You think that held the poison?"

"What else? Wasn't my brand of ice cream. I thought maybe you could come look at the container. I didn't bring it with me. Thought it would melt and maybe change composition." I handed her the piece of paper with the sleeping dogs message. She studied it.

"Looks like it came off a laser printer. Probably a Panasonic – the kind a lot of libraries use. But it's hard to tell here. Mind if I hang onto it."

"Go ahead."

"There's also another couple notes maybe you can look at. Another case – I think."

"Sure, I can look 'em over."

I searched my pockets. Realized I didn't bring Teddie's and Pilar's notes. "I don't have them with me." My heart started thudding harder. I could feel the blood rush through my veins. In my eagerness to get to Mary I hadn't thought to bring the evidence. I'd fucked up again.

"I can drop by after I'm done here, look at the ice cream and the notes. Sometime this evening."

I took the garage key off my ring. "If I'm not home, the container's in the outside freezer. In the garage."

"Where'll you be, out bracing the bad guy no doubt."

"No doubt. Except I don't know who the bad guy is."

I thanked her and started heading back to the road.

"I'm sorry, Duke, really sorry," her voice trailed off after me.

◈ ◈ ◈

Craylock's black Beamer wasn't in the driveway. I pulled around the corner. Walked back to his house and nonchalantly down the driveway, past a security company's sign. Alarm system. My Navy training would help here. I'd brought a set of tools from the car. It was easy to jimmy the lock on the alarm box. The system looked pretty rudimentary. As long as it wasn't a pulse system that would send a signal to the alarm company if the phone line was cut it wouldn't be a problem. It didn't appear to be that kind. He didn't want to spring for the cost. Sweat beaded on my forehead as I played with wires. Snip-snip. A done deal.

Getting inside was a cinch. I had the seen the kitchen before. Nothing new to report. Made my way through the house. Quiet. I could hear my own breathing. The blood rushing in my ears.

The living room was a sight. Photos of Laurie everywhere. Huge blowups. Some framed. Some poster sized, unframed. Laurie walking down the aisle of a market. Laurie getting into her car in the morning. Laurie sunbathing in her backyard.

Boxes of negligees from Neiman Marcus. Dresses from Robinson's. His and Hers T-shirts: Gary Loves Laurie. Laurie Loves Gary. Future gifts.

Laurie.

Laurie.

Laurie.

A shrine to Laurie Hoffman.

A frilly quill pen sat in a holder on a blotter on an antique desk in the corner. On phony parchment paper, he'd written, calligraphy style, the lyrics to *Got to Get You into My Life*, an old Beatles love song. He was in love all right. Also crazy.

Looking at his paean to Laurie made me sick. Angry. I hoped he wouldn't come home now. I didn't know what I'd do. I knew what I was capable of. I thought about turning him into the cops, but I knew they wouldn't do anything – couldn't, until Craylock made his move. And then it would be too late. It's a great system we've got.

I gently tossed the whole house, making sure to put everything back as I'd found it and keeping an ear out for a car pulling into the driveway. A thought dawned on me. I checked the freezer. No ice cream of any kind. Looked around the house for poisons. No cyanide. No insecticides that used the stuff. Didn't mean anything. He could be clever enough to hide the stuff.

One bathroom had been turned into a darkroom. Pictures of Laurie hung to dry. I pulled them down. Ripped them up. I didn't care anymore about covering my trail. I tossed the darkroom harder than I had the rest of the house. Put a match to the negatives and let them burn down to my fingers. Then tossed them on the floor. Watching all that fire glazed my eyes. Fixed me in a trance. It was cathartic. After a few seconds I stomped the fire out, but I was tempted to let it burn the whole damn house down.

The only camera I found was a Polaroid? He must have had his other camera with the telephoto lens with him. What did that mean? He was out shooting pictures of Laurie now? His true love. Thinking about it made me crazy. I wished he'd come home. Prayed for it.

My prayers were answered. A car drove up. I couldn't tell if it was in his driveway, next door or out on the street. When I heard the back door open, I knew.

Footsteps quickly padded through the house. He probably smelled smoke. I stepped behind the tub curtain in the darkroom-bathroom. The door popped open. A backhanded fist swung out from behind the curtain and busted him in the jaw. He dropped the small red fire extinguisher he'd brought to save his precious artworks. The blow jolted him back into the doorjamb. Son-of-a-bitch didn't know what hit him.

I jumped out of the tub, the shower curtain derailing around me. He tried swinging at me. It was hard for me to defend myself, wrapped in the curtain. His swings were weak. Ineffectual. He popped me in the jaw, a glancing hit. Hardly hurt. I came back at him, both fists flying. He didn't put up much of a defense. Kept falling back. Out the door, into the hall. Against the wall. I pummeled his belly. He gasped for air. Doubled over. I didn't stop. Grabbed his hair in my left hand, pulled him up. Kept pounding away. Blood trickled from his nose and the corners of his mouth.

I broke contact. He was almost smiling. I socked him in the mouth. He stopped smiling. I let him fall to the floor. He curled up, fetal-like. Got to his knees and vomited on the lush hall carpet. When he was done he sat back against the hall wall, knees to his chest. He was white. His eyes weren't focused. Hands were shaking. He was just how I wanted him: scared.

"How 'bout some dessert?" I said, yanking him down the hall, into the kitchen. Opened the freezer door as he fell to his knees. His unfocused eyes looked at me, questioning as best they could.

"What's your favorite brand of ice cream?" I landed a kick on the side of his head. He fell over. Righted himself.

"I, I don't eat ice cream. Too much cholesterol. I eat yogurt."

"What brand?"

"Dannielle's Proprietary."

That wasn't the brand of the ice cream. Not that it mattered anyway.

"Y'you're crazy." His voice shook. Hands trembled. Fear radiated out of him. I pulled him up. Walked him to the living room, pushed him down on an uncomfortable looking chair.

"You like pets?"

He wrinkled his brow? What was this crazy man talking about now? I walked up and down his bookshelves, looking for Dickens. Or even Bartlett's.

"Pets? You like 'em?"

"Sure. They're fine."

"Dogs?"

"Yeah."

"How come you don't have one?"

"No one to take care of it. I'm out a lot. Working."

"Taking pictures of people who don't want their pictures taken. When they don't know you're doing it." I swept my hand across the room. Went to a wall. Pulled a framed 8X10 of Laurie off, crashed it to the ground. Shattering glass. He jerked back in the ugly chair.

"Whadda you want? I haven't hurt anyone."

"Leave Laurie alone." I crashed another picture to the ground.

"I'll call the cops."

"No you won't." I picked up the camera with the foot long telephoto lens on it that he'd left on the desk when he came home and smelled the fire. There was a 50mm lens in a case. I switched it with the telephoto. Snapped pictures of the room. Proof, if the cops ever asked. When the roll of film was finished, I rewound it, put it in my pocket.

"Leave Laurie alone." I slapped him across the cheek. "She's not interested in you."

"Okay. Okay." He covered his face with his hands, cowering back in the chair.

"Have you ever been arrested?"

"No."

"Tell me the truth. It's easy enough for me to find out."

"No, goddamnit. No."

"How long have you been stalking? Is Laurie your first?" Jeez, it sounded like a first date. First kiss. First lay. First stalk. Society was crumbling around me. And Nero fiddled on.

I grabbed his collar. Shook him.

"No, she's not the first one."

"How many others?"

"I'I don't know. Two. Three." He paused. Took a deep breath. "Women like me. I can't help it. They like it when I shower them with affection. It's just part of their act, playing hard to get, to pretend like they don't want it."

"When was the first one?"

"About four years ago."

"What made you do it?"

He looked at me like he didn't know what I was talking about. Do what? You could see it in his eyes.

"What makes you do it? Why do you hound these women? What about the first one?"

"Hound them?" His hands covered his face. Rubbed his temples. His eyes were red. Teary. A revelation hit him: "I'I don't know. She didn't really like me I guess. I wanted her to so bad I made it up. I believed it. It didn't seem made up to me."

"What happened?"

"She moved away."

"'Cause of you?"

"Yes, I think so." His voice shook. Reality breakthrough. The truth was hard to take.

"Why? Why do you do it?"

"I don't know." He gulped air. "I guess 'cause no one likes me." His whole face seemed to drop when he said it. Shattered. Reality infused with his dream world. He didn't like the reality.

"You know any other stalkers?"

He laughed. "What, do you think we have a society? Stalkers Anonymous?" His laughter was uncontrollable. I shoved a picture of Pilar Cruz in his face. He wiped his eyes.

"You know her?"

"Never seen her."

"Her?" I put a picture of Teddie down for him to look at. He picked it up. Held it close. Recognition crossed his eyes.

"I, I've seen her before. Movies. TV. Can't remember." He held it closer. Pulled a pair of glasses from his pocket. Looked at it again. "Didn't she get–"

"Yeah."

"Shit. I don't know anything about it."

I believed him. He was scared enough at this point to tell the truth.

"Stay away from Laurie."

"Yeah."

"And don't harass anyone else either." I headed for the door.

He was muttering behind me: "It's not stalking. It's–"

I was too far out of range to hear what he said.

The drive home was uneventful, cruise control smooth, except for a thought that kept roiling my mind: Was I any better than the rioters? I also used force to get what I wanted. I figured mine was for a better cause. I was trying to help someone. A couple of people. The looters just wanted free candy. They may have had some legit grievances. Looting wasn't the way. Was bracing Craylock? I don't think he would have talked otherwise.

CHAPTER 21

T he answering machine light flashed. One message. Rita. I didn't call her back. Crashed on the living room sofa, strands of golden hour sun beaming in through the Levelors. It was quiet. Every part of me ached with exhaustion. I wasn't a SEAL anymore.

Dancing sunlight.
Candlelight dinners.
Dinner with Rita.
Dinner with Lou.
Breakfast with Mrs. Matson.
Ice cream.
Baron.
Mary.
Craylock.
Lou.
Jack.
Firefight.
Firestar.
Blam.
Blam.
Blam.
Warren.
Warren?
Weasel.
Cruise control smooth.
Cruz, Pilar.
Cruz, Ben.

Martinez, Ramon.
Martinez, Anna.
Teddy bears.
Teddie Matson.
Teddie.
Teddie.
Teddie.
Image shards crash my brain.
Dreaming.
The good life is just a dream away.

◈ ◈ ◈

Door slamming. Startled awake. Grabbed the Star off the couch. Walked noiselessly to the back of the house. Press against the walls, peek out windows. Room to room, ready to fire. No one. Nothing. Unlocked the backdoor, drove it open with a foot. Charged out. Aim left. Aim right.
Noise.
Straight arm the gun at the noise.
Trigger.
Squeeze.
Shit.
Heart stop.
Lay off.
Mary came out of the garage holding a crinkled bag. Seeing the pistol aimed at her gut wiped the smile off her face – fast. I'd forgotten about her, or thought she'd already come and gone.

"It's only me. Friend. Not foe. The wind slammed the garage door shut." Her voice was cheery. Her eyes were scared. I lowered the gun. Some people have been known to pull a trigger unintentionally in a moment of crisis from the tension in their finger. I was relieved I wasn't one of them.

"I heard a noise. I'm a little jumpy."

"Who isn't?" She lowered the sack, revealing a chrome-plated .32 automatic aimed at my heart. I wondered if fearful eyes betrayed my cheery voice, as she slipped the gun into the black leather purse that hung on her shoulder.

"I'm pretty sure it's cyanide," she said, opening the bag for me to see the ice cream container. "But I'll run it to make sure. I'll also run the laser note you gave me. Don't think it'll be much help though."

"Why not?"

"There's a million laser printers in the naked city. How you gonna track one down? Sure, I can tell you the brand and model number most likely. But after that it's almost impossible to find whose it is. It's not like the old movies. Unless you have access to the machines and can compare them, there's no way."

We sat on a bright white wood-slat bench in the yard. Birds sang. I remember thinking about them singing, thinking it was corny. I liked it anyway.

"I don't have a lot of friends," I said. It just came out. I wasn't sure why.

"You know people all over."

"Close friends."

She was silent a moment. Then: "I know what you mean. People you can bare your soul to. People who, if you haven't seen or talked to them in years, you can pick up right where you left off." She put her hand on my knee. "People like Baron."

It was a silly thought, thinking of Baron as a person. It made perfect sense to me. Maybe that's why I kept Jack on as a friend, I thought. No pretenses there. No bullshit. He said what he thought. I said what I thought. No judging. Other people may think he's a bigot and worse. But he was a good friend. That's what counted. Same with Mary. I'd known her a long time. And we'd gone for long periods when we hadn't talked or seen each other. But we always drifted back together, our friendship undiminished by the time gap. And here she was now, doing me a favor, her hand on my knee. A good friend.

◈ ◈ ◈

In the heat of the moment with Mary, thinking about Baron and cyanide, I'd again forgotten to give her the notes to Teddie and Pilar. It was a stupid oversight, one that I hit myself for, but one that I wouldn't let stand long.

By now, the riots were officially over. You wouldn't know it by the troops on the street and the fights breaking out everywhere. And the looting that continued. And the name calling from politicos covering their fetid asses. It was such a nice L.A. day, I decided to go for a drive. To East L.A.

Over the river and through the dale to ganger's house we go. To Indian country. Another world. Signs in Spanish. Graffiti everywhere. The rental car rambled down the last street Pilar Cruz had written in her address book for Anna Martinez. Above it, her address had been crossed out and rewritten seven times. Took up a whole page in the book.

Some newer Toyotas and Nissans mixed in with plenty of faded yellow or shit brown or bright orange junkers, ancient Oldsmobiles, Chryslers, Fords, and more Toyotas and Nissans. I pulled up in front of an old stucco house. One story. Small. Locked the car, walked to the front door. Before I got there, someone popped out of the driveway.

"*Que quiere?*"

Someone else to deal with. On the one hand this was getting old, on the other I could understand people being wary of outsiders in their neighborhood. Mine was the same.

"Hi." My Spanish wasn't very good. I think he wanted to know what I was doing there. He wore a white tank top and lowrider pants. Had nervous hands, moving this way and that, stringy biceps flexing as he did. Coal colored eyes. Solid. Steely. No emotion in them. A raggedy black moustache adorned his upper lip. "I'm looking for Ramon and Anna Martinez."

"*Quien?*"

"Ramon and Anna Martinez?"

"*Ramon y Anna Martinez? No los conozco.*" He shrugged.

I thought he was giving me a line. Not so much from what he said, but how he said it. He was playing me. I wasn't in the mood to be played. I also knew better than to try anything. I was out of my turf. Couldn't speak Spanish. At least not well enough to talk to him. I needed something. Something I didn't have. I used what I did have:

"I'm looking for Pilar Cruz?"

His eyes showed nothing. They were as dead as the Dead Sea. I backed away from him. Headed for the front door. Rang the bell. A haggard Mexican woman opened the door.

"*Habla Ingles?*" My Spanish was rusty but I could get that much out.

"*Poquito.*"

"I'm looking for Pilar Cruz, or her friends Anna and Ramon Martinez."

The woman's dark eyes became liquid. Almost young. Before she could say anything the boy from the driveway stepped between her and me.

"*No Mama, Ramon sera enojado.*"

"*No me dices que hacer. Soy tu Madre.*"

"*Yo decire a Ramon que usted hable con este gringo. Le decire todo.*"

"*Ya vaya a decirle. Que mas puede hacerme?*"

I thought I understood the gist of it. Junior was threatening to tell Ramon if Mama blabbed. Mama didn't intimidate easily."

"Why," she said, pleading in her eyes, "why you want Ramon? *Policia?*"

"No, *no policia. Yo estoy* looking for Pilar Cruz. I thought Ramon could tell me where she is."

"What do you want with Pilar?"

I could understand her reluctance. If things went down the way I figured Pilar might have had a stalker. To her family I might look like another one. I showed her my PI's license, told her I was looking into Teddie Matson's murder. She was quiet a few moments, then finally spoke.

"Pilar." The liquid in her eyes spilled over, running down her cheeks. You can fill a pool only so high, then one ice cube and it's over the edge. My guess was that the old lady – Ramon and Anna's mother? – had been holding a lot in. Wanted to talk to someone. She was clearly afraid of her younger son, who stood menacingly in the background, flashing gang signs with his hands to no one.

"*Ramon es un muchacho bueno, pero* he, how do you say, gets off on the wrong foot. He comes home only when he wants. Not when his mother wishes to see him."

"What about Anna?"

"I have not seen her since Pilar has left."

"Are they together."

"I do not know."

"*Callase Mama.*"

She shoved him aside with a strong forearm. He didn't stand aside long.

"I'm not after Ramon or Anna. I want to find Pilar Cruz. To help her."

"*Gringos* don't help *Mejicanos. Bastardos,*" the kid said.

I understood that. I wanted to slug the kid. Jack would've slugged the kid, then told him to go back to Mexico if that's how he feels. He needed someone to discipline him. I figured his mother tried to no avail. Not her fault really. He needed a father. Of course, I'd had a father, and it wasn't a lot of fun growing up around him. There are no pat answers I guess.

"I've talked with Pilar's father, Ben. That's how I found you. He trusts me. He gave me Pilar's address book. He wants me to help. *Ayudar.*" I pulled it out of my pocket, showed it to her. She clutched it in her hands, then gently flipped through the pages, stopping at her daughter's name. Staring. Lost in a past that wouldn't come again, and a hoped-for future that wasn't ever going to come.

"Where can I find Ramon?"

"*No le dice nada, Mama, o yo dicere a Ramon.*"

"*Mira en que manera tu tratas a tu Mama. Sinverguenza. Si estuvimos en Mejico, no pudieres desgraciarme asi.*"

"*Mejico, Mejico. Si le quiere tanto, porque no le vuelve alli.*"

That stung Mrs. Martinez. She had probably come here for her kids, a better life for them, and this was her younger son's gratitude. She wasn't looking as old now. The lines around her eyes and mouth were softening. Even her hands appeared more supple. Thinking about the way things might have been, thinking about how it was when her kids were young and happy and carefree. Innocent. It was the power of memory. The power of love. Her own private fountain of youth. I had nothing to base this thesis on. It just seemed right.

She handed back the address book, looked squarely in my eyes: "Ramon goes *to una cantina, La Revolucion,* on Whittier Boulevard. He is there a lot."

"*Muchas Gracias.*"

"*Cuidado.* Be careful. Lots of bad people there."

I tipped my non-existent hat to her, retreated to my car to the sounds of yelling from her younger son. The front door closed, muffling the sounds.

◈ ◈ ◈

I drove by the bar. It was a nasty neighborhood. Rough. Dirty. Even the rats were afraid to come out at night. Not a *gringo* in sight. Not on the streets, not driving by in cars. Nowhere. What did they know that I didn't? I drove to a payphone, parked close and put my quarter in. Suspicious eyes followed me, from the gas station, from the street. I put on a look that I hoped said, don't mess with me.

"Jack."

"Yo, old buddy. Where are you? Sounds like you're calling from a sewer."

"I'm in East L.A."

"Didn't I say sewer?"

Whether or not one considers East L.A. a sewer, it was uncanny how Jack could sniff these things out.

"How'd you like to party this afternoon? I found a great bar."

"Not down there, I hope."

"Hell no. Pick you up in half an hour."

"Thirteen hundred. Check."

CHAPTER 22

P arty time," Jack said, gruffly. I didn't think he had believed me about the bar. But he was wearing dress slacks, a black silk shirt and snake skin cowboy boots. "I need somethin' to relieve the tension after the past few days-a this shit."

Beethoven's Ninth blasted from the CD player. The volume made my ear drums cringe. I felt sorry for his neighbors. Jack's apartment was microscopic, cramped – the iron lung he called it. One room with a kitchen and dining area off to one side, a small bathroom on the other. A Murphy bed, now folded away. Busts of Beethoven and Mozart on end tables. Posters of Dewey Weber, from the glory days of surfing, and Hobie boards, on the walls. A picture of the old Team on a small desk. In one corner, a six foot board and a mini, twin 38 SCUBA tanks and a weight belt. Stacks of books in the other corners. He read everything from trashy romance novels to Kafka to How-To books on just about anything. A small 9" television sat on the dining table, hooked up for cable TV.

Jack's kit bag sat on the dining table. "Let's go," I said, picking it up to toss to him. It was heavier than usual. I wasn't prepared for the weight and almost dropped it. "Jeez, what do you have in there, a cannon?"

Jack pulled out a Colt .45 Officer's model. Grinned at me.

"You never carry a piece, man."

"Nobody's gonna Reginald Denny me. They might get me, but I'll take a few of them with me on my way down. 'Sides, I hear hell ain't so bad. 'at's where all the fun people go." He said it with a straight face. No irony there. "Segue, man. Segue." He didn't want to talk about the gun. I tossed him the bag and we jammed out the door.

We pulled away from the curb. He took a cassette out of the kit bag. Stuck it in the player. *Peer Gynt: In the Hall of the Mountain King.* He cranked up the volume. We sat at a light between competing blasts of Nirvana and Ice T. Hell, it all melded together like an artillery barrage of sound. We won.

We headed downtown: The streets looked bombed out. Charred skeletons of buildings hulking over dead sidewalks. Ravaged. War torn. Was this really the U.S.A.?

"Hey, where is this great club?"

"Party time, Jack."

"Yeah, but if I knew it was gonna be this kinda party I wouldda worn a different shirt."

"Maybe you can take it off and ask some pretty young lady at ringside to hold it for you."

He snorted. "Will there be any pretty young ladies where we're going?"

"Doubt it."

"Well, you owe me bro. A hot time on the old town one night." He sounded pissed. I knew he wasn't serious. Jack loved a good fight. I was hoping we'd avoid one. But if it couldn't be helped I wanted him there.

I filled Jack in on the mission. We got lost east of downtown.

"Man, it was easier in the bush or in the sandbox than finding your way around these damned city streets."

I needed directions and the tank needed filling. Pulled into a gas station. Jack pumped while I fumbled with a map.

"How do you get to Whittier?" he asked the attendant after topping off the tank.

"No hablo Ingles."

As soon as I heard those words, I slid a touch lower in my seat. Didn't want to look in Jack's direction. Didn't have to. I knew what he looked like when he got this way – the veins in his neck sticking out. His mouth curling. Eyes narrow. Hands balling up into huge fists.

"Well, does anyone here *habla Ingles?*"

"No, no hablo Ingles."

A police black and white drove by.

"Then why don't all you tamale eaters go back to Mexico if you don't want to learn our culture? Our language."

I slunk deeper in the seat. Jack had a way of picking the wrong time and place for things.

He got back in the car, slammed the door, rolled up the window.

"Drive on, James."

The attendant was beating on the window. *"El dinero. El dinero."*

"You haven't paid?"

"They wouldn't give me directions."

"Maybe they really don't speak English."

"Don't gimme that shit. They speak-a da English." He rolled the window down a little. "I'll give you your money when you tell me how to get to Whittier Boulevard."

Jack was right. The attendant had miraculously learned English awfully fast, gave us the directions, and we were on our way.

◇ ◇ ◇

La Revolucion was a dingy place on the outside. Looked like an old industrial building, small machine shop or something. The bottom half of the stucco wall was painted a dark, though chipping, forest green. Top half was white, or used to be. Grime and dirt crept all the way up to the roof. Made you wonder how it got that high. A handful of men stood outside talking, playing dice and drinking. We parked a few doors down. Jack dumped the contents of the kit bag on the floor, swept them under the seat, all except for his credit card, drivers license holder and the .45, of course, which he put back in the kit and stuck under his arm. We walked back to the entrance. Several pairs of intense brown eyes followed us up the sidewalk.

The door was open, sort of. It was blocked by a large Mexican with a round face and rounder belly in a sweat-stained T-shirt. He grinned at us. Held a pool cue across his chest at port arms.

"Wha's he think he is?" Jack said softly. "The Master at Arms."

We stepped into the doorway. Round face took a short step forward. Pushed the cue out a couple inches.

"Stand aside," Jack said.

"You don't order us around down here."

"Nobody's ordering you around," I said. "We just want a couple-a beers."

"No beer in here. No liquor license."

"Don't give us a hard time."

"I ain't. I'm tryin' to help you. This building's been condemned. You could get hurt in there." He shrugged, squinting his face into a fake smile.

"We'll take our chances."

Jack shifted the kit bag from one hand to the other.

"Nice purse."

"Thanks. My boyfriend gave it to me," Jack minced.

The Mexican grinned deeper, baring pointed yellow teeth. He stepped aside. We walked in in front of him.

"You ain't the police," he said. "This guy dresses too good. Like a *vato*." Several others inside overheard and laughed. Seemed they spoke English.

The floor was covered with sawdust. The bar tin, dented. Dull yellow lights flickered across the ceiling. It was dark and yellow inside. Jaundiced.

"We're the hit of the party," Jack said, as we walked up to the bar, leaning in. Eyes followed us. Bodies too. It was hot in there. Sticky. No windows. No air conditioning. You could smell the sweat on the men who played pool and drank all day and all night.

The bartender ignored us. No one else was giving us that much space. Jack laid his kit bag on the counter.

"If you ain't the *policia*, who are you? And how brave you are, coming into the barrio alone? Two *gringos*."

"Two white bread boys," another Mexican said.

"This ain't like the movies. You ain't Eddie Murphy in a pussy redneck bar now."

"Speakin' of pussy." A short Mexican with a stubbly beard grabbed for Jack's kit bag. Jack caught him by the wrist. Twisted. There was a snapping sound. The man winced with pain.

"We're looking for someone," I said.

"This ain't the lost and found."

"Lost *Gringos*, over here."

"Lost Mexicans, this corner." They had a good time, partying and chugging beer.

Jack sat facing the rear. He could also see behind the bar. I sat with my back to him, scanning the front of the dive and the other half of the bar. They might come at us, but we'd see them coming.

"And jus' who might you be lookin' for?"

"Ramon Martinez."

"Man, you know how many Ramon Martinez's there are? Sort of like John Smith."

"Yeah, well this one has a sister named Anna."

"Another uncommon name."

"Look, we know he hangs here."

"Hangs. Cool talk. You been *hangin'* 'round the niggers again? That's how they talk, *hang. Gringo's* been *hangin'* with the niggers again."

"Whachu want this Ramon for? Beat 'im up? He rape your sister and you know no Mexican–"

"That's Mexican-American, ain't it?" Jack said.

"Yeah, man, no Mex-American can *hang* with a white bitch."

The circle around us grew tighter. A noose of people, hot sweaty bodies. The liquor on their breath stank.

"White man's law don't count in here."

"In a few years won't even count in Ca-li-forn-aye-a. We're takin' it back."

"Can't wait," Jack said.

"Well we don' know no Ramon Martinez, so you better go. You never know what a *borracho Mejicano* will do."

"We'll wait. We've got plenty of time."

"White men with no job. Didn't think it was possible."

Someone in the back of the crowd put their hands in their pockets. I heard a very soft click. The safety being shifted on a pistol?

Jack jumped off his bar stool. The Port Arms man we'd met in the doorway stepped in front of him. Jack swung his kit bag hard and straight, right into the man's jaw. That .45 hitting him must've stung. He fell back. Jack whipped the gun from the bag, letting the bag fly. The men surrounding us drew back. The man in the back who had slipped the safety off his pistol drew it –

too late. Jack charged through the crowd, which parted to let the crazy *gringo* with the gun go by. He jammed the .45 up to the other man's head, disarmed him. Backed to a side wall. I moved next to him, Firestar drawn. He handed me the man's .32, which I slipped in my belt, and held the man in front of him, the .45 still jammed into his temple.

"Now," Jack said, "We'll do a little talking. Or a little waiting. Whatever turns you on. *Comprende?*"

"Ramon Martinez," I said. No response. "My friend here is crazy. That's why I bring him along. He doesn't mind killing. He doesn't mind doing time. *Loco.*"

"And I don't like Mexicans. 'Specially Mexican-Americans." Jack spit. "You wanna be American, be American, goddamnit. Learn our language."

I nudged him: segue. Might not have been bad to have him spouting off. Might make them think he's crazy enough to do anything – and he would, if he thought he could get away with it. But I had lied. Jack could take anything, but jail time. He'd go crazy in stir. He would kill if he had to, but not here, not unless it was truly a matter of life or death. More than anything, he didn't want to land in jail. Small as the iron lung was, he could come and go as he pleased. Eat the slop he wanted and listen to his classical musical all day and all night. But he wouldn't be able to adjust to being penned in, taking orders from people he thought were morons. He didn't have trouble taking orders in the Navy because, with an exception or two, he thought the people there were sharp. When he bucked them and landed in the brig, he nearly tore his eyes out, until our lieutenant could get him free.

Jack shoved the .45 harder into the other man's temple.

A large man, not fat, but well toned, pushed through the crowd. "*Ya basta*. Ramon comes in here just about every day."

Murmurs of disapproval shot through the crowd.

"We'll wait," I said. "Nobody leaves."

I made sure the back door was locked. Everyone, including the unfriendly bartender, sat at tables that had now been pushed to the back of the room. Everyone but Jack and his hostage. They stood near the wall inside the front door. A spot where they couldn't be seen until someone had already entered. I sat on a bar stool on the other side of the door, scanning back and forth between our guests and the front door. I guess we could have been brought up on kidnapping charges had anyone complained. But we didn't want anyone getting out and warning Ramon off.

Any time anyone entered, they were escorted to the rear and sat to wait with the rest of us.

And that's what we did. We waited.

CHAPTER 23

We didn't have to wait long. About an hour. It seemed more like a decaying eternity in a condemned house, as we ushered in more guests, seating them in the back of the room.

"Hey, my *mamacita* wants me home," a long-haired man shouted. Jack and I didn't respond. Our eyes fixed on our designated cover spots. I was glad I didn't have to hold that heavy .45 up to someone's head for an hour.

The door opened. A wash of late afternoon sun poured in. I knew it was him as soon as he stood in the doorway. I knew it was him even in silhouette, from the sun bleeding around his shoulders and head. He held himself like he owned the place. His shoulders were powerful, bulging underneath a black short-sleeved skin tight shirt with rolled cuffs at the ends of the sleeves. Tats up and down his arms. If he knew something was wrong, he didn't let on. Stepped inside.

In the dim yellow light of the bar, I could see his face. The same as his younger brother. Harder looking, more creases. More coldness around the eyes, if that was possible. But the same. A little taller. A little more filled out. But the same raggedy black moustache. Acne scars. Another scar. Longer. A thin slit. Knife. Tough *hombre*.

He sauntered in, easy gait. Cool. Blase. I saw it before he cleared the vestibule. The rectangular butt of an automatic pistol outlined in his waistband under his shirt. Our guests in the back of the room were silent. Probably praying that Ramon would have come in blasting, two gun style, like in the old B westerns. No such luck.

He jerked his neck to his left, saw Jack holding his prisoner. Jerked the other way. His hand flew to the open bottom button of his shirt. Before he could pull the gun out, Jack yanked his prisoner in front of him, leveled the .45 at Ramon. The wheels were spinning in Ramon's head. Should he run for it? Shoot it out? Who were these *gringos* anyway? What did they want? He let his hand drop to his side. Walked deeper into the room. Turned around to face Jack and me.

"Looks like what we have here, *amigos*, is what might be called a Mexican standoff," he said with a trace of Mexican accent. Our guests cackled. Even Jack cracked a smile. My face was immobile. I didn't want to give anything away. "My brother said a couple-a *gringos* was lookin' for me. What'd I do, rape your sister?"

"You guys all learn the same script?"

"It's the script we're given, *amigo*."

I didn't like the way he said *amigo*. He sure as hell didn't mean it.

"Let's talk." I motioned him over to my end of the bar." The Firestar was in my lap. He didn't have a chance with his gun and he knew it.

"I don't have time for your *gringo* bullshit."

"You can leave. You can leave now. But aren't you just a little curious about what we're after?"

"Un poquito." He walked toward me at the bar. Didn't lean against it. Stood tall. Hands at his sides. "Somethin' about my sister."

"We're looking for Pilar Cruz. I thought maybe you or your sister could help us find her."

His eyes swam. Debating. "Man, why should I help you? White man been nothing but trouble for both of them."

"What do you mean?"

"Nothin', *amigo*. Nothin'. I'm just a dumb Mexican. Talk when I shouldn't." His voice wasn't very loud, as if he didn't want the others in the rear of the bar to hear what he was saying. I got the feeling the macho act was as much for them as for us. "What can you do for us, *amigo*?"

"I'm a private detective. I'm trying to find someone that might have known Pilar Cruz."

"How's that gonna help Pilar?"

"Same guy that might have been after my client might be after Pilar." I was beginning to believe it.

"Shit. No one's after Pilar."

"Then why is she hiding?"

The cold eyes warmed. Only for a flash. Long enough for me to know he believed what I was getting at.

"'s bullshit, man. 'Sides, I haven't seen Pilar for a couple-a years."

"What about Anna?"

"Don't see her neither."

"Look, if you're not gonna help us, fine. We'll leave."

I handed him a business card. He rolled it in fingers. "*Un hombre grande con un* bees-ness card." His audience laughed on cue. He glanced at the card. Tore it in half.

Jack and I headed to the door. He walked towards it, pulling the hostage with him. I backed to it. We weren't taking any chances. He shoved the hostage forward and we were out the door.

◈ ◈ ◈

"You sho' know how to give a party, bro."

"Stop bitching. You love it."

"Know I do."

"You really took off after that guy."

"I see a gun, I take defensive action."

The tires squealed as we pulled out. No one had followed us from the bar, but I didn't wait around to see what would happen next. I wondered what Ramon had thought of us. Did he expect it to be so simple? Did he expect us to brace him? We'd have had to brace the whole place. It wasn't part of the plan, but we'd had no choice when they came at us.

"Fuckin' Mexicans. Don't know what's good for 'em. You're tryin' to help 'em out. For what? They don't give a shit. You'll never hear from that sucker."

I felt I owed Jack dinner at the least. We went to El Coyote. He may not have liked the people. He loved the food.

◇ ◇ ◇

I made it home in one piece. When I'm out with Jack I never know if that'll be the case. I settled in. The phone felt cold to my touch. I was going to dial Rita. Changed my mind. I needed an evening alone. Time to think. Sort things out, about her. The case. My life. It rang. Mary.

"Duke, I was right. Panasonic Laser printer. Model KX-P4410. No good way to trace them. And the ice cream is definitely laced with cyanide."

"Easy to get?"

"Easy enough? Some rat poisons have it. Some–"

"I get the idea. I appreciate the fast work."

"Only for a friend."

We hung up. I thought about friends. When I first met her, I had considered Mary more of an acquaintance than a real friend. I was wrong. A friend was someone you confided your innermost secrets to. Someone who would accept you faults and all. Jack considered me his best friend. Sometimes I thought I was his only friend. I accepted him. I didn't like the way he thought about certain things or the way he acted. But I let him be himself. He repaid the favor by accepting me. On the rare occasions I confided in someone it was in him. And that wasn't that often. There was no one else. Did that make him my only friend? If so, what was I hiding from?

With that thought roiling around in my brain, I downed a jigger of Scotch and went to sleep.

I woke up the next morning refreshed. The first good night's sleep I'd had in days. The first thought on my mind was Rita. Could she be a good friend? Could I be one to her? Would our racial differences make a difference? Would they get in the way? So far we'd enjoyed a diverting relationship – mostly on the surface. It seemed we were both giving each other safe harbor during the storm. Telling each other, by our presence in bed together, that things weren't so bad. The country wasn't – and wouldn't be – falling apart. That the races could get along with each other some day. We proved it by our mere presence together. Or was it all just surface? Were we still really strangers? Was she just an *acquaintance*?

There were no answers. Not then. I hoped there would be. Soon. I liked her. She was different. And I was probably different to her. It would all have to come to a head. Or it might just fade away. I wouldn't hear from her. She wouldn't hear from me. It would be over. Nothing said. Nothing resolved. I didn't want it to end that way. Didn't want it to end at all. But I wondered if our differences were so great that without fires raging in the street to push us together, nothing else would.

I got up. Showered. Those thoughts kept circling in my head. I had an onion bagel for breakfast with some melted cheddar on it. It was enough to satisfy me. It was seven-thirty in the morning. The whole day lay ahead. I thought about going down to the ocean for a swim. Or laying on the raft in the pool. I sat in the living room and watched the sun streak in through the leaded glass window. Picked up the book I was reading, *L.A. Confidential* by James Ellroy. Couldn't concentrate.

It felt like I was getting closer. Closer to what? Was I trying to trick myself into believing I was onto something? Trying to avoid being the fuckup of my dad's mind? My mind. Ramon had told us nothing. I thought he knew, but if he wouldn't talk then what? The Jack method? Brace him? Beat the shit out of him? The Craylock method. Ply him with candy? Liquor? Drugs?

He knew where Pilar was. I was sure of that. She was hiding. But why? From who? I figured I'd contact him again – maybe – but it couldn't be at the bar. We – I – couldn't risk it again. We'd been lucky that first time. Might not work out so well again.

What was the connection between Pilar and Teddie? Teddie wasn't here to tell. Pilar was. Somewhere. I had to find her. Without her there were nothing but deadends.

They were both actresses. Both women of color. Was that it? The acting thing seemed more likely. Someone liked actresses. Thought they liked him back. Was rejected. That made sense. It was in the letters. Had to be. A beam of light spread across the floor, a favorite spot of Baron's. For a moment I saw him there, then nothing.

I spent the rest of the day scouring the letters again. The only connecting points were the two *sparks* notes.

Had both been attached to a teddy bear? I only had one bear. Should I do the movie thing and see where the teddy bear was made and sold? Track it that way. That seemed as useless as tracking down Panasonic laser printers.

Should I go back to the Perlman's? See if the old lady had forgotten something? See if there was anything I could glean in Teddie's apartment? What about going back to Mrs. Matson's? Not much there, I figured. Except maybe Rita. That would be worth a trip to South Central. What about Ben Cruz? No, he didn't know anything. Back to the motel where the Weasel had stayed. I could ask Tom Bond to look at mug books. I made a note to do that.

Something was missing. The keystone. What the hell was it? The only thing that made any sense was going back to Ramon. He wasn't the keystone. But he could tell me where to find it.

My eyes were glazed over. Too much reading. Too much thinking. The phone rang again.

CHAPTER 24

Laurie read the words from *Got to Get You into My Life* unemotionally, without any of the rhythm of the song. Things weren't going so well for her either – only I didn't know it at the time. Craylock had sent her a note with these Beatle lyrics. The same note I'd seen in his house.

He didn't give a damn. He'd get her into his life whether she wanted it or not.

"He sent me another note."

"Craylock?"

"Who else?"

I saw her point. It was a stupid question. I had a good excuse. Dazed and glazed. I didn't bother explaining.

"He doesn't take a hint," I said. The line was silent. I could hear breathing at the other end. Slight. Even.

"I thought about buying a gun, but they have a moratorium on gun sales." Her voice twisted like two braided power lines turning around each other, sparking off each other. She was pissed.

"I'll lend you one of mine."

"I don't know, I've never used a gun before, I'm scared."

"I can take you to a range. Teach you to shoot."

"I don't know. I guess I probably wouldn't be able to hit the target."

"All the more reason to learn."

"God, I don't believe this. Me, the person who can't stand to watch violence even in a Saturday morning cartoon, and here I am discussing guns with a detective." There was a sob at the other end of the line. "Do you believe how I'm talking? I used to be for gun control, till I realized through painful experience that it only controls the good guys. The bad guys'll always have their weapons."

"You oughta meet my friend Jack." I was serious too.

"I don't think I'm ready for another man right now. Jeez, what am I saying, *another* man. I don't have a man now. Just one who thinks he's mine and I'm his. This is a crazy world."

I picked her up and we drove out to the range in Tujunga. I liked it 'cause it was an outdoor range and I could fire my Ruger Mini 30 rifle there without a problem. We continued our conversation from earlier:

"And it's gonna get crazier." I caught myself sounding like Jack again.

"I think I know what you mean. I'm starting to see things differently. I used to think that the police would protect us and that if you lived in a nice neighborhood you'd be safe. Maybe that sounds naive, but I always felt pretty secure. I mean, to look at Craylock you'd never think he was capable of doing anyone harm. Now I guess I don't trust anyone."

She had planned to buy a short barreled .38 Colt revolver. Not a bad choice for someone unfamiliar with guns. A revolver is good since it's easier to use and clean than a semi-auto. .38's not a bad size bullet, especially if you go with a Plus-P. If she'd asked me, I would have recommended a .357 and maybe a little longer barrel. Short barrel's good for concealability, which she wanted. But less accurate. Everything's a tradeoff.

The flat hard pops of guns being fired startled her at first. She stood well back from the firing line. I didn't like the looks of some of the folks at the end of the range nearest the parking lot. Backwards baseball hats. Lowrider pants. Tats up and down their arms. Looked like bangers. They were firing everything imaginable. Including AKs. I wondered if they were registered. I thought I knew the answer. We moved upwind.

We started with the targets at twenty-five feet. "But," I told her, "you'll most likely be firing at even closer range." She nervously picked up my .38 Smith and Wesson. It was an older gun that had belonged to my dad. I showed her how to load the gun. She tentatively took it, tried for herself. Hefting it first. Then deliberately inserting each bullet. I'd teach her how to use speed-loaders later. She raised it to the target, hands shaking.

"Go ahead. Pull the trigger. Gently. Squeeze."

She fired the first shot. Winced at the kick. Backed up.

"Steady. Both hands now."

She went back to the firing line, capped off the other five shots. Jerked the gun wildly. I took it from her. Showed her how to hold it. How to position herself properly. She reloaded, fired six more times, shaking less with each shot.

"Now imagine that the target's Craylock. He's broken into your house. He's coming toward you."

She tensed the muscles of her face. Clenched her jaw. She fired. One. Two. Three. No bullseyes. Better than before. Four. Five. Six. Not bad. She looked at me. I nodded approval.

She reloaded, spun the cylinder like she'd seen in the movies. Giggled.

I let her run through a Firestar magazine. Four out of seven hit the target.

We played for about two hours. She got a little better. Not much. The biggest improvement came when we switched from bullseye targets to man-silhouette targets. She started hitting about seventy percent. She didn't want to try the Mini 30.

"After I get comfortable with a handgun I might try it," she said. "It's, it's so ugly."

"Looks are only skin deep."

I wanted to stop at Tommy's Hamburgers on the way home for something to eat. She wanted to get home.

"I'll loan you my .38 till the moratorium is over," I said as we pulled up to the curb in front of her house.

"I'd appreciate that." She started to get out of the car. "Why don't you come in? I'll fix you something to eat." Her voice was taut, a stringed instrument tuned too tight.

I wanted to get home, get back on the Teddie and Pilar letters or something. She sounded upset. I agreed to come in for a late lunch-early dinner.

The sun was still up. It was dark inside. All the curtains drawn, the blinds closed tight. A lonely shaft of golden hour sunlight slithered in here and there giving the room an eerie glow. Particles of dust floated on the slivers of light like so many tiny angels pirouetting along the vector.

She grilled hamburgers on the Char-glow. I made a salad. There wasn't much dialogue during the meal. We watched the sun set through the cracks in the blinds and with it her feelings of security and well being. As I rinsed dishes and put them in the dishwasher, I could see her pupils expanding with fear. The fear of the hunted animal. Night was falling. She was the prey. Craylock the hunter.

Dishes done, I reached for my windbreaker.

"Do you have to go?"

I knew what she was getting at. I didn't bite. Maybe I should have. I wasn't trying to make it hard for her. There were other things I wanted to be doing. Rationalizations floated through my head: if you help Laurie you can make amends for Teddie. Didn't work. Nothing would make amends for Teddie. Perhaps I could help avert another tragedy. But I couldn't be with her all the time.

"Maybe I should pay Craylock another visit on my way home."

"Can't you stay a while? We could rent a movie." Her voice was breathy. Desperate.

"If I stay a while, you'll ask me to stay a while longer."

"Won't you stay the night? I haven't slept in days. I'm not trying to blackmail you or make you feel guilty. I'll pay you for your time. I–"

"He hasn't done anything violent yet, probably won't."

"How do I know he won't? He's obsessed. I'm scared."

There wasn't really a choice. I agreed to stay the night. She would sleep on the floor in her bedroom on the far side of the bed from the window. I would sleep on the couch in the living room, weapons at the ready. There was already a pillow and blanket on the couch. She brought fresh ones. I thought of Rita and felt a twinge of guilt, but there was no real attraction between Laurie and me.

"It's awfully quiet in here," I said.

"The bell on the phone's turned off. Answering machine in my office picks it up."

We checked the machine. The tape had run out. Fear ate at her eyes, the corners of her mouth. Craylock's voice wasn't on the tape. Only music. Semi modern torch songs from the Beatles' *Love Songs* album. We knew who it was. It wasn't enough for the police and he obviously knew that.

"Is there a trap on your phone?"

"No."

"You might think about getting one."

"The phone company tells me I need to go to the police. The police tell me I need to talk to the phone company. Nobody wants to help."

"It's not easy, I know. But it can be done."

She said goodnight. Went to bed. I sat on the couch, thumbing through her magazines. Seems she subscribed to just about everything there was, from *Omni* to *Essence*, *Atlantic* to *Spy*. Lonely? One hand flipped pages. The other curled around the Firestar. The safety was on. Good thing. The way I was hugging that piece of metal with my fingers it might have exploded from the pressure. I hardly realized what I was doing, till I cut myself on the trigger guard, something I would have thought impossible. At that moment, I could have started a fire just by rubbing my two fingers together. I wanted Craylock. Wanted him bad. Bad enough to go outside the law? Bad enough to risk jail? Bad enough to live with myself after I'd done it?

I checked the bedroom. Laurie was curled up in a pile of blankets on the floor. Her breath came in short bursts. At least she was sleeping. I sat back on the living room couch, hoping Craylock would show. If I knew how to pray I would have prayed for his arrival. I wanted the son-of-a-bitch. I wanted an excuse to vent all the anger and rage I'd been storing up since the Weasel did his deed. Since my dad had done his deeds. I used her phone to check my answering machine. No messages. No Ramon. No Rita. The room was stifling, everything shut up as it was. I pulled the blinds up a few inches at each window, opened the windows. A gentle cross breeze made the room tolerable. I sat back on the couch, Firestar in hand, and drifted off to sleep in a few minutes. My senses were acute enough that I would have wakened at anyone tramping about outside the house. I slept through the night.

202 – Paul D. Marks

CHAPTER 25

L aurie would have preferred I stay with her the next day. It wasn't a horrible proposition. If I didn't have other things to do, I might have. Guilt and wanting to do penance had made me stay the night. I didn't think Craylock would come at her during the day. Roaches like him hide from the light. I could have been wrong. Nonetheless I couldn't stay with her twenty-four hours a day. I wasn't a bodyguard. Was this a rationalization? Justification for my leaving.

I went home, showered. Didn't know how I would spend the day. I felt Teddie slipping farther and farther away. Or was it Rita? I hadn't heard from her in a couple days. Of course, she hadn't heard from me either. Why? I put it out of my head.

The phone rang.

"Duke, Tommy here."

"I take it the South Central Olympics are over. You sound tired, man."

"Haven't slept in days. And I'm on duty again. At least the riot's over and things are settling down, sort of. Just don't believe what you see on the news. It's a hell of a lot worse out there. They're trying to make it like everything's back to normal. Ain't so. At least tonight I'll get to go home and sleep."

"Sweet dreams."

"Thanks, bud. I'm back at West Hollywood station. C'mon down. I'll look up the stuff you want."

I figured I was just about in my rental car before he hung up. West Hollywood station wasn't far from my house. Would take me ten or fifteen minutes to get there. Traffic was still light. Lots of people staying home behind locked doors.

The station was guarded more like a military installation than a sheriff's station that day. It was hell getting through the heightened security. When I finally did, Tommy could barely raise a smile.

"Glad to see you, bud," he said. Dark circles engulfed his eyes. His uniform looked like it'd been run over by a truck, not the usual crisp look. He pulled out several thick mug books, dumped them unceremoniously on a desk.

"Stalkers. Let me know when you're done with them and I'll get you some more."

I flipped through the dog-eared pages. Black faces. White faces. Brown and yellow faces. No discrimination here. No Weasel either. I wasn't really looking for Craylock, but I kept an eye out for him too. Didn't expect to find him. And didn't. Tommy came back.

"Hey, Tom, how 'bout we look up some stuff on the computer?"

"I shouldn't be doing this for a civilian."

"Aw shut up. You've been watching too many crummy TV shows."

He flicked a button on a keyboard. A computer monitor lit up. He punched some keys. "All right, whadda you want?"

"Check out a guy named Jim Talbot or James Talbot, J. Talbot. Even Talbot James." Hell, the Weasel might have been stupid enough to give me his real name or a variation of it. Several histories, even computerized photos, popped up. None looked like my Weasel.

"Doesn't mean he ain't done nothing. Only that he's not in our system. He local?"

"Yeah. Now anyway. I don't know his background."

"Well, he ain't done nothing in California."

On a whim, I also had him punch up Gary Craylock. He hit more keys. A simple message popped up: "Unknown."

"What a bust," I said.

"Now you know what we go through. Day in. Day out. Hell, even when we find the bastards our hands are tied. Gotta treat 'em real nice. Especially now."

He then ran Talbot and Craylock through the FBI computer. Nothing there either. A couple of ciphers.

"Late bloomers," Tom kidded. It was his way of saying sorry he couldn't be of more help. We promised to go out to dinner soon. He and his wife. Me and my flavor of the month.

Before leaving, I called Martin Luther King Hospital to check on Tiny. He was in X-ray a nurse told me. I left a message of well wishes.

Instead of heading home, I drove Laurel Canyon to Mulholland. Mulholland to Coldwater. The arroyo was crowded with the forensic crew. Same cop as the first time. He recognized me, passed me through. Mary was crawling on her hands and knees in a trough three feet deep. She was pawing at the dirt with a small mesh screen. She found the carcass of a rat. Picked it up in her gloved hands. Examined it. Bagged it. She looked up, a sparkle in her eyes, happy to see me. I gave her a hand up and helped her out of the trough.

She went to a red and white Igloo cooler, pulled a wrinkled brown paper bag out and two Orange Crushes. She handed me a drink. Opened the bag, handed me a sandwich as we headed to a low berm to sit on. She bit into her sandwich with ferocity. Washed it down with the sweet orange soda. I hesitated. Even though the sandwich had been in a plastic bag she touched it with her gloved hands.

"Go ahead. Eat the damn thing. It won't bite you."

"That's not what I'm afraid of."

"Look, I've been doing this how many years now. Haven't got sick once." She ripped another bite out of her sandwich.

"I don't want to take your lunch from you."

"Chicken."

It was a challenge no macho male could ignore. I clamped my teeth on the whole wheat bread, bit off a chunk. Roast beef with mayo. I hated mayo, rat flavored or not. Couldn't put the sandwich down though. She wouldn't believe me about the mayo being the only reason. She would lay it off to the rat. I forced the thing down quickly, washed it all down with Orange Crush and wished for something hot and spicy. The mayo left a pasty taste in my mouth.

"I don't have anything new to report," she said.

"I didn't think you would. Just wanted to run some things by you." I told her about looking for Teddie Matson's killer without the part about my involvement. Told her about Pilar Cruz, possible connections there. Then: "I brought the notes. Can you examine the handwriting?" She took them from me.

"I'm no handwriting expert. I could show them to someone though."

"Yeah."

"They do both say something about 'sparks.' Sparks flying and the like. That makes me think there's something connected with them. You could also call Teddie's family. Maybe they know if she got a teddy bear."

I had thought about calling them. And had avoided it. I didn't want to impose on Mrs. Matson again. I didn't want Warren to impose on me. And if Rita was there, what would I say to her?

We discussed Craylock. I told Mary about his house. His obsession with Beatle lyrics. His knuckling under and obsequiousness when confronted.

"I'd like to help you there, Duke. I'm no shrink though. It's so far out of my area that I don't have any ideas at all. I'd recommend that Ms. Hoffman move."

"She can't do that. Then he wins."

"Why does it always have to be a thing with winning and losing with you men?"

"That's not me talking. It's her."

Mary blushed. She tried not to show it. Couldn't help it. Dead air filled our corner of the arroyo. Finally, she said: "You're feeling guilty, aren't you?"

My head jerked in her direction. She'd hit a nerve. I hadn't told her my part in Teddie's death. What the hell was she talking about?

Fuckup. It raced through my head, swirling, insinuating into every corner.

Fuckup.
Fuckup.
Fuckup.
Did she know something?
Was she a mindreader?
Psychic?
Racing heart.
Sweaty palms.
Tense shoulders.
Constricting veins.
Short breath.
Don't let her see.
Don't let her know.
Don't tell her.
Don't give it away.
Fuckup, pal.

You are a fuckup.

"What're you talking about? What kind of guilt?"

"You think you should have stayed with Ms. Hoffman today?"

"Yeah, part of me does."

"Guilt."

"You can't protect her forever, Duke."

"I know. But she came to me for help. I shouldn't just leave her alone."

"She didn't hire you as a bodyguard. Even if she did, you can't do it twenty-four hours a day."

"I can try. The police sure as hell don't give a damn."

"You have the other case to worry about. Teddie."

"Yeah, Teddie."

"There was a peak in your voice."

"What're you talking about?"

"Sounds like you're taking this Teddie Matson to heart."

"It's just another case." But I knew it wasn't, and she probably figured that out too.

She stared hard into my face. I had to turn away. "Maybe it isn't Ms. Hoffman you're feeling guilty about?"

"Whadda you mean?"

"Maybe it's Teddie."

"You're crazy. I came on that case after she was–"

"Don't mind me. I like to play little puzzle games in my head. Do it all the time. That's how I put together pieces of rat turd and pieces of bone and come up with a murderer."

"Maybe you can market it as a board game."

"It is a good idea, isn't it?"

◈ ◈ ◈

I left Mary wondering if she had more pieces to my puzzle than I knew or wanted her to have. Driving into the city over Coldwater, my mind darted back and forth. I felt like I'd hit a brick wall. Didn't know where to go from here. Everything was turning into a dead end.

There was one message on the answering machine: "*Hola amigo.* Maybe we should talk. Don't try callin' me. An' don' come to the bar. You do and you'll never hear from me again. I'll catch you sooner or later." The caller didn't leave his name. It couldn't have been anyone but Ramon.

The cordless phone sat on the deck by the pool's edge as I floated into a Never Never Land of drowning dragonflies, woodrats and Weasels.

CHAPTER 26

Ramon had said not to come looking for him.
What else could I do? I headed to East L.A.
Drove by *La Revolucion*. Circled the block
several times. Parked across the street and watched the
place for hours. I couldn't just sit home waiting for a
phone call. When he didn't show at the bar, I drove by
his mother's house. No sign of him there either.

I was at wit's end. Didn't know where to turn.
Everywhere were deadends and metaphorical streets
with no outlets.

"Fuckup," I said to myself as I headed back to the
westside. "Fuckup. Fuckup," I shouted. The man in the
car next to mine rolled up his window. Did he think I
was yelling at him? Did he think I was crazy? Gonna
blow him away for breathing. A riot-ravaged citizen
who'd lost his marbles?

Start over. That's what I had to do. Retrace my steps.
Retrace Teddie's steps. Might she have known the
Weasel? Where would they have met? Did he simply
see her on TV? It was impossible. I slammed the
steering wheel, hard.

Driving the L.A. streets was like driving through
Beirut. Soldiers. Bombed out buildings. Debris
everywhere. Instead of turning off to head home or to
the office, I kept going to Fairfax. It was the only thing
I could think to do: start over.

I was in luck – but I certainly wasn't lucky. Mrs.
Perlman was home. Her husband wasn't. She was

wearing one of those old-lady dresses, a midnight blue number with tropical fish on it. Her blue-gray hair was nicely coiffed. Maybe she'd just come home from the beauty parlor. She was running a hose on the bushes in front of her apartment building.

"Hello, young man." She remembered me. That was a good sign.

"Hello, Mrs. Perlman."

"Did you find Teddie's killer yet?"

The *yet* cut through my heart like a knife.

"No. I'm still looking though."

"I thought you must be or you wouldn't be here. Unless you were coming to tell me that you had solved the case."

"I'm making some progress. Thought I'd check back with you. See if you remembered anything you hadn't told me. Or maybe you came across something in her apartment that her family left behind."

"I can't think of anything."

"You never saw the man that killed her around here before?"

"Not before that day."

"So you don't think they knew each other."

"Not to my knowledge. Anything's possible though. I'm not a nosy neighbor."

I had my doubts about that.

"We did come across some of her things. Put a box in the garage. Her family hasn't come for them yet."

"Mind if I see them?"

"No. Not at all." She turned the hose off, led me down the driveway. "Seems like the police aren't doing much. After the first couple days, they haven't even been back here."

"Why doesn't your husband want you to talk?"

"He's overprotective, the dear."

"Maybe he's afraid you'll get the credit for cracking the case." I grinned. She smiled back.

"I suppose he simply doesn't want us involved in all the hassles with the police, the media. You know what I mean. But I feel it's my civic duty. Not to mention a responsibility to Teddie."

The garage was dusty. Spider webs filled every corner. Mrs. Perlman pointed to a box on a shelf in the rear. I got it down. Started going through it.

The contents were ordinary. A book on acting. A small actress' makeup case. Some stationery. Nothing unusual. Nothing that gave me a hint in any direction. I put the contents back in the box.

"I could bring these to Mrs. Matson."

"Don't get me wrong, young man. I don't think that's a good idea though. It isn't that I don't trust you. I think that the Matson's should get it themselves. That way it's their responsibility in case anything—"

"I understand."

I put the box back on the shelf. We headed up the driveway.

"Thank you again, Mrs. Perlman."

"I'll let you know if I think of anything. I still have your number."

"Can I see her apartment?" Grasping at straws.

"I'm sorry. It's rented again. The new tenant has already moved in. There wasn't anything to see. It was empty. Completely empty."

Teddie's body was hardly cold in the ground and they'd already rented the place again. There might not have been anything to glean from seeing her apartment again. Didn't matter. I wanted to see it. Be there. To tell Teddie that I was sorry. Very sorry. And I wanted to visit Teddie's grave. It would have been cathartic for me. It wasn't going to happen. At least not now. Right now it was more important to find the Weasel.

I was about to open my car door: "Did Teddie have a teddy bear?"

"Oh, why yes. Of course. She had lots of teddy bears. Her fans were always sending them to her. Teddie – Teddy Bear – get it?"

Just what I needed to hear. "This one looked like Smokey the Bear."

"It doesn't ring a bell. I'm sorry."

So was I. I had hoped harder than hell that there'd be some new shred at Teddie's apartment. Nothing. "Fuckup," I thought as I drove away.

❖ ❖ ❖

I stopped at a gas station for a fill-up. I thought that these small foreign cars were supposed to get such good gas mileage. This one didn't seem to be. Or was I driving more than I thought I was?

I needed the fillup because I wasn't going home. I took another trip through Beirut, U.S.A., heading toward South Central. Toward Mrs. Matson. Warren. Rita.

I had told Mary that I didn't want to impose on Mrs. Matson. That wasn't the whole truth. I was afraid of seeing her. Thought she could read something in my face. Guilt. Responsibility for her daughter's death. There was another reason: Rita. I'd been avoiding her. I still wasn't sure why. For some reason, I hadn't returned her calls. Hadn't called her on my own. It kept gnawing at me. Why?

The Matson's neighborhood was peaceful. Quiet. Kids played on front lawns. I parked in front of Mrs. Matson's. Rang her bell. She answered the door, surprised to see me.

"Mr. Rogers."

Pleasantries were exchanged. She invited me in. We sat in the living room, sipping tea. The house was warm. Cozy. A friendly place to be. A strange feeling came over me. I felt safe there. At home. Like it was my home. Not the house I grew up in, but a place where I could run to escape the outside world and find myself in *Leave it to Beaver Land*. In the real world my father had been a manipulative bully. But I always had my room. The same room Rita had used as a guest room. The same room we had made love in.

The conversation with Mrs. Matson was trivial. Surface. A little awkward. She finally looked me in the eye: "Did you think of something else? Something you might want to look at. Talk about?"

"I don't know."

A spiritless silence filled the room. The air hung heavy. The walls closed in on me. Mrs. Matson got up from her chair. Came and sat next to me on the sofa. She put her hand on my forearm.

"We appreciate what you're trying to do."

"I'm not doing it very well."

"You can only do your best. If you're doing that, there is no more."

Was I doing my best? I thought I was. But I kept running into blind alleys and dead-ends. I was a fuckup. My dad had been right.

Right now, Ramon was the only plausible lead I had. And that was probably a dead-end too.

"I'm doing the best I can. Problem is it isn't good enough."

"You're following your leads. Talking to people."

"Yes."

"What else is there to do?"

Noises in another part of the house. Someone padding around. Warren? Rita?

I didn't want to whine and complain. She'd been through enough. "Did Teddie have a teddy bear?"

"Oh yes, many."

"That fans sent her? One that looks like Smokey the Bear."

"I can't recall it. She got so many stuffed animals and other gifts, she used to give them away to the local hospitals."

The light in my eyes went out. Cold.

Mrs. Matson continued: "She might have had some things at her apartment that I never saw. Or she might have kept something like that, a special one."

"What about the things Warren and Tiny brought back from the apartment? Anything in there?"

"To be honest with you, I haven't had the heart to go through all of her things yet. In the boxes I have gone through there were no teddy bears."

There was more shuffling in the back of the house.

"Do you think Warren would talk to me?"

"I don't think so. Please don't take it personally."

No, don't take it personally. He probably treats all white men the same.

"What about looking through the boxes?"

"I'm afraid now is not a good time."

I figured I shouldn't take that personally either. Warren, guardian of the boxes, Guardian of Teddie, was home. Not a good time to look into them. I thanked Mrs. Matson for the tea. Headed out to my car.

Guess who was waiting for me curbside.

"Whyn't you leave my mother alone? Chill, man."

"I'm not bothering you. If she wants to talk to me that's her business. You hear everything or only the good parts?"

"She-it. There waddn't no good parts." He flashed a toothy smile. "Why you gotta be comin' back to my hood all the time? Can't we get no peace from the likes-a you?"

"Free country. Come to my hood sometime. We'll talk." I shoved a business card in his hand.

"I come to your hood, I get busted. Man don't like me in yo' neigh-bo'-hood. Guess it ain't such a free country at that."

"All depends how you see it. Rita doesn't have a problem."

"Rita, she-it."

"Tiny either."

"Fuckin' Oreo, man."

I walked around to the driver's side of my rental. "Talking to you is a waste of time. You wanna help me find your sister's killer, give me a call sometime. You don't wanna help. That's okay too."

◈ ◈ ◈

On the way home, I stopped at a 7-Eleven, bought some magazines, swung by Martin Luther King hospital. Tiny's throat was still swollen, but he could talk a little now. And he wasn't gasping for air.

"Hey, man, wha's happenin'?" Tiny jerked his hand up for a high five. I slapped his palm. Held up the magazines for him to see. "Don't you know niggahs can't read."

"Guess I was misinformed."

"Or maybe you figured I could just look at the pictures."

"Yeah, that's right." I slapped the magazines on his bed. "You're looking pretty good. What're you doing in bed on a nice day like this?"

"Man, it's the nurses. They won't lemme leave. Just love ol' Tiny."

"When are you getting out?"

"Get my parole tomorrow. From what I hear my business is still standing."

"There's a few of 'em."

"Not many. Crazy business all this. "He pointed up to the TV. "Man, I didn't even have to watch it on the tube. All I had to do was look outside my window."

"How's the food?"

Tiny looked at me. Unsmiling. The corners of his mouth and eyes started to bend. He began laughing. Hard. Harder. "It ain't soul food, that's for sure."

◈ ◈ ◈

When I got home, there was another message from Ramon on the machine. "Fuckup," I shouted, pissed at missing the call again, slamming the machine into the wall.

CHAPTER 27

There's always a scene in B westerns where the cowboys or the cavalry are trekking through a craggy ravine or the desert flatlands, a ridge of mountains in the background. It's hot. Dusty. And silent. One tyro always says something like, "Sure is quiet out there. Indians must be miles away." The grizzled old scout comes back with: "Too quiet." He scans the horizon. Sure enough, there's a horde of Indians on the move. Or looking down on the troop from the ridge above. That's how I felt. After picking up the pieces of the answering machine, I sat on the living room sofa. It was too quiet. Much too quiet. None of the usual neighborhood noises. I sat for at least ten minutes. Not a sound. Not the breathing of the wind or the tinkling of windchimes. No music from down the street. No traffic noise. Utter silence. It was eerie. Otherworldly.

Someone was watching, breathing down my neck. I checked the perimeter of the house. Secure. The grounds. Same. It was making me crazy. It felt like *I* was being stalked.

Ribbons of sun bled in through the windows. I thought about Baron. He had been a great companion and friend. I'd raised him from a pup. He had wandered up to my door, cold, hungry. His coat was mangy. I took him in. We adopted each other. I took him to the vet. Took care of him. He also took care of me. The feeling I had now was the same empty feeling I'd had when I discovered Baron's body.

I felt the presence of someone else. I walked the house back and forth, checking every room. Every closet and window. The only sound was my shoes squeaking on the hardwood floors.

I patrolled the yard again, looking in and under bushes, behind everything. In the garage. Even inside the incinerator. Nothing. I was alone. But it didn't feel that way.

◈ ◈ ◈

Deidre Ireland – could it possibly be her real name? – was one of the biggest TV producers in Hollywood. You could tell that by her office – huge. Separate sitting and work areas. Mahogany walls. Plush carpet. Three TVs, four VCRs. I wondered if any were from the recent street sale. My appointment had been at 11:00 a.m.. She was there. Didn't allow me entry till almost noon. If it had been for anything other than learning about Teddie I would have split long ago or I would have barged into her inner sanctum, telling her what a hypocrite I thought she was. But then this was Deidre Ireland. Big TV producer – produced both of Teddie's shows, *Holier Than Thou* and *Day Timers*. Major contributor to the Cause of the Month Club. Major union backer, except on her own set, where she busted the union, kicked them out and hired scabs.

She pursed her thin lips, swept back her limp brown hair and stared at me across the great divide of her table. "Mr. Rogers, as I told you on the phone, I'm not sure I can really offer anything on your investigation."

"Just a few questions."

She sighed loudly. I wanted to pick up the Emmy on her desk. Crash it through her plate glass window. Not only for her hypocritical politics, but for the lousy TV shows she foisted on the public. Remembering what Rita had said, I wanted to ask her if her kids went to public or private schools. I bit my tongue, literally.

"Did Teddie have a fan club?"

"Yes. Most of my stars do."

Her stars. Her property. Another possession like a new Beamer or cellular phone.

"Do you know if there were any fans, in or out of the club, that were, shall we say, getting overly friendly? Overly familiar?"

"I really don't know of anything myself. Perhaps Ralph Clauson, our head of security might know something."

"Had Teddie ever complained about receiving any threatening mail or phone calls?"

"Isn't that the same question as before? You need a good rewrite man."

"You don't seem very interested in helping solve this case."

"Of course, I'm interested." She stood. I stayed put. "But I'm very busy. I think Ralph would be a better bet for you."

I was out of the office after only a couple minutes. My chat with Ralph Clauson didn't last long either and netted the same results.

◈ ◈ ◈

Jack's bike was parked in Laurie's driveway. I had called him earlier to see if he wanted to make a few bucks bodyguarding her at night. He was leaning against the wall, fiddling with an unlit cigarette. Jack had smoked in the Navy. Quit the day he exchanged a uniform for mufti. It was a rare occasion he toyed with a cigarette in his fingers. I hadn't seen him do it for months.

"Hey, Dukie."

"Gonna take up smoking again?"

"One-a these days I just might."

"Tobacco companies'll be glad. Let 'em know. Maybe you can be a poster boy."

He did his Adonis pose for me.

"Uptight about the gig?"

"It ain't the battle or firefight makes me nervous. You know that. It's the waiting. You said you was up most-a the night. Just listening. That's what I hate. The waiting."

"I know what you mean."

"Makes me nervous." He rolled the cigarette between his thumb and forefinger until it tore open, shreds of tobacco plummeting to the ground. He tossed the cigarette, what was left of it, on the ground, crushing it under his heavy black motorcycle boot. Took his kit bag and sleeping bag from the back of the bike. Went to the front of the house, knocked. It didn't take Laurie long to answer.

"Laurie Hoffman, Jack Riggs."

He put out his hand for her to shake. Hers was on delayed action. Her eyes were wide, unfocused. Staring. I should have prepared her for Jack's appearance. I had thought it might scare her off. I was having second thoughts. She finally managed to push her arm away from her body and shook Jack's hand.

"Don't judge a book by its cover."

"Yeah, I'm really a teddy bear inside," Jack said.

Laurie invited us in. We sat in the living room. She and I went over the history of her being stalked. Jack nodded politely, as if he were bored. He probably was.

"Don't worry," I said, "His bite's as bad as his bark."

"And *his* bite's bigger than his bark," he said referring to me. Laurie tried not to laugh. Couldn't help it. I was relieved. The ice was finally broken.

Laurie told us about her latest encounters with Craylock: "He keeps calling me at work, pretending to be a client. Then he won't let me off the phone and if I hang up he calls right back. The receptionist doesn't want to bother with him so she passes him onto me. The boss said if I don't get my personal life in order I won't get a promotion I'm up for. That I've worked hard for." Laurie's eyes danced with fear.

Jack set about unloading his kit bag. Toothbrush, hairbrush, razor sharp Ka-bar knife. Colt .45. 9mm Beretta backup gun. He was ready. Laurie reached for her purse, pulled out the .38 I had loaned her. Jack dived for the deck, rolling, coming up with the .45 aimed point blank at Laurie's mid-section.

"Whoa, boy. A little fast on the trigger."

"See a gun, take defensive action."

The fear returned to Laurie's eyes. Would she be safe with this madman for even one night? I made excuses to leave. She walked me to my car.

"Are you sure you can't stay? Cost isn't a problem."

"I know. I'm sorry, I'm working this other case day and night. It's not fair to you. Jack's a good man. Don't let his looks fool you. He's a little crude on the outside, but he's okay."

"It's not the looks that—"

"He didn't fire at you. He knew what he was doing."

"Yes, but he seems a little—"

"—Insane? If he's insane, so am I. Don't worry."

She looked like she wanted to say something. Her lips curled into talk-mode, then retreated. Again.

"Say it."

"I, I don't even know *you* that well."

"So you don't know who you can trust? Me? Jack?"

She nodded.

"But you know who you can't trust: Craylock. And I'm telling you, the cure – Jack – isn't as bad as the disease – Craylock. If you don't trust him, or me, say the word, he'll leave with me now. And we're outta your life. Or tell him later. He'll leave."

"I guess I'm just not very trusting right now. Because of what's happened."

"I understand."

"I guess I need to learn to fend for myself. Stand on my own two feet."

"You're learning. People aren't born tough."

"I'm going to do this even if it kills me."

"We won't let that happen."

She thanked me.

I drove to Mary's apartment in Santa Monica. The sun was sinking over the horizon. It reminded me of the giant ball that's dropped every New Years in New York. There were no noisemakers or confetti for this descending ball.

The streets hadn't yet come back to their full capacity. There was traffic. Not as much as usual. I still had the feeling I was being followed. I changed lanes. No cars behind me made a move. I continued down Santa Monica Boulevard, toward the beach. The feeling didn't leave. I told myself it was nerves, stress, anxiety. All those good things that people buy paperbacks by doctors and quacks to cure. I changed lanes again. No one made a move. I turned down 26th Street. Several cars followed suit. If I pulled over to the curb, the tail, if there was one, would suspect I knew I was being tailed. I didn't want him to know that. I kept on 26th. Turned right on Washington, left on Princeton. A couple cars followed down Washington. No one turned on Princeton after me. I pulled up in front of Mary's apartment building, parked and waited. After five minutes, with no one suspicious to take my attention, I went up to the front door, rang the buzzer. Mary buzzed me in.

The building was modest. One of those cheap '50s stucco jobs. Of course, the name wasn't so modest: *Le Grand Villa*. The apartment was comfortably, though cheaply furnished. Mary was saving for a house. No sense throwing money away on rent.

She favored prints of classic paintings. Everyone was there, Rembrandt, DaVinci, Gainsborough. She offered me something to drink. I declined and sat at the dining table.

"I showed the notes to my friend, the handwriting expert." She continued on through a merry melange of her history with this guy. I didn't care. I was trying to be polite. My fingers were dancing on my thighs. She finally came to the part that I wanted to hear. "Anyway, he says they're both from the same hand?"

"One hundred percent?" My heart raced. This was the first real breakthrough I had on the case. Something to tie them together. Teddie and Pilar. A definite connection.

"Nothing's a hundred percent," she said. "He said there's a ninety-nine percent probability they're by the same hand."

"Close enough."

She put the two notes on the table side by side. "Notice the way he makes the loops on g's, y's and the like. And the way he crosses his t's, dots his i's. Also, the same slope of the letters. They fall at the same angle. It's very close."

Silence filled the room. She looked at me: "Are you still with me?"

"Yeah. There's a connection now. You proved it. So the Weasel knew them both, or if not knew them, knew of them."

"But there isn't really a connection yet."

"No?"

"You don't know if these notes are from the Weasel."

"I've got something with his writing on it. A piece of paper he dropped in the hallway of Teddie Matson's apartment building."

"Then you'll know for sure."

"I'll still be nowhere. Okay, so I have him tied to the two actresses. What then? It doesn't help me find him."

"Talk to their families."

"Easier said than done. Much easier. They're stonewalling me. Even the ones that talk don't tell all."

"They don't know you."

"It's not that. They're hiding something. I have no idea what."

"It's a start."

"Yeah. Hey, what about that old movie trick of trying to figure out where the paper came from, tracing it that way."

"Unless it's a very unusual specimen that's a waste of time. And I don't think it's that unusual."

"I had to ask. I'm grasping for straws at this point. It does give me a direction to head."

We made small talk for a few more minutes. Jack used to bug me about my friendship with Mary. Why hadn't we clicked? We'd met on a blind date. We went to Yamashiro's, overlooking the city. Then drove up the coast. With anyone else it would have been a very romantic evening. With Mary it was a course in forensics. Checking the sushi for traces of heavy metals. Worrying about the mercury in the ocean. We never even kissed good night. A week later she called me about a little research she needed for a case she was working. We decided we actually did have something in common, even if it wasn't in the romance department. After that we became fast friends. Mary's one of the two people I trust completely. Jack is the other.

Heading out to my car, I scanned the street. It was dark. A street lamp was out at the north end of the block making it even harder to see. Nothing out of the ordinary. No one sitting in a car, waiting. Stalking.

I drove off down the road. I had to find Pilar. Had to find out what the connection was. I was too wired to go home. I could go to the office or get a bite to eat. Wasn't hungry. I wanted news. I needed news. I jammed the pedal to the floor. Burned rubber, heading east on Olympic. Heading back to Beirut.

There were less cars on the road now. I could count them all. I still couldn't see anyone in particular. But I still had the eerie feeling that I was being followed.

CHAPTER 28

L*a Revolucion* was jumping. People in and out. Mostly men. A few women. Whores from their appearance. Ramon would more likely be here than at home. It was dark. I hung low in my front seat, just over the dash. Enough to see who was coming and going. Popular hangout, for everyone but Ramon. Unless he'd gone in before I got there. No way could I check out the bar myself. After the last visit, my company wouldn't be welcome. And I had no backup.

California law says you have to stop serving liquor at 2:00 am. Maybe they did. They sure didn't close the doors. People kept on coming. Still no Ramon. When the sun crested the sooty building across the street, I decided it was time to go home, get some sleep. At that hour, the drive was quiet. No rush hour traffic yet. A few cars here and there. Nothing out of the ordinary. And still I felt a pair of eyes on my shoulders. If I turned right, they turned right. If I slowed, they slowed.

Paranoid visions.

Monsters in the rearview.

Jam on brakes.

Shrill howl.

Brakes squealing.

Lay rubber.

Skid marks.

Hand on Firestar.

Cursing drivers.

Slamming brakes.

Fingers flying.
Flipping off.
Swerve around me.
No guns pointed.
Lucky me.
Accident avoided.
Lucky me.
Suspicious persons.
Everyone.
No one.
Sign of the Weasel?
Nowhere to be found.
Craylock?
No shiny new beamers.
Not down here.

❖ ❖ ❖

By the time I got home, my eyelids were held up by perseverance and muscles that were locked in place. Sugar plum fairies danced on the lids, closing them tighter. Tighter. Park the car. Auto pilot to the house. The bedroom. Crash. Sweet dreams, sweet prince.

❖ ❖ ❖

Ocean waves swim over me.
Schools of fish brush my shin.
Depleted bubbles rise to the surface.
The direction I should be heading.
No.
Nitrogen narcosis.
Diver's disease.
Loss of orientation.
Swim down when you mean to swim up.
Deeper.
Deeper.
Into the abyss.
Dark chasm.

Gaping open.
Bidding: enter,
Sweet prince.
Enter.
Never to return from here again.
Oxygen tank spent.
Muscles exhausted.
Drift.
Drift
Into the darkness.
Where light doesn't penetrate.
Where men fear to tread.
Dark waters.
Cold.
Angry.
Surround you,
Sweet prince.
Suck you down.
Papier mache Neptunes fire spears at you.
Swim for the surface.
Exhaling all the way.
Don't get punished with the bends.
Drop your weight belt.
Clear your mask.
Pop your ears.
Save yourself.
Shoot to the surface.
Exhale.
Exhale.

◈ ◈ ◈

In the Navy I never got tired. Wasn't allowed to be tired. The stress had served me well. I knew how to carry off long operations. This was different.

The ocean had permeated my thoughts on the drive home. Another world. With its own inhabitants. Its own set of laws. An escape. I was always at home in the water, from the time I was a baby. Could swim before I could walk. Fish out of water. Yet when I dove into a deep sleep after the all night stakeout, the ocean of my dreams sucked me in. Under. Couldn't see. Couldn't breathe. Couldn't find the surface. I'd swim up, but I was really swimming down. That had never happened before. Not even in a dream.

The unexamined life may not be worth living, and the unexamined dream may not be worth dreaming. No way was I going to analyze that dream. Not now.

Dropping weight belts.

Nitrogen narcosis.

Papier mache Neptunes.

What a paranoid dream. I was glad to be up.

Paper. I had to find the note the Weasel had scribbled. Compare the handwriting. Shower. Shave. A quickly devoured onion bagel. Daylight streaming in the windows. Nothing unusual. Yet still the feeling. Eyes watching. Was I a puppet on a string being worked by an unseen puppeteer?

No time for that BS now. Where was that damn paper, if I had it at all? Home? The office? My car? Still at Tiny's. The car would be the last place to look. Might not still be a car. Might be an empty charbroiled hulk.

Had I saved the paper?

Last I remembered seeing it was in my car right after Mrs. Perlman had given it to me. Damn car again.

Where had I gone after the Perlman's? The William Tell Motel. If I left it there it was long gone. Did I bring it to my office? Home?

And why wasn't the damn phone ringing? Where was Ramon? Did he have a spy in the sky letting him know when I wasn't home so he could only call then? It was getting to me. The whole case was getting to me.

I tore through the drawers in the kitchen where I sometimes put things when I got lazy. No paper. Began working my way through the rest of the house. In a hurry. I wasn't putting things back. By the time I was finished, it looked like a hurricane had ripped through the house. Make it easy for whoever's spying on me. Everything out in plain sight, including me.

"Come and get me, you bastard," I shouted. "I owe you a little payback for Baron." I shook my head to clear it. Continued through the house. Damn paper wasn't anywhere. I was about to head for the office when I thought I should look in my clothes. Might be in a pocket somewhere.

What was I wearing that day? Couldn't remember. I hadn't sent any clothes to the laundry or done any laundry myself in several days – too busy working the case. That gave me hope.

Jackets. Shirts. Pants.

Tear 'em inside out.

Nothing.

Laundry hamper.

Zilch.

Damn.

Car.

I raced out to the driveway. Jerked open the rental car's door. My windbreaker sat on the front seat. I turned the pockets inside out. Hard candy wrappers. An old piece of paper from the spiral notebook I carry. Paperclip. Shriveled piece of paper. Unfold it carefully. Smooth it out. Eureka!

The notes to Pilar and Teddie were in a large envelope I had with me. I spread them on the hood of the car next to the Weasel's scribbled note. Examined them for several minutes. The letters that looped below the line looked the same. T's and i's crossed and dotted the same. To my untrained eyes it was a match. Mary and her friend could confirm it later.

My heart did somersaults. The case was closing. Things were coming together. Finally. It was a good feeling. It lasted about ten seconds. Until thoughts of Baron flashed my mind. The joy turned to anger, which turned to determination. I'd get the S.O.B. I still wasn't sure if the Weasel or Craylock or someone else had killed Baron. Short of the two of them, there were no major suspects. Possibles: Warren. Ramon. Someone I'd found for a previous client. Someone who hadn't wanted to be found.

I had an unlisted home phone number and address. It wouldn't have been easy for them to find me. But then it shouldn't have been easy for the Weasel to find Teddie Matson. Anything was easy if you knew how to do it, or someone who could do it for you.

There was always the possibility that some maniac had done Baron. That was the least likely possibility. A maniac doesn't go around with cyanide. He would have cut the dog's throat or ripped his eyeballs out with his bare hands. Maniacs were at the low end of the totem pole.

The phone rang. I gathered up the papers, ran inside. Ramon. It had to be Ramon.

"Hello, Duke. This is Lou."

CHAPTER 29

My heart dropped. Almost stopped. Lou could only want one thing.

"Time's up."

"I need a few more days."

"It's always a few more days with you, Duke."

"A couple days. I'm getting close."

"I'm getting uncomfortable. The police should know what's going on."

"Lou, I could lose my license."

"And I could lose my job. You're not getting anywhere."

"I am. It hasn't been easy, but I'm finally making some progress. Don't cut me off now. The police'll always be there."

"The trail'll be cold."

"The stuff I give them will warm it up for them, if it gets to that point." I thought about telling her that I was being stalked now. Get some sympathy. If it were true, I might have said something. Without proof, there was no point. Lying wasn't my forte. Silence. She was softening.

"I don't know why I let you talk me into these things."

"Because I take you to El Coyote."

"That's as good a reason as any. I'll give you a few more days, but I really am getting nervous. The cops are getting nowhere. They might have information you don't. Don't you have a friend on the force?"

"Yeah, but he's been kinda busy lately." My voice trailed off.

"Well, good luck."

"I'll need it."

More silence. "I thought you were getting hot."

"I am, but I ain't there yet. Can always use luck."

We said our goodbyes. I felt as if I'd been reprieved from a jail sentence. Time to get moving.

Should I hire an answering service? They could keep Ramon on the line while they beeped me. Sounded like a good idea. The Yellow Pages were full of them. Eenie meenie miney moe, Larry, Shemp and Curly Joe. I needed one that could take my MasterCard number over the phone, set me up right away. Found it, Diane's Dial. Cute. They'd have me set up within the next couple of hours and I could stop by to pick up a beeper. They were expensive. The Weasel's money would cover it. The plumber would have to wait.

Jack called. "Quiet as a mouse, buddy."

"How's she feeling?"

"Scared."

"You gonna be there tonight?"

"I feel rejected, man. She said she could handle it alone."

"I thought you said she was still scared."

"Yeah, man. I think she wants to try it on her own. Knows she can't have someone babysitting her all the time."

"It's like the toothache that goes away when you go to the dentist's office. Maybe I'll stop by there later. *Adios.*"

"Hey, buddy, sleep with one eye open."

◈ ◈ ◈

Jack always slept with his eyes open. Spooky. He wasn't going to let anyone sneak up on him. To look at him you'd have thought he was dead. To approach him, you could easily have your series canceled.

Dropped by Diane's Dial. A hole in the wall in a medical building in Beverly Hills. Several operators busy taking calls. Jeremiah, he of the blue suede shoes – for real – gave me my beeper, showed me how to use it. There was no Diane. Ever.

For the first time in a couple days it didn't seem like anyone was following. Guy had to sleep sometime. I felt free.

Laurie wasn't home, must have still been at work. Her house looked still. No missives or fancy-wrapped packages on the porch. Of course, she might already have taken them in. Doors secure. Windows locked. Her work wasn't too far away. I found a phone booth in a gas station. The payphone – I needed a car phone – smelled of dried urine and God knows what else. I didn't want to know. The receptionist at Laurie's office put me on hold. Laurie took my call immediately. Insisted she wanted to try it alone that night. I gave her the beeper number and told her if she called my home or office to let it ring at least seven times. If I didn't pick up, it would switch over to the service, who could also ring through to the beeper, saving her an additional call.

Streets almost back to normal. Traffic bursting up to the curbs. People a little more courteous. Afraid to run a red light or cut someone off. Afraid of getting shot.

Beeper beep. Anticipation. I read out the number of the person who called. Familiar digits. Familiar warmth. Rita. Glad I'm in the car. Afraid to call her. Why?

Where to go? Head to East L.A. so that if Ramon calls I'll be close by. No. Heart racing. Hands drumming steering wheel. Driving in circles. Head swimming. Pull over to the side of the road. Relax. Don't forget to breathe.

Don't forget to breathe.
Silver shadows.
Rearview mirror.
Gleaming chrome.
Snarling black enamel.
Pulls to the curb.
Spaces behind me.
Clutch the wheel.
Squeezing tight.
Tail?
Sitting in his car.
Not moving.
View blocked.
Cars inbetween.
Sitting.
Sitting.
Tail.
Angry fingers.
Grasping gritty steel.
Safety off.
Poised.
Delicate balance.
The waiting game.
Make my move.
Let him make his.
Waiting.
Biding time.
Tension fills.
Angry blood.
Coursing veins.
Hold steady.
Steady now.
Ditch the car.
Roll to the street.

Crouching run to his car.
Yank open driver's door.
Startled look.
Wrench him from the car.
Throw him against hood.
Spread eagle.
Frisk.
Who are you?
Who the fuck are you?
Why are you following me?
I'm not following you. Never seen you before in my life.
Relieve him of his wallet.
William D. Kinnear.
What's your business here?
Fuller Brush Man. Are you a cop?
Shut up. This isn't a residential neighborhood.
I'm stopping to pick up a pair of shoes.
Search his pockets. Find the receipt.
Then what were you sitting in your car for?
Since when did that become against the law?
Don't let me catch you behind me again.
Walk away.
Paranoid motherfucker.
Don't take the bait.
Get in the car.
And drive.
Don't forget to breathe.

◈ ◈ ◈

I was getting as paranoid as Laurie. It scared me. There probably wasn't anyone following me. There was nothing objective to support that theory. The case – cases – were getting to me.

C'mon and beep you damn thing.
Beep, Goddamnit.

Beep.
Back to the office. Clean out old files. Dust the desk.
Windex the windows. Keep busy. Nervous energy.
Someone on the stairs. Heading down the hall.
Shadow cuts across the pebbled glass.
Ready.
Waiting.
Safety off.
Cocked and locked.
Weasel?
Stalker?
My stalker?
Front office door swings open.
Framed by the door:
Warren.

◈ ◈ ◈

I visually scanned him for weapons. Hands: empty. No baggy pants today. He had dressed for the white man's hood. Slacks and a sport shirt. Shiny black shoes. Overly shiny. I could've used a pair of sunglasses. No jacket. No place to hide a gun, unless it was a small one. I kept my eyes on his hands.

Watch what people do, not what they say.

"I'm clean." He watched me watch him. Held his hands out, palms up. "Left the Uzi in the car." Didn't even crack a smile.

"I see you made it all the way up here without *the man* busting you."

"The man. Chill, man. Don't try to talk like us okay. You'll never keep up. No one talks like that anymore."

"Fine. We'll talk straight English."

"White man's English."

"Call it what you want. We have to settle on something. You don't want me talking your language."

"For one, you don't know it. For another, you steal everything we have. Leave us our language. Hell, Vanilla Ice. That's a rapper? What mean streets he grow up on?"

"I don't know. Plenty of white kids have their own mean streets."

"Ain't no mean streets like nigger mean streets."

"All right. Let's get down to business."

We walked through the outer office and into the inner sanctum. He sat in my chair behind the desk.

"If you're waiting for me to tell you to get out of there, you'll be waiting a long time. That's the most uncomfortable chair in the place." I sat on a wing chair in front of the desk, right where the Weasel had stood.

"You're the man now."

"The seat of power." He spun in the chair.

"Not much power here."

"You white. You got power."

"I don't buy it. Not today."

"You're as prejudiced as the rest." His eyes roamed my office. There wasn't much there to scream power or anything else.

"'Cause I don't agree with you? That's an excuse."

"I been hearin' excuses all my life."

"I don't give a shit."

"That's the problem."

"That's not what we're here to talk about."

"What are we here to talk about?"

"I don't know. You tell me. You came to me." I didn't need his BS. If he wanted to talk he would, but I was getting tired of his games.

Silence.

"Why you so interested in my sister's murder?"

"It's a job, man."

"Figures. Tha's all it is to you, man. A job. Wouldn't be helpin' no niggers 'less there's money in it."

"I don't have time for this. Whadda you want?"

"You're tryin' to find out who killed my sister. I want to find out who killed her too."

"A partner."

"Ain't talkin' no partner shit. But you need me to help you."

It's about time is what I wanted to say to him. I held it in.

"But first I want to know why you're so interested. Yeah, it's a job. Who you working for? She's just another dead *Nee-gress*. No big deal."

"Who I'm working for is privileged information."

"So you're doing it just for the money."

"It's more than that."

"Ah, the Great White Knight. Great White Hope."

"Talking to you makes me feel like the Great White Dope. Maybe I should just give up. Let the guy run."

"It don't seem like just the money with you. Seems more. Personal."

I hid behind a veil of chatter and officiousness. His dark brown eyes tore holes in my veil. But he said: "I know, man, it's just a job."

"Listen, Warren, I want justice."

"Noble words, man. So did we when those cops got off."

"You keep coming back to that stuff."

"That stuff is our lot in life. Okay, if you want to help – noblesse oblige and all that – who am I to say no. Didn't know a nigger knew such big words, huh?" He'd lost his street accent.

I hadn't responded to his speech in any way. The veil was still drawn. Then: "You know what your problem is. You can't stand being treated like a human being by a white man. You want to be treated like a nigger so you can go around pissed off all the time."

He jumped from his chair. I didn't get up. I could feel his hate. It grabbed me by the throat and wouldn't let go. I glared back. A Mexican standoff, except neither of us was Mexican.

"You don't have to like me Warren, 'cause I'm white, or 'cause I'm a private dick or 'cause you like the way I part my hair. But we are after the same things. Might as well work with each other instead of against."

"You're right, I don't have to like you," he said and I could see a softening in his eyes. I didn't think we'd ever be friends, but we didn't have to have our knives unsheathed either. He went on, "But we are after the same thing. Sort of."

His eyes were tentative. Debating. His hand shot out for me to shake. We would never be friends. At least we didn't have to be enemies.

"What can I do to help?" His voice cracked. The helpless squeak of a small child who'd held in a ton of hurt not knowing how to express it. He wasn't about to unload on me, not in any meaningful way. At least we'd moved closer together.

It took about five minutes to tell him about the teddy bear, the handwriting. Ramon. Pilar. How I'd like to find her. I didn't tell him I came upon the Weasel's piece of paper.

"Don't remember anyone named Ramon. And she had lots of stuffed animals. Lotta teddy bears. Don't know about Smokey. So many things. I can tell you it wasn't with the stuff we took from her apartment. I'll look around the house, see if there's anything there. Teddy bears. Notes from fans. Anything looks interesting, I'll give you a call."

"Thanks, Warren." For the first time, I felt hope. I gave him the beeper number. "Call any time, day or night. I'll come down and pick the stuff up."

"You don't wanna come to my neighborhood at night. Not even when there ain't no disturbance."

I was waiting for him to bring up Rita. He didn't. We tried for some normal conversation, sports. Movies. It was almost pleasant. So pleasant you could cut the air with a cleaver.

He got up to leave: "Any white guy that would hang around my neighborhood during the rebellion must have balls."

We shook again. It was warmer this time, for both of us. Not friendly. *Detente.*

As he walked through the outer office, I asked: "Do you like dogs?"

"Say what?"

I didn't want to confront him directly. I figured if he was guilty it would show. What showed was that he thought I was out of my mind for bringing it up.

He stepped out into the hall. Turned back: "Did you know Teddie?"

"Never met her."

◈ ◈ ◈

No point in staying at the office. Things were quiet. With the beeper I was in touch everywhere. Next thing I'd have to get was a cellular phone so I could order pizza while driving. On the way to the market, the beeper beeped. It was the answering service; I stopped at the first payphone. They said they had a caller on hold for me. They put me through.

A hazy voice answered.

It was familiar.

CHAPTER 30

H*ola, amigo.*"

◈ ◈ ◈

MacArthur Park is midway between Hancock Park, not a park, but an upper class neighborhood, and downtown L.A., a neighborhood in search of an identity. When I was a boy, my grandparents used to take me to the park. We'd rent rowboats and paddle through the lake, tossing bread crumbs to the birds. The park is a different place today. You can still rent paddle boats – if you want to paddle across the lake while talking to your dealer. Sometimes on Saturdays or Sundays immigrant families still try to use it as a park. Most of the time, it's a haven for pushers, crack addicts, hookers and worse. Even the police don't like treading there. If they were scared, who was I to play Rambo?

The rental car slid easily into a parking place on Alvarado. Click – locked. Of course that wouldn't keep out anyone who wanted to get in. The Firestar was in my belt, under a loose fitting Hawaiian shirt that was left untucked. Wet grass sucked under my feet. As long as it didn't suck me under I was okay.

"Meet me by the statue of *el general*," Ramon had said. The statue of General Douglas MacArthur is in the northwestern corner of the park where there was, naturally no place to park. Cutting through the park was not a good idea. I walked along Wilshire Boulevard, past garbage and litter and clusters of men, teens really. Some young men in their early twenties, in white tank top undershirts and baggy pants, charcoal hair slicked back off their foreheads. One man danced a nervous jig by himself in a corner of the pavilion building. Crack dancing.

No one approached me to buy or sell drugs. Probably thought I was a narc. Maybe saw the silhouette of the Star. MacArthur had seen better days, both the park and the statue. Graffiti camouflaged the general's stern visage. No one there cared who he was or why there was a park named after him.

No Ramon.

I stood on the corner. Waiting. Trying to look nonchalant. A black-and-white cruised slowly by. Mirrored eyes scrutinizing. What's the white man doing there? Is he buying drugs? Do they see the gun? Were they calling for backup? Fingering their triggers? Seconds passed like hours. The car drove by. Gone. I felt lucky. Luckier than I had walking the length of the park without getting mugged.

"*Amigo.*"

"Ramon."

He stood behind the statue, signaling me to join him.

"We finally connect, uh, man?"

Nod.

"You must be pretty desperate to be lookin' me up."

I was, but I didn't admit it.

"I used ta hang here. No more. That's why I figured i's a good place to meet. Guys I hang with now don't come down here an' I don' want 'em seein' me talkin' with you. Used to be a nice park." His arm swept across sooty gray water and expanse of green lawn covered with multi-colored garbage. For my money it hadn't been a nice park for at least twenty years, maybe more. "Let's make it quick," he said.

"Ball's in your court."

"Wadda ya wanna know? Whachu want with my sister? With Pilar Cruz?"

"I'm looking for Teddie Matson's killer."

His eyes snapped open. Impressed.

"I have reason to believe that Pilar Cruz might be able to help me find him."

His eyes half closed, heavy lids over dull bloodshot eyes. Should he tell me? Was I to be trusted?

"Pilar don' live in L.A. no more."

"Where does she live? Where's Anna?"

"I haven't heard from Anna in more than a year. Could be anywhere by now."

"Is Pilar with her?"

Silence. Thinking.

"I don't know." More silence. "I think so. Prob'ly."

I looked into his eyes. Probing.

"Don' look at me that way. An' it's not what you're thinking."

"What am I thinking?" I said.

"Never mind."

He was probably thinking that I thought his sister and Pilar were lesbian lovers. He was right.

"Where's the last place you had an address for them?"

A piece of wrinkled paper materialized from his pocket. A street address in Calexico, near the Mexican border, on it.

"I haven't heard from her in over a year."

"Are you worried?"

"Yeah, man. We used to write at least once a month. Me an' Anna. Or me an Pilar. At least once a month."

"Why didn't you go with them?"

Silence. I figured they didn't want him. Didn't want to push it.

"What are they running from?" Maybe they were two lesbian girls who felt alienated from their community. Hiding out so they could be alone – together. But then why Calexico – hardly the most tolerant place, I imagined. Maybe there was something else. Still hiding out, but not from their community. Maybe it was from one person.

He was thinking, hard. How much should he tell me? Was he betraying confidences?

"It's better if you tell me, Ramon. Better for–"

"It ain't gonna bring Teddie Matson back."

"True. But maybe your sister and Pilar can stop running. Live a normal life."

"How do I know I can trust you?"

"Would I come down here if I didn't have good intentions?"

"Depends on what's in it for you."

"Look, someone hired me to find Teddie Matson's killer. If it's the same guy that hurt Pilar I'll be doing us both a favor."

That struck something in him. "I don' even know his name. They wouldn't tell me."

"Pilar and Anna wouldn't tell you?"

He nodded.

"Tell me what you know."

"I don' know much. The girls went to stay with relatives in Sparks for a summer."

"Sparks? Sparks, Nevada?" Sparks flying. Teddie's and Pilar's notes.

"Yeah. Stayin' with relatives. I was here. Workin' a summer job when I was stupid enough to do that kinda sucker shit. Somethin' happened. I'm not sure what."

"Rape?" There was no easy way to say it.

"They wouldn' tell me. Something bad. Knew I'd kill him. Didn't want me goin' to jail. Can you believe it? I been to jail four times since then. Before that summer, Pilar and I– It was never the same. I mean, we was only kids anyways. But I loved her. She loved me. We was gonna get married. Have kids. Live the American Dream. The *Gringo* American Dream." He snorted a disgusted laugh. Sarcasm glinted in his eyes. "It was never the same."

"Did Pilar or Anna know Teddie Matson?"

"I don' know. Don't think so. How could they? She's from another world."

"In Sparks maybe."

"Don't know."

"How long were they in Sparks?"

"I don' know, man. A few months. Maybe they were fifteen, sixteen. Somethin' like that."

Teddie was a few years older than Pilar and Anna. She might have been in Sparks at the same time. Seemed like a long shot.

"Were they in any kinds of plays or something when they were in Sparks?"

"I don' know. Yeah, maybe. I can't remember."

"Is there anything else?"

"Here, man." He handed me a picture of Pilar and Anna. "If you find them, tell 'em to write."

"I will."

He started to walk away. "If you find the dude done this to 'em, lemee know. I'll take care-a him. Waste 'im, man. Then you won't have to go to jail."

"No, you will."

"I can do the time standing on my head." He lit a joint. Walked off.

◈ ◈ ◈

I drove home. It was empty without Baron. I grabbed the phone.

Calexico was a long shot. Information didn't have a phone number for either Anna Martinez or Pilar Cruz. Unlisted number? Gone?

I dialed again, Mrs. Matson this time. The phone rang seven times. I was about to hang up:

"Hello."

"Hello, Mrs. Matson, this is Duke Rogers."

"Hi Duke. Any news?"

"I'm making some progress. Wish it could be faster. Do you have a minute?"

"Surely. What can I do for you?"

"Did Teddie ever live in Sparks, Nevada? Visit there?"

"No, not in Sparks. When she was first starting out she lived in Reno though."

"What was she doing?"

"She was in a chorus line at one of the hotels."

"Do you remember which one?"

"No, I'm sorry. I might be able to find it in her things though."

"Would Warren know?"

"He might. They were very close. He isn't home now."

"If he gets in within the next hour will you have him call me."

"I'll ask him. But he, well, you know–"

"I think he might this time." I didn't go into our rapprochement. "Is there anything you remember about her time in Reno? How long she was there? Any friends she might have made? Anything like that."

"I'm afraid I don't. It was several years ago. I think it was rather uneventful. She didn't work there very long. A couple months. Three maybe."

I thanked her and hung up. Packing didn't take long. Ammo for the Star. More ammo. And a toothbrush. A small bag of clean underwear, fresh shirt. The phone didn't ring. Should I call Mrs. Matson again? See if Warren's in. Don't be a pest. Not yet.

Tanked up the car. Ready to go. I hit the road. It was early enough in the afternoon to miss rush hour. These days just about any time is rush hour. Traffic was bad. Could've been worse. I hit the Hollywood Freeway to the 10 and headed out.

Somewhere around San Berdoo, the beeper rang. Hit the first offramp. First gas station. Old fashioned glassed in booth. Greasy finger marks on the glass. Dial.

"Warren. Duke Rogers."

"Yeah, man. What's up? I haven't found the teddy bear yet."

"Keep looking."

"I will."

"Tell me about Teddie's playing Reno." The line was silent. Dead? "Warren?"

"I'm here."

"Reno."

"Yeah, Reno. Hold on."

Bang, the phone hit a hard surface. Shuffling, nondescript noises. Another extension being picked up. "Okay, you can hang up." A reverbed Warren. Click. First extension being hung up. "I'm back." His voice was low, almost a whisper. Conspiratorial.

"What's going on?"

"You wanted to know about Reno. What do you want to know?"

"I'm not sure exactly. Anything unusual about Teddie's time there?"

Silence. "Yeah, man. But my mom doesn't know. If I talk, it's between us."

"It might come out. I'll do my best and I won't tell her. I'll try to keep it quiet."

"That ain't good enough."

"It's the best I can do. Look, I could lie to you. Tell you it won't come out. I'm not lying. I'm being straight. Be straight with me."

"Okay. Guy there saw Teddie in the show, at the Crystal Palace. She was mostly in the chorus, but she also had a couple of bits. A line here, two lines there. He went head over heels for her. Wouldn't leave her alone."

"A stalker?"

"Yeah, I guess. But it was before that word got into vogue, know what I mean? He'd send her flowers and candy backstage. Notes. All kinds-a stuff."

"Teddy bears?"

"Yeah, I think so. I'm lookin' for it. Really. Can't find it." More rustling. "But even before the shit got so heavy I didn't want her seeing him."

"Why not?"

"He wasn't good for her."

"You're being oblique."

"Good whitey word there."

"Cut the shit."

"He wasn't good for her."

I started to say something. Warren cut me off: "He was white." As if that was enough.

"What else?"

"I don't know. It was a long time ago. Teddie and I were close. Real close. But I'm not sure she told me everything."

"You think she might have liked him? Led him on?"

"Get off, man."

"Might he have raped her?"

"She never said so. I thought maybe."

"Maybe?"

"She wouldn't tell me for sure. Knew I'd kill the guy – didn't want me landing in jail. Already been – would have been really hard time." He lowered his voice even more. "Don't you mention none of this to my Mother. It would kill her."

"Any chance you remember the guy's name."

Silence. "I think his first name was Jack. John. Maybe Jim."

"Jim?"

"Yeah, something like that. One-a those J names."

"Last name."

"Can't remember?"

"Talbot?"

"Doesn't ring a bell."

"Did he ever contact her after she made it on TV?"

"Might have. I remember she did get something that upset her. Some kind of gift. I never actually saw it. Might have been the bear. She could've thrown it away."

"Would Rita know anything?"

"Shit, man, this ain't goin' nowhere. Let's get out. Hit the streets."

"You've got to be methodical. We're taking it as best we can. Now, tell me, would Rita know anything?"

"I don't think so. I was closer to Teddie than Rita."

"Did she know a Pilar Cruz?"

"I don't know. Why?"

"Anna Martinez?"

"I hate beaners, man. They're comin' in here, takin' over all our hoods. Grabbin' the power and they won't even speak English."

"I didn't ask your opinion of them. Did Teddie know either of these girls?"

"I don't know. Doesn't ring a bell."

"Anything else you can think of?"

"Not now. If I do, I'll let you know."

"I'm gonna be out of town for a couple days."

"I'm comin' with you."

"I'm going to be hard to reach. Leave any info with my service. Detailed message and tell them to make sure they get it right."

"Yes, sir, massah." There was a silence at his end of the phone. Then: "See you in Reno." He slammed the phone down. I pulled my map box out of the trunk. Nevada. Sparks. Reno.

Bingo.

Sparks was a suburb of Reno.

◈ ◈ ◈

As I was leaving the booth, the beeper beeped again. Read out a number. Familiar. Rita.

I cleared the beeper. Headed for the car.

Something nagged at me. Why was I avoiding Rita?

CHAPTER 31

Dust swirls engulfed the car. Calexico. A desert border town. Like something out of the movies. A cross of cultures. Or maybe a clash of them.

First thing, gas up. While they filled the tank, I checked the phone book. Lotta Cruz's. Lotta Martinez's. No Pilar Cruz's. No Anna Martinez's. Several A. Martinez's. One M. Cruz. Rip. Tore the page out of the book for future reference if the address Ramon gave me turned bust.

Small house. Faded yellow planks. Faded brighter yellow trim. Two car garage at the end of the driveway. Window in front. Sound of the vacuum cleaner shooshing back and forth. Knock-knock.

"Who's there?"

"My name's Duke Rogers, I–"

"Don't need anything."

"I'm not selling anything."

The door jerked open. "Then waddayou want?" Older woman. Red, puffy skin. Mid fifties maybe. Maybe younger. It was the moo-moo and alcohol lines that made her look old. Might have had a figure at some time. Not now. And if she did, who could tell under the cow tent?

"I'm looking for Anna Martinez and Pilar Cruz." I showed her the photograph of the girls.

"Sorry, you must have the wrong address." The smell of alcohol spit from her mouth like fire from a dragon.

"Well, maybe they don't live here now. But they used to."

"I've owned this house for seventeen years. No Anna Cruz or Pilar Martinez ever–"

"Anna Martinez and Pilar Cruz."

"Whoever."

"You never rented a room or–"

"–Or nothin'. I'm busy now, please."

"Thank you."

Hissing sound. Before I reached the curb, sprinklers doused my pant legs with unfriendly water. As an ex-frogman, I'd thought of all water as friendly. Not so this H_2O.

Simon Bolivar rode a magnificent rearing white steed in front of the cheap motel bearing his name. Both he and the steed were covered with magnificent graffiti *art*. The room was small. Clean. Double bed with a tapestry spread. TV had to be fed quarters. A phone in the room cost extra. It was worth it. I started dialing the names from the phonebook pages. No one had heard of Anna or Pilar, at least they claimed not to have. Both had common enough Hispanic surnames. It was possible that none of the Cruz's and Martinez's in the book knew them. It was also possible they were covering up.

After exhausting the phone pages, I fed four quarters into the TV for an hour's worth of mindless pabulum. *A Team* reruns were the only thing I could stomach – best of the lot. With the sound low, I lay back on the bed, hands folded under my head, and stared at the ceiling.

Ramon could have given me the wrong address to send me on a wild goose chase. I didn't think so. He knew I didn't have much to go on. He'd tried too hard to get in touch with me. Meet off his current turf. I believed the address was correct. He might have copied it down wrong. That was a more likely possibility. Another possibility was that the lady of the house, whose name I'd forgotten to get – fuckup – was lying. The garage had a small curtained window in it. The car door looked sealed shut. There was a people door cut into it. A garage apartment?

The question was, were the girls living there now? Had they moved? Had they ever lived there? Using their own names. Aliases? Mental note: go back there.

Night fell, a crisp desert evening. The town kept bustling. Hustlers on the sidewalks selling everything from marijuana to Rolex watches, or "*un bueno* facsimile," as one of the vendors had so honestly put it.

The smell of dope coupled with the reedy desert air burned my nostrils. A sunburned bearded man in a trenchcoat and ratty knee-high moccasins was digging through a garbage can. He turned, standing square in front of me. Smelled like his skin was decomposing on the spot.

"Got any spare change, man?"

"I gave at the office."

He called up a loogy from the back of his throat, ready to spit a projectile in my direction. I pivoted out of the way just in time. The spittle projectile darted past me landing bullseye on a telephone pole. My nature had me wanting to fight. My judgment said no. I didn't want to touch this guy. Lice and diseases he might be carrying were something I didn't need. I'd made a deal with myself several years ago not to hand out money to anyone on the street. It was dangerous and most likely they'd use it for booze or drugs instead of food or shelter. I gave to a couple of the missions in downtown L.A. every year as well as to the Salvation Army. I figured that was the best way to go. I guess my friend in the trenchcoat didn't agree.

Castle's Bar was a dive. A comfortable dive. And apparently the swankiest dive in town. A washed out blond with black roots in a sequined black velvety dress sang and played piano for tips. It was so low cut everything hung out, almost falling onto the keyboard when she leaned over to light a cigarette. I'd only been in the bar half an hour and she'd already played Billy Joel's *Piano Man* twice, changing the words to *piano girl*. Must've meant something personal to her as no one around the piano seemed to be making any requests.

I ordered a light beer and some conversation from the bartender: "Been here long?"

"Does it matter to ya?"

"I'm looking for these two women. Ever seen 'em?"

He perused the photo of Anna and Pilar. Shook his head. "Mex don't come in here."

That was that. On my way out, the blond was singing *Piano Man* for the third time in less than forty-five minutes. It might have been the only song she knew.

There were several bars on the street. There were several bars on every street it seemed. Good business, drinking at the border. No one in any of them, Anglo or Mexican admitted knowing the girls.

It was almost one a.m. by the time I headed back to the Bolivar. The trip down to the border had been uneventful. No feeling of being spied upon. But now it was back. Faint footsteps, several paces behind me. I slowed, they slowed. I sped up. So did they. Pretending to window shop, I stopped in front of a bridal store displaying outlandish bridesmaid costumes in dayglow orange with green trim in the window. The footsteps stopped.

From the corner of my eye, I saw a shadow in a recessed doorway three doors back. I headed in that direction, retracing my footsteps. The shadow pulled deeper into the doorway. Disappeared. I walked past the doorway, not looking to the side. My peripheral vision told me someone was hunched up against the door in the farthest corner. I walked past. Quietly, I turned around. Headed back to the doorway. Didn't step in front of it. If I was as quiet as I thought, he hadn't heard me.

I waited.

After about three minutes, a sigh escaped the doorway. The man stepped forward. Foot out. I tripped him. He fell into me. I grabbed his collar and pulled him back into the darkness of the doorway. A police car cruised by. Didn't see us.

"Who are you?"

He shrugged. He was taller than me by two inches. Skinny as an I-beam. And as muscular. But he didn't know how to fight. I shoved him back against the door.

"Why are you following me?"

His teeth wanted to chatter. He wouldn't let them. Couldn't stop his hands from shaking though.

"La photo."

"Speak English."

"*Si*, this side of the border, English. I saw the picture you are showing in *la cantina*."

"You know those two girls?"

"They used to come in there sometimes, Castle's."

"Used to."

"*Si*. No more."

"How long since you've seen them?"

"Maybe a year. Maybe less."

That jibed with what Ramon had said.

"Where'd they go?"

"*No lo se.* I don't know. I have not seen them in town for that long, not only the bar."

"Were they hurt? Leave town?"

Shrug.

"I know where they live. Lived. I show you for ten dollars."

"You show me first." I pushed him out onto the street. We walked for several blocks, from the main drag to the residential section. He took me to the faded yellow house. Pointed.

"There. In the back." He pointed to the garage. Bingo. Moo-moo was lying. I pulled a ten from my pocket, gave it to him. We walked to the corner.

"How do you know they lived there? How did you know them?"

He shrugged. Backed away, ready to run. I caught his collar. He seemed to shrivel into his shirt. "I, I follow them here one night. I have, how you say, a liking, a–"

"–crush."

"*Si, un* crush on one of them."

I pulled the photo out. "Which one?"

He pointed to Pilar. *"Ella es muy bonita, no?"*

"*Si.* Did you ever talk to her?"

"No."

I believed him. He was wimpy enough to have followed her around and not say anything to her. "Did she have any boyfriends? Talk to anyone else in the bar?"

"There was *un hombre*, Hector. But I have not seen him around either."

"Was Hector married?" Fishing. Were Pilar and Anna lovers? Something else. What was going on?

"Si."

"His wife gone too?"

"Yes."

"Any of the people in Castle's tonight know them, the girls?"

"I do not know. People come and go so much here. Many migrant, is that right word, workers."

Mental note: Check back at Castle's.

I asked for his phone and address. Said he had no phone. Gave me the name of a farm outside of town where he was currently working. He said he was usually in this area, but not necessarily at the same farm or ranch. I gave him ten bucks; he shuffled down the street in the opposite direction of the yellow house. I headed back to it.

The lights were off. House next door was dark too. I nonchalantly, as if I owned the place, walked down the driveway to the back. Couldn't see through the curtain in the garage window. Walked around the side. Two more curtained windows. I pried at them. Didn't budge. Same with the door. No windows in the back. The fourth side, along the border with the neighbor, was walled in. No way to get to it.

What if someone else was renting there now? A little burglary might enliven their life. The windows on the side were big enough to crawl through. I pulled my boot knife and went to work on them. No need to worry about an alarm here. The window was easy. I was inside in less than a minute.

Musty. As if no one'd been in for a while. Dark. No flashlight. I pushed the curtains aside. A sliver of moonlight shot in. I stood silently, waiting for my eyes to adjust to the dark. Moved to the next window. Opened the curtains there. More light. Enough to see silhouettes by. A sofa-bed against the rear wall. Closed. No one on it. I felt my way to the tiny bathroom in the back corner. Turned on the light. The outside walls of the bathroom faced the neighbor's wall and the rear of the property. No one in the main house would see the light on. Gloomy light filtered out to the main room. A kitchenette in one corner. Coffee table in front of the sofa. I closed the curtains I'd opened, just in case. Set about tossing the place.

Drawers: empty. Shelves empty. Low shelves immaculate. Upper shelves dusty enough to write your name in. Open up the sofa-bed. Nothing in the sheets, under the mattress. Nothing in the sofa. Kitchen: clear. Bathroom: one half-full bottle of Suave shampoo. Nothing else. Not even a hair left on the tile. Why the bottle?

The place was empty. Except for the bottle. Did it mean anything? I couldn't fathom a guess. I turned off the bathroom light, put the windows back the way they were. Split.

◈ ◈ ◈

Back at the Bolivar, I fell asleep to *The Philadelphia Story* dubbed into Spanish. I wondered if it lost something in the translation.

I braced Castle's again in the daytime. Again no one owned up to having known Pilar or Anna.

Went back to the yellow house. Vacuum was going again. The woman had a clean fetish. Maybe that was why the guest house had been so spotless except for the bottle of Suave.

Rang the bell.

"You again."

She tried to close the door on me. Too slow. Too late. I was already inside. Ratty furniture. Old Motel 6 stuff that'd seen better days. Creepy floral patterns. By the numbers paintings on the wall. But all as clean as could be.

"You lied to me."

"Get outta here. I'll call the cops."

"I'm tired of being lied to. The wheel spun round and landed on you. You're gonna tell me the truth." I walked up to her. She was my height. Probably outweighed me by twenty pounds. She didn't back off.

We stood eye to eye. Glare contest. She took a step forward. I didn't move. Our noses touched. Hers was warm, greasy. She finally backed away. I thought I'd give her more space. I stepped back too. She reached behind a large upholstered chair, grabbed a baseball bat. Swung it at me. I ducked. Grabbed the bat. Her grip on the bat was tight. She wouldn't let go.

Twisting the bat in her hand, I freed it. Tossed it across the room. Pushed her into a chair.

"Sit."

She did. Neither one of us spoke. I pulled the Star, held it on her, while I peeked into the kitchen, dining area and hall, without leaving the living room. No sign of anyone else.

"Tell me about Pilar and Anna."

"Leave them alone. They just want to be left alone."

"Who do you think I am?"

"I don't know. I do know, they was bothered. Just wanna be left alone."

"From who?"

"Everyone. Wanna do their thing in peace."

"How long since they've been gone?"

"About three, four months, I think."

"You cleaned up their place pretty good."

"Got nothing better to do. 'Sides, a clean house is a–"

"–clean house."

She glared at me.

"I'm a detective. I'm not out to hurt them."

"They wanna be left–"

"I know. Did anyone else come around looking for them?"

"You're the detective."

"Don't get cute. I'm trying to help them."

"Why?"

"Anna's brother, Ramon, gave me this address. He wants me to find them."

"Yeah, I remember him. Came around a few times."

"Who else came around?"

"You're the cop, you ought to know."

"I'm not leaving till I get the information."

We sat in silence for minutes that passed slowly. She picked up a long, slender cigarette holder from the end table next to her. Stuffed a cancer stick in one end. Lit it. Drew in the smoke. She didn't quite fit my image of the cigarette holder type. "I don't know much. They were scared-a something," she exhaled.

"Someone?"

"Yeah."

"Who?"

"Guy that liked Pilar I think. I don't know his name."

The Weasel.

"You ever see him?"

"Nah. But they told me if he comes around tell him they don't live here."

"How would you know who to tell that to?"

"They told me what he looked like." She described the Weasel to a T.

"Did they tell you his name?"

"Sure."

My heart raced. "What is it?"

"It's been a long time."

"Did you write it down?"

"I don't know. Maybe." She stared at me over the end of her cigarette holder. "Maybe you're working for him."

Not anymore, lady.

"I'm not. I'm investigating the murder of Teddie Matson."

"Poor girl. I used to watch her show."

"We have reason to believe that there's a link between her murder and Pilar. The man that killed Teddie could be the same man who's after Pilar. Are you forwarding mail for them?"

She moved to get up. I lowered the gun. She went to a small table near the front door. Handed me an envelope on it. It was from a loan company, addressed to Anna. A line through the address for the yellow house led to a handwritten note: "No forwarding address known." "I was going to send it out with the mail."

She couldn't have thought ahead this far to prepare something like this. Besides, the letter was postmarked only a few days ago. I handed her my card.

"If you think of his name, come across a paper with it, or think of anything, please call me. The girls are in danger."

"I know. I didn't talk to you 'cause I was trying to protect them."

"I'm on their side. I'm licensed." I pointed to my license number on the card. "Bonded. Check me out. If you think of anything, no matter how trivial you think it is, call me. Leave a message with my service." I didn't plan to keep the service forever. Only until I could replace the machine. "Call me."

"I will."

"By the way, what's your name?"

"Mrs. Laren. There is no Mr. Laren anymore. That's another reason I was cold to you. Never know who'll show on your doorstep."

"You're right to be careful. I'm sorry I barged in like this."

"Maybe I'm too distrustful."

"Keep your guard up."

I headed to my rental car parked at the curb.

"Hey, wait a minute. I think his name started with a J. I'm not sure. James, Jeremy. Something like that."

"Thanks."

"Don't hold me to it. It's been a long time. But I think it was a J-name."

I got in the rental, headed back to L.A.

CHAPTER 32

Instead of heading back to L.A., I turned off on 395 and headed for Reno. The road was a roller coaster of up and down hillocks and valleys. Heat waves melted into the asphalt giving it a sleek sheen of black dye.

Copses of Joshua trees meandered off on either side of the road. *Little men,* hunched over their work, tending the desert garden. I felt eyes on the back of my neck. Was I being followed again? Had I ever been followed?

A gaggle of cars pressed around me, front and rear. There was open road about a mile ahead. I decided to run with the wind. Dodging in and out of traffic. Each car a land mine to be avoided.

Honk. Sorry, buddy, didn't mean to cut you off. Thanks for the bird.

Open road. Check the rearview. No one making any sudden lane changes.

Hoboes count ties, I counted broken lines in the road. Hypnotic. Don't drift. The road began to look the same. Same trees, same fast food joints, gas stations and quick-stop stores clustered in bunches. Same white lines.

L.A. Beirut felt as far away as the real Beirut. It might as well have been across an ocean. The sky was clear, no settling ash from the days of fire and firefights. No lines of people waiting for their ration of food and food stamps. No attitude.

Not far outside Reno: Weird dude on a three-wheeled bicycle. Tattered trenchcoat, in the high desert heat. Stubbly beard. Hat. Saddlebags on either side of the rear wheels and a box on top of it. Heat musta got to him. Pedaling along. Rear view: Stopping. Getting off bike. Bending over. What the hell's he doing? Still no sign of a tail.

I made Reno with only one stop for gas. Checked into the Edsel Motel. Gleaming chrome and polish. Ten Edsels lined up, five on each side of the walk to the main office. Edselmania. I hoped the motel had a better history than the car. The room was cramped. Clean. Repro photos of Henry Ford, Edsel on the walls. Various shots of Ford cars from the Model T through the late '50s porthole Thunderbird. A TV you didn't have to put quarters into. Bathroom glasses wrapped in *sanitary* wrap. "Do Not Throw Sanitary Napkins In Toilet" over the tank.

Beat. Wanted to crash. Couldn't do it. Shaved. Showered. Put on clean shirt. Wished I'd brought more clothes. Called Laurie. No answer. Jack. No answer.

The Crystal Palace Hotel and Casino. Look up gaudy in the dictionary: Crystal Palace. Flashing, clashing neon lights. Lit up like a sunny afternoon in the dark of night. No clocks. Always high noon.

Genteel ladies with blue hair feeding hungry slots. Businessmen in Michael Milken toupees and thousand dollar suits playing five card stud and Baccarat. Long-legged women in fishnet stockings and lowcut *uniforms* serving free watered down drinks to the customers to keep them playing past their bedtimes. Past their limits. Big spenders wearing shorts and flipflops. I felt right at home in my jeans and sport shirt.

Neither Warren, Mrs. Matson nor Ramon could tell me any of Teddie's or Pilar's friend's names from their stays in Reno. It would have been so much easier if I'd had a name. Now I had to start questioning people blindly.

"Thanks," I said, taking one of the free drinks offered by a *hostess*. She smiled, started to walk off. "Wait, please."

"Yes."

I maneuvered her to a corner. She looked slightly uncomfortable. It was hard to tell if it was real or part of the show. "There was a young woman who worked here a few years ago. I'm trying to locate anyone who might have known her."

"I'm sorry. I've only been on the job a few months."

"Who's been around a while?"

"Was she a hostess? Dealer?"

"I think she was in the chorus in the show."

"The show's producer is Jeanette Lyon, but I don't think she's been here that long either."

"Can I talk to her?"

"I'm sorry. I wouldn't know. I have to go now. They don't like us spending too much time with any one customer and they watch through the ceiling." She nodded to a row of mirrors above us. She smiled again, walked off. I headed for the showroom.

The first show of Follies Crys-tal was already in progress. It was more than an hour till the midnight show. Between shows seemed like a good time to find Ms. Lyon. I figured the show'd been rehearsed a dozen times, played for an audience a million. It probably ran by itself. Lyon might not even be around.

A stiff tuxedo, pressed and spit-shined, stood at the door to the showroom. When I headed toward it, the tuxedo nodded and smiled a rehearsed smile at me.

"I'm sorry, sir. There's no admittance until a break in the show. If you have tickets for this show I can arrange to exchange them for—"

"I don't want to interrupt such a lovely and well-practiced speech, but I don't have tickets for the show."

A frown overtook his face. He wasn't prepared to ad-lib.

"I'm looking for Jeanette Lyon. Is she here tonight?"

"Do you have an appointment with her?"

"No. But I think she'll want to see me. An old friend said to look her up."

"If you tell me who that is, I'll look and see if she's here."

"No can do. It's got to be a surprise."

"No can do," he said, mimicking. Nodded his head. Before I could blink, three large men surrounded me. None of them smiling.

"Three for the price of one," I said.

"Can I help you, sir?" the largest said in a meek voice that was more Pee-Wee Herman than Hulk Hogan. Still, the *sir* oozed from his tongue like hot oil slithering from a crank case.

"I'm not sure why you gentlemen were called. I merely told this fellow that I was looking for Jeanette Lyon."

"Miss Lyon is a very busy woman. She can't be meeting with just anyone who wants to meet her."

I wanted to talk to Lyon. I didn't particularly want these hulks to know my business with her. The lid had to stay on the can of worms for now.

"It's nothing really. An old friend of hers asked me to look her up. I didn't think it would be this much trouble."

"No trouble. We take care of our people."

Like they did in the Soviet Union.

"If you tell us who the friend is and where you're staying, we'll have her get back to you. In fact, why don't you step back to my office and we'll see if we can reach her right now?"

Out of sight of the public, are you kidding? "No thanks. It's not that important to me. I'm just doing a favor for a friend."

I started to walk off, into the casino. The four of them stood, guarding the entry to the showroom as if I was stalking Jeanette Lyon. I played a few hands of blackjack, figured I'd better quit for the night and headed back to the Edsel. It was about a three block walk. There were plenty of people on the street. I felt followed, didn't turn around. After making a couple of detours, hoping to lose the tail, if there was one, I finally hit the Edsel. Before hitting the bed, I checked the phone book. No Jeanette Lyon. I called information. Nothing there either. The wild hair was making me crazy. What the hell, I figured and called the Palace, asked for Jeanette Lyon. The phone rang seven times. A raspy woman's voice answered:

"Hello."

"Ms. Lyon."

"No, this is her assistant. She's in a meeting now. Can I take a message?"

"I'll try back later," I said. My head hit the pillow and my brain hit dreamland.

◈ ◈ ◈

It wasn't as good as Dreamland on Coney Island, but it was all I had.

Joshua trees.
Cactus plants.
Blue skies.
Clean air.
Smooth breath.
Breathing like a baby.
Crazy dudes on bikes.
Talking tuxedos.
Desert rats.

Need desert cats.
Keep the rat population down.
Spinning wheels.
Red and black.
Put your wad on a number.
Hope it comes back.
The game is rigged.
Nothing to do.
Do the best with what you've got.
Showgirls and showtime.
Kicking high.
Dancing disco dollies.
Fans waiting in the wings.
Eager to lavish their favorites with flowers.
And candy.
And teddy bears.
And–
Never alone.
People following.
From L.A. to Calexico.
Calexico to Reno.
Good at hiding.
Crawling under the woodwork.
But there.
Always there.
Stalking.
Stalked.
Sleep.
Perchance to dream.
Perchance to nightmare.
Sleep.
Sleep.
Sleep.

◈ ◈ ◈

The sun lunged in through a crack in the drapes, piercing my eyes with hot white light. Enough to wake me up. It was after eleven in the morning. I called the front desk, told them I'd be staying another night. My body telegraphed its desire to go back to sleep. The receiving station was down, the wires had been cut by the men in black hats. The brain wouldn't listen. Forced the tired body out of bed and into a cold shower. That put the connections back together in a hurry.

Before I left the motel, I got a shoe box from the desk clerk, put the Star and my private dick's license in it and had them lock it in the safe. The clerk assured me that the safe was secure and had never been broken into or had anything stolen from it. That was good enough for me. Besides, crooks had better places to steal from than the Edsel.

Bright sun belied brisk weather. I couldn't stand my clothes anymore. It felt like I'd slept in them, because I had. I was sure that there were discount places in Reno, shopping malls, department stores. But I wanted to buy my new clothes at the stores in the Crystal Palace. Why spend a hundred bucks for a suit when you could spend three hundred?

The Palace's casino was booming. More little old ladies with blue hair than the night before. None of the tables were empty. I scanned the room for the Three Tuxeteers. Not around. Must be the nightshift. Other Tuxeteers abounded, but I figured they didn't know my face and wouldn't pay it any mind, especially after I got my new outfit.

Jerome's Men's Wear was a pretty good sized ye olde shoppe for a hotel. It had nice big MasterCard and Visa logos on its front window. That made me happy, since I hardly had enough cash for breakfast. Plastic money I could live on till the year 3000.

The man himself helped me. I was the only patron in the store. He was eager and only too happy to please. His hair was neatly trimmed and slicked down above a beak-like nose. His own suit reeked of fine and expensive taste and fine and expensive perfume, er, cologne. Instead of a tie he wore an ascot. What would Jack have thought of that?

Two other salesmen rearranged stock on racks and shelves.

"Hmm, a dark suit," Jerome said, after I told him what I was looking for. "Does it have to be black or might we go with a dark blue or gray?"

"Doesn't matter. But something sharp. No brown."

"Of course not. Brown, no way."

After measuring me, he pulled a couple suits off a rack. Had me try on the jackets. I needed a good suit. Jerome may as well have my business as anyone else. This was quality stuff. Maybe this was where the Weasel got his suit.

Jerome spent over an hour with me. We finally settled on a double breasted gray suit, kinda snazzy, as mom would have said. While we were trying out various ties and shirts with it, another customer came in. Jerome beamed. One of his salesmen attended to the customer, while the other continued with the racks.

"The pants are a tad long. I can have them tailored for you in a couple of hours, I think." He smiled. Happy for the business.

"Sounds good."

He marked the cuffs with chalk and pins. As I was changing, handing clothes to him over the short dressing room saloon door, I asked if he knew Jeanette Lyon. I wished I could have seen his face when he responded.

"She comes in once in a while to buy something."

"She around today?"

"Haven't seen her."

I came out of the dressing room. His expression was calm enough.

"Are you a detective?"

"That's a strange question." It was. It got me thinking. "Hell no. I'm just trying to look her up for an old friend in L.A. But last night when I was asking around, some big dudes got in the way."

"Yes, they're very protective around here."

"Over-protective if you ask me." He handed me the charge receipt to sign. "Listen, don't tell anyone I'm looking for her. I don't need any trouble."

"I won't, unless you want me to tell her."

"Sure."

"I'll see what I can do. Might be a couple days."

Great, a couple more days at the Edsel. "Great." I left him my room number at the motel. The other customer left without buying anything.

◈ ◈ ◈

I spent most of the rest of the day wandering around, trying to nonchalantly ask if anyone had known Teddie. A couple times I even asked about Pilar. She'd been too young to work at the hotel, but it couldn't hurt to ask. I checked messages at the motel. No calls. And the only ones who should have known I was there were Jerome and Jeanette, if he'd reached her.

About 4:00 p.m., I picked up my suit. Changed into it at Jerome's to see how the tailoring had come out.

"Magnificent," he said. I agreed. I looked pretty good. He offered to have my shirt and jeans washed and pressed and sent to the motel the next morning, no charge. It was an offer I couldn't refuse.

He volunteered: "I looked around a bit for Jeanette. She didn't come in today."

"Will she be here tonight?"

"I imagine. She's here most nights. I'll hang around a bit after closing. See if I can latch onto her."

"Thanks, Jerome." I felt like I should have bought another suit. Maybe two. Up the hall from Jerome's was a shoe store. Men's and women's. The selection wasn't the greatest. I needed a pair of shiny black shoes to go with the suit so I bought the cheapest pair of loafers I could find with the shiniest paint job. The kid who waited on me had only been working there a week, his manager a few months. Neither knew Jeanette. Neither cared that I'd asked. And neither would bother to call the Tuxeteers.

◈ ◈ ◈

The hotel's coffee shop hamburger was soggy, but it would do. There was no point trying to get backstage to see Jeanette. Calling her office only got the raspy voice again. Again I left no message. The Tuxeteers spotted me playing blackjack. Kept an eye on me, but kept their distance. I called the motel a couple times to see if Jerome had reached Jeanette. No messages.

An acne-scarred pit boss, in a black suit with a black and white striped bow tie, closed down the blackjack table I was playing at. Everyone, including me, started to disperse.

"Hang loose, buddy," he said.

When the table was clear the dealer picked up cards and money. The pit boss stood behind the table, beady black holes staring at me. "Why you lookin' for Jeanette?"

"News travels fast."

"We're just one big family." He grinned. Two gold teeth gleamed at me from the top of his mouth.

"Happy no doubt."

"No doubt. We don't like strangers comin' and–"

"There is no and. I told your pals last night, I'm looking her up for a friend. That's all. It's not that important to me so I stopped asking and now I'm just playing."

"Cheap stakes blackjack."

"That's my game."

"You're not staying at the hotel."

"I'm sure you like taking my money anyway." How'd he know I wasn't staying there? Had I been followed last night?

"Cop?"

"No. But I'm getting awfully sick of this place."

"The air is a little bad in here. Bad circulation. Maybe you should stay out."

"You mean my money isn't good enough. I like it here."

"Plenty of other casinos. Some with better odds. Try Harrah's or Bally's.

"Hey, all I did was ask to see the lady. I didn't send her a pipe bomb. Didn't follow her home. What is it with you guys?"

"Better odds down the street."

◈ ◈ ◈

The odds weren't that much better down the street. Three to one in fact. The Three Tuxeteers were waiting for me in my motel room. As soon as I opened the door I knew something was wrong. I'd left the bathroom light on and the drapes open. It was off and they were closed. It could have burned out. I didn't think so. They grabbed me, threw me on the bed face down, spread eagled. Frisked me.

"No gun."

"I.D.?"

"Marion Rogers. Los Angeles."

"Business cards?"

"Nope."

"Whadda you do for a living, Mary-un?"

One Tuxeteer held my feet down. Another my arms.

"Hey, man, it's a new suit. Bought at–" I thought better about telling them I bought it at Jerome's. If they knew, they'd come down on him. I shut up. They didn't seem interested.

"Well, we'll try not to wrinkle it," Hulk Wally said. A line of pain ran up my left leg. Then warmth. Wet. He'd slit my trouser leg up to the butt with a razor sharp knife – my own, which they'd taken off me when they frisked me. That wasn't the only thing he slit. "Wanna tell us why you're here?"

"Vacation."

"And don't you like the fringe benefits of your tour plan?"

I was glad I'd put the license and gun in the safe. "Who're you looking up Jeanette for?"

"Shouldn't that be, for whom are you looking up Jeanette? Don't want to end with a preposit–"

The fist with the knife slammed into my mouth. Luckily not the blade end. My mouth began to bleed. I didn't want to think what the other end of the knife would have done.

"We checked your car. Piece-a-shit rental job. We just don't know enough about you. Wanna cut the jokes and be friendly now?"

"I don't know what else to tell you since the truth doesn't cut it."

"Who's the friend in L.A. wants to look up Jeanette."

Blood gurgled out of my mouth. It was hard to talk. I figured that worked in my favor. I also wished I'd called Rita and gone to see her instead. "Jamie. Jamie Tanberg. She asked me to look up Jeanette. See if she's still here. If so, get her number, or give her Jamie's and see if they want to get back together." I didn't know where I pulled that name from, but it sounded familiar.

"Ja-mie Tanberg. One n or two?"

"One."

He wrote in a small pad. "We'll be seeing you, especially if Jeanette doesn't know anyone with this name." He threw two one hundred dollar bills on the bed. "Get yourself a new pair of pants and some mercurochrome. Have a nice day. The Three Tuxeteers left my Edsel of a room, leaving me with the taste of blood in my mouth and the memory of Jamie Tanberg, a girl I'd had a crush on in fourth grade.

CHAPTER 33

The Tuxeteers hadn't found out anything and I wasn't sure they wanted to. They wanted to scare me off of talking to Jeanette Lyon. They hadn't succeeded in that either. The cut on my leg was only surface. The bash on my mouth wasn't bad either. I borrowed alcohol from the front desk, cleaned the wounds. I had a swollen lip. Nothing else noticeable. I also retrieved the Star and my P.I. license from the safe, slept sitting up against the headboard of the bed. Anyone who tried breaking in would get a severe headache.

I overslept the next morning. It'd been several days since I had a full night's sleep. I checked my service. No messages. I kept waiting for Warren to show up. At my door? In the casino? In a dark alley? Called information for Jerome's Men's Wear in the Palace. Before I could call him, the phone rang:

"Mr. Rogers. This is Jerome."

"Jerome's Men's Wear?"

"Yes, of course."

"You have my pants ready?"

"Yes, but—"

The Tuxeteers might have bugged the phone. I didn't want Jerome giving anything away. I interrupted: "Why don't we meet for breakfast. There's a coffee shop across the street from my motel. Arnold's. Bring the pants and breakfast's on me."

"But—"

"See you there in half an hour. No smoking section." It dawned on me: The Tuxeteers had sliced my only other pair of pants. I caught him before he hung up. "Jerome, meet me at the motel. Bring the jeans. Room 106."

I showered. Shaved. Waited. Towel around my waist. Exactly half an hour later: a knock on the door. I grabbed the jeans, started to put them on. He sat in a chair by the front window.

"I talked to–"

My hand clasped over his mouth. I shook my head. Released my hand. "Thanks for bringing the jeans here." I held up the shredded pants. He noticed my lip.

Whispering: "What happened?"

I put my finger across my mouth: ssh. After I dressed, I landed the gun in my pants. Covered it with the windbreaker. His eyes popped on seeing it. I ushered him out.

◈ ◈ ◈

Smoke from the Smoking Section infiltrated the No Smoking Section. The Star could've solved that situation, but it's impolite to shoot smokers in restaurants. We sat in a corner booth in the back. No one was in the booth next to us. We were both quick to order. The Double Breakfast, pancakes, hash browns, bacon and eggs. OJ. And a double side of cholesterol.

"What's going on?" he said, aflutter. He loved every minute of it. The intrigue. The suspense. A chance to do something more exciting than sell suits. "Some of the hotel security men were asking about you?"

"Anything in particular?"

"No. Just what you bought."

I hadn't noticed them watching me there. More two-way mirrors? "Anyone follow you to my hotel?"

"I don't think so."

"Between you and me?"

He nodded.

"I'm trying to find people who knew Teddie Matson."

"The TV star that was just murdered?" His eyes lit up like Vegas after dark. I guess he just wanted to be part of something.

"She worked as a chorus girl at the hotel a few years ago."

"Yes, I remember hearing about that. And that's what you want to talk to Jeanette about?"

"Would she have known Teddie? Seems a lot of people come and go."

"Lotta drifters. Some-a the pit bosses been around a long time. I'm not sure about Jeanette."

"You?"

"Me? I've been in the hotel a couple years. But I never met Teddie."

"At the motel you started to say you'd talked to someone. Who?"

"Jeanette, of course. She was going to call you in your motel room."

"Why didn't you tell me? We might miss the call."

"You didn't want to talk on the phone. Think the lines are bugged?"

"Maybe. I don't know."

"I can call her. Maybe we can go to her place."

I popped a quarter in his hand. He got up, headed for the phone. I hoped he wasn't calling hotel security. What was their interest in all this anyway? He came back just as the breakfasts were being set down.

"She says we can come by."

I jumped up.

"What about breakfast?"

"We'll get it to go."

"She's not dressed yet. She said in an hour."

Long enough to dress. Or long enough to get the Three Tuxeteers over?

"She live near here?"

"Not far. In Sparks. It's a suburb of Reno."

I was hungry. I could hardly keep the food down.

◈ ◈ ◈

Jeanette Lyon's house was one of those flat-roofed, cheap boxes that developers in the '60s seemed so fond of. No ornamentation. A few cactus plants in a gravelly dirt bed around the house. We parked in front. She met us at the door. Bright red hair stood up on her head, cascading down in back. It looked natural. Her skin was peaches and cream perfection. That white-white skin redheads often have. Very striking. She wore a black body suit and high heeled pumps.

Before we entered, I double checked the street. No sign of a tail. There hadn't been one all the way over. The Tuxeteers probably figured they'd scared me off.

The living room was tastefully decorated. A couple Diebenkorn prints. A mock fireplace with mock wood. Sliding glass door opening to a dead-grass plot of land a little larger than a double burial plot. Rusted swing set. No other sign of kids.

Introductions were short and sweet. Then:

"Jerome says you're looking for people who knew Teddie Matson when she worked here."

"Yes." I showed her my license.

"You looking for her killer?"

"Yes, but I can't go into any details." Were the Tuxeteers going to burst from behind a closed door and try to make me?

"What do I get out of it then, if I don't even get to know the dirt?"

"You get the glorious good feeling of knowing you helped someone." I smirked.

"Good feelings don't pay the bills."

"I don't have any money to offer you. If you know something and want to talk, I'm all ears. If not, I'm outta here." That's when I expected the Three Tuxeteers to erupt through the door. Nothing. Maybe they weren't there.

"People are asking about you. Saying to stay away."

"So why'd you invite me here?"

I sat on one end of the couch. Jeanette on the other. Jerome in a chair facing us. His head didn't move. His eyes followed us back and forth, as if he was at Wimbledon.

"Curiosity."

"Curiosity killed the cat."

"Is that a threat?"

"No. It's an attempt at levity."

"It's not funny." She thought a moment, debating whether or not to go on. Then: "I did know one girl who knew Teddie. Eleanor Hildreth. Was in the line when Teddie was. She quit. It was all very weird."

"Weird?"

"Like there was no reason for her to quit. And now the security guys are asking all kinds of questions. Weird. I don't know anything really, but I can give you her name and number."

"I'd appreciate it. I'd also appreciate it if this meeting never happened as far as anyone else is concerned."

"Yes, I agree," Jerome said. "With them asking all those questions, it's better if our involvement isn't known."

"No problem there," said Jeanette. "I like my face." She stared pointedly at my fat lip.

❖ ❖ ❖

Jerome didn't say much on the way to the Crystal Palace. He did offer to replace the slit pants free. Business didn't look good at his place and I told him just to stitch up the pair I had. I went to the lobby. Checked my service. No messages. Called Eleanor Hildreth. She sounded sleepy. It was noon. She invited me to come by.

She lived in a medium sized – maybe thirty or forty units – apartment building. Another of those flat-roofed, flat facaded boxes painted what I can only call shit-brown. The color of an obvious narc car. She lived in the back, next to the laundry room which made a rumble of white noise in her living room, blotting out other outside sounds.

She looked to be in her early forties. Unkempt, greasy strands of hair fell on her face and shoulders. Flowered robe and chain smoker. The lines on her face said it had seen some of life's little *joys*. Jeanette had described Eleanor as being quite a beauty, although she hadn't seen her in a couple of years. Her beauty had seen much kinder days.

I showed her my license. "How do you know Jeanette?"

"I've known her forever." She almost sounded boozy, but she wasn't drinking. "She went to New York, tried out for the Rockettes. Almost made it too. After a few years in the Big Apple, she came back here. I got her a job on the chorus. In less than a year they made her choreographer, then producer of the show."

"Why'd you quit?"

She retreated into a protective blanket, huddled inside her robe. She didn't want to answer.

"Jeanette said she thought you knew Teddie Matson. Worked with her."

Her face was a stone mask. "I knew Teddie. That's what you're here for?"

I nodded.

"What do you know?"

"Nothing. I've traced her back here. Don't know much else."

"Her murder is such a shame. She was a nice girl. But hey, so was I – back then."

"What happened? To you? To Teddie?"

"Jim Colbert happened."

Jim-Talbot/Jim-Colbert. Made sense. He'd kept his first name, a name he'd respond to when called by it. Phonied his last name.

"Tell me about him."

"He was this punk kid. Used to hang around the shows. I guess he was old enough to get in. Had a thing for the girls in the line, especially coloreds, know what I mean?"

"He had his eye on Teddie?"

"More than his eye?"

"Did they go together?"

"For about two weeks. But she thought he was too weird. Broke it off. He wouldn't stop coming around. Kept sending her candy, flowers."

"Orchids?"

"Yes. He liked to impress them by buying expensive things."

"Did he ever give her a teddy bear."

"Yeah, I think so."

"You said he wouldn't stop coming around."

"He'd hang out by the stage door. That kinda thing. Nothing dangerous."

"Did he ever do anything dangerous?"

"Teddie only worked a few months. After she left, he tried to find her. Write her. Couldn't get anyone to give him the information, so he eventually forgot about her, lit on another girl. Domino. That was her real name. Domino, can you imagine? I don't know where black folks get the names of their kids."

I figured when Colbert saw Teddie on TV it rekindled his spark for her, if it had ever truly dimmed. He got the bright idea of hiring a dick. He knew the show was filmed in L.A. She had to be there. So he came to me.

"How long did he go with her?"

"Not long. A little longer than Teddie. Maybe a month. Then she broke it off. He just came on too strong. Anyone could see. He wasn't for her, or Teddie. They were just kids. I was a few years older than them. Hell, I'm only thirty-four now. You wouldn't know it looking at me."

"Do you know where I can reach Domino?"

"Sure do. 1715 Del Gado Boulevard, Sparks."

"Near here?"

"Not too far."

"Phone number."

"She doesn't have one. Doesn't need it. 1715 Del Gado is the Del Gado Cemetery."

CHAPTER 34

What was it about him that the girls couldn't stand after a week or two?"

"He was smothering." Her eyes glazed over as she left the present and ran a movie memory of it all from a long time ago.

"In more ways than one," I said, figuring she'd get the implication.

"He wanted all of their time. Day and night. To be with them. It's not like he was evil. At least not then. But he was sort of – nerdy. Nice guy nerdy. They liked him. But he wouldn't let go. Called them all the time. A hundred times a day. At least it seemed like it. Wanted them to spend every minute with him. Just wanted everything they had and more. And he was jealous. I know he asked Teddie to quit the line. He didn't like all those men in the audience looking at her."

"Did he know she was from L.A.?"

"I think so. I'm not sure."

"I'm curious why he didn't follow her if he was so in love with her – follow her to L.A.."

"I don't know." She shifted uncomfortably. "I think he thought he'd try his luck with Domino. I don't know if it was the actual person that counted or the idea of her."

"What happened with Domino?"

"She wanted to break it off. It bruised his fragile male ego I guess. He stalked her, wouldn't leave her alone. He caught her backstage one day. Chased her into the catwalks. They fought. She fell and died – a bloody mess." She drummed a nervous beat with her foot. "Everybody knew it was murder, but because of the way it went down it could be interpreted differently."

"The hotel covered it up?"

"Didn't want the bad publicity. Nice folks."

"So if anyone comes around asking questions–"

"They take it into their own hands."

"It'll come out sooner or later."

"No, not with these people. They keep everything inside the family – if you know what I mean."

"Didn't you or anyone else put two and two together when you heard about Teddie's death?"

"My math isn't very good. 'Sides, you live around here long enough you learn to leave things alone if you want to be left alone."

"What happened with you? Why'd you quit?" I wanted to ask: Why'd you age beyond your years? Didn't.

"Teddie was a friend of mine. So was Domino. It was just too much. That and the pressure. Having to look perfect every goddamn second. Painted on smiles and kissing customers' asses even when they treated you like shit. Made you feel worthless. But I got back at 'em. All of 'em. I'm on disability now. They can pay for me the rest of my life."

I figured her disability was a payoff from the hotel, but there was no point bringing it up.

"Anyone else know Teddie or Domino?"

"Most of the girls are gone and I wouldn't advise you bothering the ones in the line now. 'Sides, I've lost touch with them. No numbers. No nothing. At least they ain't in the Del Gado Cemetery.

"Did the hotel pay off Domino's family?"

"I don't know."

"Why did Colbert like black girls?"

"Black, brown, green. Didn't matter."

"But no whites?"

"Not that I saw. But I don't know why he liked them. Maybe he didn't feel good enough for a white woman." She snorted a laugh. Jack would have appreciated her thought. What did it mean about Colbert?

"He from around here?"

"Colbert. Far as I know. I think he's from Sparks. He left town though. I mean, he could be back, but I don't think so."

"Why not?"

"That was part of the deal. Get outta town, and the cops and D.A. look the other way. Hotel's big enough to pull that kinda weight."

I asked if I could borrow her phone book. Looked up Colbert. There were a handful. I gave her ten bucks and started making calls. None of the Colberts admitted knowing Jim.

"No luck?" she said, offering me a box of saltine crackers.

"No."

"There's an odd dude might know Jim Colbert. Collects bottles and cans and any other junk he can find. I think he used to be a friend of Jim's or something. Funny to call it a *bi*cycle when it has three wheels, but it's hard to imagine a grown man riding a tricycle. That's for three year olds, isn't it?"

"Where does he live?"

"I don't know. But you can't miss him."

I remembered seeing him on my way into Reno. It had to be the same guy.

"Just hit the highways. You're bound to run into him sooner or later."

"Any idea which roads he favors?"

"Nope."

"What's his name?"

"People 'round here just call him Lobo."

❖ ❖ ❖

I gassed up the car. Hit the road. Since I'd seen him on my way into town from the south that's where I headed. After driving two hours out, I turned around and headed back. Made a couple detours on side roads. No luck. Next I ventured east, only going one hour out. That was sixty miles. Hard to imagine Lobo pedaling more than sixty miles in a day. Of course, he might not have lived in Reno, but somewhere outside. Anyway, it was the same thing. No sign of Lobo within an hour of town.

South. East. North. I hit the roads to the north of Reno and Sparks. Heat waves shimmied up from the ground, dancing on air. An hour out of town, I hit a greasy spoon diner, its parking lot filled with trucks. The greaseburger hit the spot. And stayed there. I asked the waitress behind the counter if she knew Lobo. She did. Had she seen him today? She hadn't. A trucker with snakeskin cowboy boots, a ten and a half gallon hat and three day growth of beard turned to me:

"Lookin' for Lobo?"

"Yeah."

"Law?"

"No. Private investigator. I'm trying to see if he's the relative of a client." I flashed my I.D.

"I saw him out on Highway 80 about an hour ago. Heading for the interchange with 95."

"Thanks." I plopped down enough money to pay for my meal and his.

Golden hour hit the desert like a spray of falling rain – bright specks of dust floating in the air. A rainbow of gold dust. Warm jasmine waves of sun lending the scene a soothing surreal quality. No sign of Lobo on 80. I headed out a little farther. Nothing. U-turn. On the way back I saw a silhouette at the junction of 80 and 95. Pulled over. It was the same grizzled guy I'd seen on my way up here. From what people had said it had to be Lobo.

"Howdy," he said. Looked about fifty to fifty-five give or take a handful of years. I wasn't so proud of my age-guessing ability after being so wrong about Eleanor. Hell, Lobo might have been thirty or seventy. I settled for fifty.

"Hi."

"Need directions?"

"Not really. You Lobo?"

"Lookin' for me? Hardly anybody comes lookin' for me. What can I do for you?" He squinted into the setting sun, his hand on his brow, Indian-style.

"I understand that you knew Jim Colbert."

His mouth narrowed to an angry gash. He backed away toward his bike. Opened a saddle bag, tossed in a couple Dos Equis cans he'd been picking out of the scree when I approached him. Closed the bag, straddled the seat. He didn't look in the mood for conversation.

"Don't go, please. I'll only have to follow you and I don't want to wear out my new shoes."

He settled into the seat, resigned to not leaving. "Whadda you want?"

"It's obvious from your reaction that you know him."

"Jim Colbert, Junior or Senior?"

"I don't know. I'd guess he's in his mid to late twenties."

A dejected shake of his head. "Junior. What do you want him for?"

"I need to talk to him."

"I figured someone'd be askin' about him sooner or later." He reached onto the crossbar of his bike, took a plastic bottle filled with green liquid from it. Swigged. He offered the bottle to me. I declined. He got off the bike. Nestled himself into a rock, stared into the sun. It looked almost as if he was trying to burn his retinas.

"Shouldn't look into the sun like that. It'll hurt your eyes."

"Doesn't matter. They've seen too much anyway."

"Tell me about Jim Colbert, Junior."

"He was a good kid. Never got into trouble or anything. I guess he musta been holding it all inside."

"Holding what inside."

"I don't know. Never did learn. Anyway, he liked a couple girls in the chorus over at the Palace. I'm sure you know the story."

"I know a little of it. Why don't you fill me in."

He did, without adding much to what I already knew.

"Why didn't he follow Teddie to L.A.?"

"I don't think he had her L.A. address. Never needed it. She was here. And when she decided to leave she wouldn't give it to him and neither would any of the girls in the chorus. I seem to remember he started out to L.A., got all the way to Bakersfield and then turned around. Came back. Never did know why. That's when he started dating that Domino girl."

"Do you know why he liked women of color?"

"Why are you looking for him?"

"It's confidential."

"If I'm to give you anymore information I think I have the right to know what this is all about. And if you don't give me the truth, I'll clam up. I promise you that."

I decided to tell him. "I think he may have murdered Teddie Matson."

The angry gash opened a tad. The anger replaced by sadness. "When I heard about that, I wondered if it could have been him. Do you have any proof?"

"Someone saw a man fitting his description at the scene. If it's him they can identify him. If not, he's got nothing to worry about." It wasn't necessary to tell him I'd also seen him. Aided and abetted him.

"Is it because of what happened here?"

"I didn't even know about that when I first learned about him." I sat down on a rock across from him, staring at the endless landscape of sage and juniper, figuring it would make him more comfortable if I wasn't standing over him.

"I knew Jim from a long way back. Farther back than most of his friends and such." He took a deep swallow of air. Just watching him made my throat dry. "His mother was black. You wouldn't know it to look at him. Or her. She was very light-skinned. You could hardly tell if you didn't look very closely at her features. She died when he was a kid. Around seven. I think his seeking out black and brown women was his attempt to deal with losing her."

"Tell me about Pilar Cruz."

"She was another of his crushes." His voice was guttural, hoarse. Filled with desert wind and sand. He took another swig of the green liquid. "She came up here for a summer. They met in some summer acting program at the local high school. This was before Teddie even. And it was the same story with her. He fell all over her, head over heels. Suffocated her with good intentions and love. He just couldn't see that it was too much for anyone else to want. He thought they wanted all that attention. He thought if he lavished them with it they would be his forever. He didn't know that people need space. Freedom." He waved his hand at the expanse of high desert valley, surrounded by snow-capped mountains. "I think the rejection, from Pilar, Teddie, Domino, and a couple others, got to him, especially on top of his feeling rejected by his mother. Wasn't her fault. She took ill with pneumonia and died."

The sun began to sink over the mountains in the distance. Red, orange and magenta ribbons of light spread out along the horizon. Golden hour was done for and twilight settled over the highway.

"Do you have a current address for him?"

"I have an address I can give you. Haven't heard from him in some time though."

"How long is that?"

"Several weeks at least. We used to write pretty regularly." He pulled a grimy notebook from the back of his faded corduroy pants. Pulled a piece of paper from it. Copied the address from the paper onto another sheet, tore it out and gave it to me. It was a Santa Barbara address. I'd hit it on the way back to L.A. "Y'know, I used to think it was nice of the hotel to hush things up and get Jimmy off without any trouble. It's Nevada you know. Mob ties and all that. They bought off the girl's family. But I don't think so anymore. At the very least he should have gotten some kind of psychiatric help. I'm sorry about that now."

There was no point in commenting to him that it was too late.

"I hope you find him," he said. "But be gentle. He's a good kid at heart."

"I'll do my best, Mr. Colbert."

He looked up when I said his name. That was confirmation enough. That and the same piercing blue eyes, the nervous demeanor.

It looked like he was crying. It was hard to tell in the dim light.

◈ ◈ ◈

I closed out my account at the Edsel, gathered my things. Met Jerome outside the Crystal Palace. He gave me a new pair of suit pants. Said he'd ruined the others trying to stitch them up. I didn't believe him, offered him money for the new pants. He wouldn't take it. I thanked him and headed out of town.

Stopping at a phone booth about a block from the hotel, I called Eleanor Hildreth. She confirmed my suspicion that Colbert, Sr. had been an executive at the hotel at the time of Domino's death, though she said she never realized he and Lobo were one and the same. I thanked her again and started to get in my car when I noticed one of the Three Tuxeteers on the sidewalk. I came up behind him, bar-armed his throat, dragged him into the shadows.

His hand shot for the shoulder holster under his expensive Armani jacket. It didn't make it. In fact, I grabbed it, twisting, and broke his wrist.

"What the fuck's this all about?" he said. "You're fucking with the wrong people."

I shoved him into the wall. Down to the ground. Slammed my foot into his mouth. A tooth fell to the ground. Blood flowed out. There was a part of me that wanted to keep going. The more sane part said to quit.

"Have a nice day," I said.

CHAPTER 35

The Santa Barbara address was a bust. The apartment manager said Colbert had moved out two months ago without leaving a forwarding address. I felt like I was back to square one. My leads had taken me there. And there was nothing. I called Martin Luther King Hospital from a payphone.

"Hey, dude, or is that Duke? What's happening?"

"You sound good. Better than before."

"Can't keep me shut up forever. Hey, I'm gettin' out."

"When?"

"Today."

"If you can wait a couple hours, I'll pick you up. I'm in Santa Barbara."

"Don't come back to this mess on my account."

"It'd be my pleasure."

I grabbed a cheeseburger at McDonald's and headed out to the 101 and the drive back to L.A. Tiny was glad to see me. Gave me a bear hug.

"Looks like they patched you up pretty good."

"Can't keep me down. I'm too mean," he growled.

"Feeling feisty."

A nurse wheeled Tiny to the curb and my waiting car in a wheelchair. There was nothing wrong with Tiny's legs. Why do hospitals always have to do that? Insurance?

"Glad to be outta that place." He looked around. Blackened buildings. Charred remains of others. "Or am I?"

We drove by his rental company. Still there and untouched. Which is more than I could say for my car. The tires and hubcaps were gone and what remained was a burned out hulk. There wasn't even enough left to tow away. It sent a shot of sadness mixed with anger through me, but nothing like what I felt for the loss of Baron.

"Whew! But I don't think I want to go in today. Tomorrow'll be plenty of time to do that. Let's go have a beer." He directed me to a small restaurant. I felt odd. I was the only white. Whispers floated our way. Were they wondering what a white man was doing here? Now?

I caught him up on the progress of the case. He offered his help. I told him he needed to rest. I asked him about Teddie. He couldn't give me any new information that would have been helpful. Then: "I'll get your car fixed up."

"You don't need to do that."

"Was on my property. I feel responsible. 'Sides, I know some good people who'll do it for a price."

How could I argue? After a couple beers, I dropped him at his house.

◈ ◈ ◈

Before going home, I dropped by Laurie's. Locked up tight. No sign of Jack's bike. I rang the bell. No answer. Rang again.

"Laurie, it's Duke. I want to see if you're okay."

Her car wasn't in the driveway and I couldn't see in the garage. I figured she might have gone out for the evening so I headed home. My answering service beeper was beeping. Turned it off. I didn't care.

The house felt strange. As if I wasn't alone. Everything appeared undisturbed. Still it was an eerie feeling.

I showered and crashed, dreaming that Baron was licking my face awake like he used to.

◈ ◈ ◈

The morning sun was bright as it streamed through window, waking me. Damn L.A. It'd be nice to have seasons. I didn't want sun on a day like this. Half of L.A. was burned to the ground. What right did the sun have to shine?

The message on the beeper was from Jack. I tried him. Couldn't connect. Called the service. Jack had left a message there too: Craylock had gotten to Laurie. She was in Cedars-Sinai Hospital with a swollen cheek and minor lacerations. It felt like déjà vu. I tried the hospital. Laurie was asleep. Jack wasn't there. Wasn't home either. They'd said she was doing fine. I wanted the details. Where? When? How? Were the police involved? No one would tell me anything.

I called Warren. He didn't have anything new to add. No teddy bear and he was as surly as ever.

"I missed you in Reno," I said.

"Yeah, well something came up."

"I thought the Big L.A. Party was over?"

"Man, some parties never end. Some dude caught me on videotape. Cops came and arrested me and I had to be arraigned. Otherwise I wouldda been there. Been on your ass all the way."

Guilt overcame me so I headed for the hospital. I was about to turn into the parking lot when I spotted a black beamer in the rearview. It couldn't be. Pulling over to the side, I let him pass. It was him – Craylock. He pulled into the hospital parking lot. I drove in behind him. He didn't notice me in his rearview mirror.

I followed to where he parked, blocking his car in with mine. He saw me. Knew he couldn't drive out. He got out of the car and ran.

I left my car blocking his. A parking attendant yelled at me to move it.

"Police," I shouted.

Craylock ran down the sidestreet to San Vicente. Dodging traffic, he dashed across the road into the giant Beverly Center shopping mall parking lot. I chased him through the parking lot, zigzagging in and around cars, to the escalators. He headed up, shoving people out of his way. One thing I never understood is why people went up when they were trying to escape. Unless there was a chopper waiting for them, there was always a deadend. I knew that if I ever had to run from someone I'd go straight ahead, full throttle.

We came out into the mall. Innocent shoppers watched two men run down the hall. He pushed a baby in a stroller out of the way. I kept after him. Mall security joined the chase, running and talking into walkie-talkies at the same time. Craylock jumped onto another escalator, heading up again. He stayed on it until he reached the top level where the food stalls were.

We played dodge-the-shopper until there was nowhere else for him to run to. I crashed into him, knocking him against the Hot Dog on a Stick's brightly striped yellow and blue walls. The fresh lemons in their lemonade machine escaped their bondage and crashed down on us, spilling sticky pink lemonade all over us.

Four uniformed guards from mall security had us surrounded. They were already radioing the real cops. I didn't show the Star. No need to hassle that. Craylock was panting. I was in a hell of lot better shape than him and I was panting too. In between gulping air, I tried explaining to the security guard in charge what was going on. "This man's wanted by the police," I said, gasping for air. He didn't care. They hustled us into a back room where we waited for the police. It didn't take them long to show up. An older L.A.P.D. sergeant, who looked like he'd seen it all, twice, and a young female officer. The mall security guys had neglected to frisk us. The cops weren't so lax. I asked Sergeant Webb if I could speak to him alone for a minute. We went into the hall.

"I'm a licensed private detective." I showed him my I.D. "The man inside is wanted for stalking and beating up a client. I saw him at Cedars, where she's recuperating, and gave chase. And I'm carrying a concealed weapon."

"Real easy now," he said, "Lean against the wall. You know the drill."

I did what he said, spreading my arms and legs. He asked where the gun was. I told him. He removed it, patted me down. Didn't find anything else – I never did get my knife back from the Tuxeteers.

"Do you have a permit?"

"No. That's why I was hoping we could work this out. I was chasing him. I felt I needed the gun."

"We'll see how it plays out. Let's go back inside." He asked for a brown paper bag, got one, and put the gun in it. No one else had seen it.

"I don't know why this man is chasing me. He's crazy."

The sergeant called the station. There was a bulletin out on Craylock. He was wanted for questioning in Laurie's beating. The sergeant got my name, address, phone number. He took my statement. "No need to come down to the station now," he said. "We'll be in touch." The woman cop cuffed Craylock, who was still proclaiming his innocence. "Don't forget your lunch," the sergeant said, handing me the brown bag.

"Thanks, sergeant."

He didn't respond, just turned to the business at hand. I told him where Craylock's car was parked, then headed off. Walking back to the parking lot across the street, I, once again, felt as if I was being followed. There were a lot of people around. Many of them had seen the chase. I passed it off to paranoia and figured people were watching me 'cause of the chase.

The parking attendants hadn't had my car towed, but more police were milling around it. I told them what had just happened. After verifying the story, they let me go without frisking me. I felt lucky.

Before getting into my car, I looked in his. Fresh flowers. He'd been bringing her flowers. People never cease to amaze me.

◈ ◈ ◈

Laurie had been off her guard when Craylock came up to her. It was the middle of the day – her lunch hour. She was walking down the street to a sandwich shop when he cut her off at an alley and pulled her into his car. He'd driven towards the freeway onramp, but hadn't made it. She was kicking and screaming the whole way. He'd tried to beat her into submission, thus the hospital stay, but it hadn't worked. She belted him in the mouth and jumped from the car.

She was home from the hospital after only one day. Craylock was safely in jail awaiting arraignment. Jack and I went to visit her.

"What's this?" she said, as I handed her a brown paper bag.

"Chicken soup. From Cantor's Deli."

"Jewish penicillin," Jack said. He had to say something. "You'll get well more quickly."

Laurie put the soup in the fridge. She poured us all diet sodas. We sat in the living room.

"I told Jack not to come around. I wanted to do it on my own. I figured, what was the point, I couldn't have a bodyguard forever."

"You did do it on your own," I said.

"I know," she grinned. "But I still want to take a self defense class and learn to shoot better. Jeez, how much longer do I have to wait to pick up the gun? I got lucky with that one punch that landed on his nose."

She thanked us. Said to keep in touch. I said we would. At the very least we'd be testifying at Craylock's trial. Jack and I split and hit a bar, downing a few beers.

"I can't shake the feeling of being followed," I told him as we downed another.

"It's just these cases, man. Both stalkers. Got you spooked."

"You're right. That and lack of sleep."

◈ ◈ ◈

I went home. Called Rita. No answer at her place. I left a message saying I'd been out of town and saying she could call me or I'd call back again. Either way. I was nervous about talking to her.

Square one.

Square one.

Square one, I kept saying to myself. Chasing all over hell and back and still nowhere. I wasn't about to quit though. Finding the Weasel had become my mission.

I dialed the phone: "Hello, Lou."

"Duke. What's going on?"

"I'm getting closer. I know who the guy is."

"You do?" She responded quickly, with anticipation.

"Yes. Jim or James Colbert, Jr. Originally from Sparks, Nevada. I think he's living here now."

"Oh no. I can see it coming."

"You have to run him, Lou. If you do I'll find him, get the police in on it."

"You're sure it's the right guy."

I told her Colbert, Junior's story.

"Sounds like it's him." There was a long pause. I could hear her breathing. "All right. I'll run him first thing in the morning. And if he's in the computer fine, you find him, turn him in. But if he's not, we go to the police with what we've got now. Deal?"

"Deal."

We made plans to have another dinner at El Coyote and hung up. My whole body ached. Stiff everywhere. All I wanted was to take a hot shower and hit the hay. Then:

A noise.

Outside.

Go to the window.

Can't see anything.

Crouch on the floor.

Peek out.

Nothing.

Wait.

Waiting hurts.

Silence.

No movement.

Am I being followed?

Maybe I'm not so crazy after all.

Still nothing.

The silence of the night.

Silence.

Calm.

Peaceful.

Too damn peaceful

Too damn quiet.

Then:
A shadow.
Moving across the garage wall.

CHAPTER 36

The shadow of a Weasel?
     A Craylock who'd made bail?
     Warren on the rampage?
Non-descript burglar, variety 27?
The guy who's been tailing me?
Safety off.
Latch off the back door.
Open slowly.
Hinge creak.
Damn.
Been meaning to oil those hinges.
Toe-walk down the stairs.
Creeping.
Shadow inching along edge of garage.
Padding forward.
A target in the light.
Could've turned the outside floods off.
Would've given myself away
Stillness.
No tranquility.
Rustling breeze.
What's that?
Breathing?
A sucking step into mud or wet grass.
Charge the garage.
Running steps.
He's heard me.
Seen me.

Knows I'm here.
Hard charging.
After him.
Around the garage.
Behind the incinerator.
Shadow on the wall.
He's over.
I'm over.
Running through the neighbor's yard.
Who's there? neighbor shouts.
I'm calling the cops.
Bolt down the driveway.
Intruder runs up the block.
Chase him.
Red lights.
Blue lights.
Cop car.
Ditch into the bushes.
Cops ride by to neighbor's house.
Don't see me.
They're gone.
So is intruder.
Damn.
Fuck up.
Fuck up.
Fuck up.
Head home.
Avoid cops.
Curse the night.

◈ ◈ ◈

What would he have done if I hadn't heard him? Spied on me? Broken in? Robbed? Attacked? Killed? L.A. cops are notorious for not catching calls quickly. My luck these guys must have been cruising nearby. Damn.

The phone was ringing as I entered through the back door.

"Yeah." Angry. Out of breath.

"Sounds like you're having a good night," Jack said.

"I'm sure I'm being tailed."

"You're being paranoid again."

"I chased the son-of-a-bitch outta my yard and into the street. Would've caught him if a neighbor hadn't called the cops."

"Should've let the cops catch him for you."

"And deprive me of the pleasure?"

"You're right. Besides, they prob'ly would've busted your sorry ass." He chuckled, pleased with his little joke. "Who do you think it was?"

"I don't know for sure. My guess is the Weasel."

"Seems weas-ly all right. Smart."

"Not smart enough. I'm onto him. I know who he is. And Lou's gonna tell me where he is."

"Well, I guess you don't wanna go out and have a few."

"Not tonight."

"Stick around, see if he'll come back?"

"Something like that."

"Want company?"

"Thanks, but no."

Jack was right. I thought maybe he'd come back, whoever he was. If he did, I wanted to be there. I slept in the hall, halfway between the kitchen and the living room. Figured I could hear anything at either end of the house that way. The Star was my pillow.

Lou's call woke me the next morning. Colbert had, indeed, moved to L.A., to an apartment about ten blocks from where Teddie lived – and died. Walking distance. That's why no one had seen a car. He had some smarts. Thank God for Lou, computers and the DMV, though some people might fault one or the other sometimes. I wondered if he knew I was onto him. Might he have called his dad? Did Colbert, Sr. even have a phone? Had he followed me? Maybe I wasn't so paranoid all along? If he had he was a damned good tail. I might have seen little hints of things out of the corners of my eyes, but I never saw him. Never anything concrete. Did he know about my meeting with Ramon? Trip to Calexico? Reno? Had he seen me with Laurie?

Had he followed me home? Killed Baron?

Lou had gone into work early to run him. She figured if she had to get up early, so did I. As long as I was up, there was no time to lose. I dressed. Headed out. It took about ten minutes to get to the Weasel's apartment. The name was prettier than the building, The Ocean Breeze Palms. There was no ocean. No breeze. And the palms were dead or dying. Just like the street they lived on. Just like the building named after them. Some Russian-speaking children headed off to school, arguing about the merits of the USA over the former USSR. I don't speak Russian, but enough of their interchange was in English for me to get the gist of it.

The water in the courtyard pool was black. Looked like it hadn't been cleaned in years. Mosquitoes might have liked it. No one else.

Number seven was ground floor, rear. The curtain in the front window might once have been white, maybe off-white. Now it was the same color as the pool water. The knocker was loose on its hinge, but it worked.

No answer.

I tried peeking in the window. He had the curtains taped at the edges. What the hell was he doing in there?

Knocked again.

A neighbor came out. "You are looking for Mr. Jim Colbert? Yes?" he said in a thick Russian accent.

"Da," I said. Couldn't resist.

He chuckled. "*Da, da.* Ver-ry good."

"Yeah, I'm looking for Jim."

"He is at working now."

Pretty early for a lot of jobs. "Do you know where he works?"

"Where he is working?"

"*Da,* where he is working?"

"He is working at produce section of market in Beverly Center. Starts to working very early. Ver-ry early."

Before leaving, I learned that Colbert had only been living there a few weeks. That he had a car and was a good neighbor. From the William Tell to here. I didn't know if that was a step up or down. Before the motel, Santa Barbara. Or something in between? Didn't matter. I was onto him now.

"Thank you." I ditched for the street and my car. The Beverly Center – seemed I was spending a lot of time there lately and I hated the place, wouldn't shop there for all the diamonds in South Africa – was only a couple minutes away. The market was at street level, with its own little parking section. I pulled in. It was half full. I parked near the front door, in a loading zone. Someone started yelling at me to move.

"No speak English," I said in an accent from a world of my own making. He threw his hands up and walked away. Inside the store, I headed for the produce section. In the back, someone was putting lettuce out. I could tell it was a man. No more than that.

I approached. Fingering the Star under my windbreaker.

The man turned around. Strike one. Not the Weasel.

"Can I help you?" he said.

"Does Jim Colbert work here?"

"Yes, if there's anything I can–"

"No thank you. Is he in today?"

"He's in back. Are you the friend who's going to help him move?"

"Move?"

"Today's his last day. Didn't even give two weeks' notice. Hell, he only worked here a few weeks. That's like a lot of them today, they just don't got no pride in their work."

Must've killed Teddie on his lunch hour. Plenty of time to do it and get back.

He stuck his hand out. "I'm Terry Lanton, produce manager."

"Nice to meet you." I headed for the "Employees Only" door.

"I'm sorry, but you can't go back there."

Before I got there, a cart pushed the swinging door open. Wider. It was him – pushing the cart. We stood about twenty-five feet apart, staring each other down. It must have lasted all of a half second. Seemed like half an eternity.

Then he bolted. Back the way he came, shoving the cart in the door at an angle that made it hard to push out of the way. I pushed. It didn't go. I flew across it, knocking tomatoes and avocados in every direction.

"What's going on here?" Lanton's voice faded in the background.

The Weasel ran through the backroom, out onto the loading dock. Jumped into the parking lot and ran for his car. I had to make a split-second decision: get in my car to chase or try to stop him from getting to his. The decision was made for me. He was already pulling out of his parking place in his lumbering old Monte Carlo.

I vaulted onto the hood of his car, trying to hold onto the side mirror on the driver's side. He bashed my hand with a large flashlight. I held on. He kept bashing. I rolled off. Got to my feet and ran for my car.

He crashed the wooden gate arm. I silently thanked him for that as that would be one less dent to pay for on the rental car.

He tore out onto La Cienega, heading north. The light changed. I caught the red. I did what so many other L.A. drivers had been doing lately – I ran it. Nearly hit a cross traffic cement mixer. I figured it would have been better than hitting a carload of gang bangers.

At Sunset he turned right, heading for Hollywood. Where were the damn cops now? Nowhere in sight. We dodged in and out of traffic to Western where he headed north, up into the Hollywood Hills and Griffith Park. I didn't know if he knew where he was going, but heading *up* the winding roads of the park wouldn't get him anywhere, except maybe to the Observatory.

He couldn't know where he was going. I think he was trying to hit the freeway and took a wrong turn. We chased up the backroads of the park, past the boy toys sunning themselves on the hoods of their cars, waiting for another boy toy to pick them up.

Finally, we turned into the Observatory parking lot. He headed around one side of the circular driveway. I cut the other way, heading towards him, hoping we'd meet at some point. If not, he just might get all the way around and take the other road down.

I gunned it around the circle. He was coming for me. A school bus was unloading children near the entrance to the building. I stopped, not wanting to hit any kids. The Weasel kept coming from the other side. Shit – I hoped he wouldn't hit anyone. A teacher saw us coming and hurried the kids out of the way.

He came flying around the circle in one direction.

Me in the other.

Engines gunning.

His old Monte Carlo with the big V-8.

Me in my little Toyota rental.

A hair's breadth before we passed, I cut in front of him. He played chicken and ditched onto the sidewalk. He thought he could go around me.

No way.

He bottoms out.

Fishtails.

Hits the statue in front of the Observatory.

People running back.

Trying to get away from us.

I jam on the brakes.

Stick it in park and jump out.

He runs around the building.

I follow.

Star out.

A park ranger comes around the building.

The Weasel barrels into him.

Knocks him down.

I jump over him.

Keep on running.

If the Weasel keeps on this way, he'll circle to the front of the Observatory.

A mother tries to pull her little boy down from a quarter observation telescope.

She yanks the boy hard.

They fall back into the Weasel.

Knock him to one knee.

He gets up.

It's enough time.

I catch him.

He throws a weak right.

I block.

Counter with a left.

Square on the jaw.

He stumbles.

Kicks me in the groin.

I drop to my knees.
He takes off.
I catch his pant leg.
Tumble him.
We roll on the ground.
The ranger limps toward us.
The Weasel throws me.
Jumps the wall.
Into the bush below the Observatory.
I follow.
Jumping.
Rolling.
Down the hill.
He limps a few yards ahead of me.
I run down the hill.
Jump off a rock point.
Dive for him.
If I miss it's the end of me.
He stumbles.
I land on him.
We roll into a tree.
Arms flailing.
Legs kicking.
I'm on top of him.
He's face down.
I'm about to use some of that old SEAL training.
Break his neck.
No. Stop.
The ranger shouts.
I stop.
Pull the Weasel to his feet.
This is your lucky day, pal.
He snorts for air.

❖ ❖ ❖

The ranger took my gun. I tried to proffer my P.I. I.D. to him. He didn't want to see it. Held a gun – my gun – on both of us, while he fished out his cuffs.

"We won't be able to climb up," the Weasel said, out of breath. The ranger looked up toward the Observatory. No trail. Just scree and scrub. Steep. He put the cuffs back in their holster, motioned us forward, upward with the gun. Escorted the Weasel and me up the hill. I helped him drag the Weasel, telling the ranger he was a wanted fugitive. Feigning breathlessness so I wouldn't have to say anymore.

"I'll get you," Colbert said to me. "I can, you know. I'll tell everyone, the papers, TV, everyone what a hero you are."

We climbed over the wall, back onto the Observatory platform. The ranger cuffed the Weasel, held the gun on me. Didn't trust either of us. Sirens wailed in the background. Cops on the way. Never there when you need them.

The ranger, Weasel and I headed toward the front of the Observatory. The ranger had one hand on the Weasel's cuffed left arm, the other holding my own gun on my back. He was pushing us forward. A crowd of children stared at us as we walked by. The Weasel looked down at them. The ranger kept pushing us forward.

The Weasel broke free, ran for the wall. Jumped to it and tottered along until he came to the point where the ground below was farthest from the top of the wall. The ranger and I chased after him. We almost got to him. He jumped. We were too late.

A piercing scream wrenched the air as the body landed on the hard ground below. A snap. We could hear it all the way at the top of the wall.

The ranger and I scurried over the wall to the twisted body below. It was too late.

◈ ◈ ◈

I hoped it didn't make the news before I had a chance to talk to Rita. If she had to find out, I wanted to be the one to tell her.

CHAPTER 37

I had wanted to kill the Weasel, not because I was angry at him, but so he couldn't talk. So Rita wouldn't find out the part I'd played in Teddie's death. The ranger's "no" had stopped me, but I think I would have stopped anyway. I hope so. Killing him would have been the chicken-shit's way out. The Fuck-up's way.

He died of a broken neck. His own making. With his hands cuffed he couldn't break the fall when he jumped and landed on his neck. Was it intentional – a way to escape jail, or was it an accident?

Between Sergeant Webb's and Tom Bond's vouching for me, the cops didn't file a weapons charge for the Star. I was lucky.

Mrs. Perlman and the gardener ID'd the Weasel as the man who had murdered Teddie. People were treating me like a hero. The news media wanted interviews. I declined. They videoed me entering and exiting the police station to give my story. Camped out in front of my house, hoping I'd give them a few words of wisdom. Jack came by and we watched old black and white movies on American Movie Classics and had a few beers. Didn't say much.

The phone was ringing off the hook. Reporters, media people. Hollywood producers. I wasn't answering, letting the service screen the calls. I didn't want to be a hero. Didn't feel like one. I had wanted to make amends to Teddie and her family for having taken a quick two hundred-fifty bucks on a scut job and having fucked up. Nothing would ever bring her back. But I felt I had evened the score somewhat.

When I checked in for messages late in the afternoon, there had been separate messages from Mrs. Matson and Warren, thanking me. Warren even partially apologized for his behavior. Chagrined, the operator read me the message he'd left verbatim: "You didn't do too bad for a white guy. I owe you one, honky." I thought the honky was affectionate. I wanted to believe it was. It sounded almost like an apology. But I didn't want his apology. Didn't need it. He didn't owe me anything. And I hoped I was square with him and his mother now, even though they didn't know the whole story. I hadn't found Anna and Pilar. I hoped they'd see the story in the papers or on TV and feel comfortable enough to come out of hiding.

Lou had also left a message congratulating me and reminding me about El Coyote. The one message I was hoping for wasn't there.

A few minutes later, the phone rang through. It was one of the service operators: "Mr. Rogers, there's a call on the line I thought you might want me to put through. She says she's a close friend of yours. Her name is Rita Matson."

◈ ◈ ◈

The reporters out front didn't realize who she was and let her through the crowd. "Probably thought I was the maid," she said with a hint of bitterness, then a smile. Jack laughed. Too hard. The smile faded from Rita's lips. She stood by the back door, her dark hair silhouetted by the golden hour sun streaming in through the pane at the top of the door. It was awkward. I could say that was because of Jack being there. It wasn't. It would have been awkward anyway.

"It's good to see you again," Jack said, gathering his overweight kit bag.

"Duke told me on the phone that you helped him. Thank you." She put her hand out. Jack took it. Shook.

"Segue," he said, disappearing out the back door. If anyone could handle the media bloodsuckers, Jack could. If they pissed him off enough, he might use them for target practice.

The sound of a Harley revving. He was gone. There was still a pall of uneasiness between us. The air felt heavy.

"Would you like something to drink?"

"No thanks. Where's Baron?" she said, looking around.

I explained what had happened and that I still wasn't sure who had done it.

"I'm sorry. Everybody's losing something these days."

We retreated to the living room, sat on opposite ends of the couch. The room was gloomy. The curtains were closed so I wouldn't have to see the leeches on my front lawn. At least they weren't making a lot of noise.

I wondered if she knew. If my guilt had shown and she'd known all along. I didn't think so. Didn't want to ask.

"My whole family is grateful to you," she said, tentatively.

They shouldn't be.

"I'm glad I could help. Still, it was my job."

"You attacked it with more energy than most people put into a job. Do you treat all your cases that way?"

I didn't want to respond to that. Thought I'd switch subjects: "I'm sorry I didn't return your calls more promptly."

"I thought you might be avoiding me. 'Cause of the black-white thing. I didn't want to believe that, so I made up my mind that you were busy working on the case."

"I was. I've been all over. Calexico. Reno. Santa Barbara."

"I read the police account in the paper. Don't you want to talk to the press?"

"Fifteen minutes of fame just isn't enough," I gave her a half smile. "Besides, they don't want the real story, they want something they can put on *Hard Copy.* Sensational. It was nothing special."

She moved closer, brushed her finger gently along my swollen lip. "Nothing special."

"All part of the job."

"That's what I'm still curious about, who were you working for on this *job*?"

"You know I can't tell you."

"Confidentiality and all that."

"It could just be a friend of hers. Someone who wanted to know."

"It wasn't the studio."

"I never said it was."

She was making me suspicious. There was no way for her to know the truth, of course, but the more she talked the more it seemed like she had figured it out. If not completely, at least partly. I thought I was pretty good at playing poker face. Maybe not as good as I pretended to myself. Or maybe there was so much guilt it couldn't help but show through.

I put my arm around her, tried to pull her closer. She squirmed. Shrugged it off. She grew colder. The warmth was gone from her eyes, mouth. Voice.

"What's wrong?" I stood up.

"Why're you putting your arm around me?"

"I didn't know it was a crime. In fact, I thought you kind of liked it."

"You ignore me for days. Don't respond to my calls."

"I was working the case."

"Bullshit."

"I got the guy, didn't I?"

"Yes, and I am grateful for that. But were you working the case twenty-four hours a day? Didn't you know I wanted to talk to you? Why would I have called so many times?"

"I'm sorry, I–"

"I don't want to hear it. I think I know why you were avoiding me. And now it's all over, and you're acting sweet and all, but distant. The case is over. Why the distance?"

"Just coming down from a rough few days."

"You know what your trouble is, Duke. You're not honest. Not with me. Not even with yourself."

"What're you talking about? What else am I supposed to do?" My voice was tense, anger-filled.

Now she stood. Each of us at opposite ends of the couch. Leaning forward, in near-pugilistic stances.

"Now that it's all over, things are quieting down. Oh never mind."

"What? Tell me what you're talking about."

"Am I your nigger bitch? Was I? Good for a roll in the hay during the riot?"

"You're crazy."

"Am I? I don't hear from you, you don't return calls. Now the riot's over you don't need my– I think it made you feel good to have a nigger-woman during the riots. Made you feel good and liberal. It was also a shelter for you, like Tiny. Hey, if you're walking through Niggertown with Tiny maybe you're okay. Maybe the brothers and sisters won't beat on you. Maybe if you're sleeping with a nigger bitch, same thing. You're okay.

Things aren't as bad as they seem. You can assuage your white guilt."

"I don't have any white guilt. I haven't done anything. But I do think you've been talking to Warren too much."

"Hardly. I've been thinking about this. All those nights when I felt so alone and no return calls from you."

"So this is your response? To lay it down to some racial thing. I'm not your master."

"And I ain't *yo'* slave," she said in poor black dialect. "But you do get your kicks sleeping with a Negress, don't you? Lotta white men do. You'd never bring one home to mommy and daddy though."

"You don't know what you're talking about, you stupid—"

"Stupid what? — Nigger?" She started to cry. The anger had been welling up in me. I could hardly control it. She was partially right, I think. She had been a safe haven in rough waters. It wasn't that I hadn't liked her, or didn't still. But it was a crazy time. I was running on adrenalin overdrive. I did like her. And it was more than the riots. More than shelter in the storm. It was more than Teddie, but she didn't know that. I don't think the word that was welling up was *nigger*. I didn't want to believe that. I didn't know what it was. Whatever, though, I'm glad she cut it off.

I stepped towards her. She put her hand out in front of her chest to hold me off. I stopped.

"That's what this search for Teddie's killer was all about too. White guilt."

"You're right." But I didn't mean it the way she did.

She looked through me with intense brown eyes. It was as if she was shocked that she'd been right. She had been right. But she'd been wrong.

"It isn't white guilt how you mean it. Colbert came to me to find an address for him. He gave me a name, Teddie or Theodora Matson." My voice had softened. She had to ask me to speak louder. "I had never heard of her. Don't watch much TV, except for old movies and news. He told me he was an old friend. Seemed like an easy gig." I told her the whole story, every detail. Sat in a chair facing the couch. I wanted to hide my head, bury it in my hands. I wouldn't let myself. Forced myself to look her in the eye.

She sat on the arm of the couch. She also didn't want to look at me. She forced herself to. "For two hundred fifty dollars. My sister. And then you slept with me." Her voice cracked. She was holding the tears back.

I went on: "I've done jobs like this before. There was no way to know. That's not an excuse. It's just the way it is."

"No. The way it is, is Teddie is dead. No wonder you don't want to talk to the media. The whole time you played me for a fool."

"Are you concerned about Teddie or about how you think I treated you?"

"Both. Warren's right. Even he softened. He shouldn't have."

"I never played you or your family for fools. I wanted to get the killer. If I'd told you the truth, you wouldn't have helped me."

She slunk down into the couch, huddled in the corner. "That's damn for sure. And then you had the nerve to sleep with me. But I guess that's to be expected. I am just a nigger."

"That's your word. Not mine."

"It's the white man's word."

"Your feelings are hurt. But that's not the way it is."

"Then why didn't you return my calls?"

"I was afraid to."

"A big ex-SEAL like you."

"Why don't you cut the crap? Let's have a decent conversation."

"Niggers can't have–"

I jumped out of my seat. She put her hands in front of her face, ready to block a blow. I wasn't going to hit her. I grabbed her. Jerked her up and to me. Held her. She tried to get away. I wouldn't let go.

"You're right. I was confused. I liked you but it was all happening so fast. I still like you, though I'm sure you don't like me anymore. That's okay. I don't blame you. I don't like myself very much when I think about it. I was afraid to call you back. Afraid to hurt you. Afraid to tell you the truth. Debating whether or not I ever should. Wondering if, after the riots, there would be anything for us. Between us. Or was it all just a *wartime romance*? Two people caught up in something bigger than themselves. Would they, we, have anything in common once it was over?"

She broke free, stepped back. I collapsed on the couch. Exhausted. Talking it out. Telling the truth had wiped me out.

"Are you all right?" she said.

"Yeah."

"We can never tell my mother or Warren."

"It's your call." I closed my eyes. "I didn't intend to hurt you or your family. When I did, I tried to make it up by finding him. There's no way to do anymore than that. I won't say I'm sorry again. Not because I'm not. Because it won't help anything."

She sat next me. Let her hand fall to my thigh. We sat like that for about ten minutes. Silent. Someone knocked on the front door. I let them keep knocking. Didn't care who it was. Probably a reporter. I took her hand and led her to the guest bedroom. Pulled out one of my butterfly collection notebooks. Handed it to her.

"I want you to have this."

"What for?"

"I don't know. I think you'll enjoy it."

"So will you. And you don't need to buy me off."

"I'm not trying to. You see, this is the problem. Now that you know, you'll be suspect of everything. I'll never be able to do anything, give you anything without your thinking it's guilt."

She took the notebook. Clutched it in her hand. She even looked beautiful when she cried.

◈ ◈ ◈

She left a few minutes after that. We had decided to wait a while before talking to each other again. No set time. If one of us decided to call the other, then we'd call. Until then, we'd wait.

◈ ◈ ◈

I never did find out if it was the Weasel or Craylock or some crazy person off the street who did Baron. But I would keep looking until I found him or knew he was dead already. And I never found out who was following me, but I'd wager the mortgage it was the Weasel. It would be nice if things were neat and tidy, but they never are. I also wondered what became of Pilar and Anna. Thought I might give Ramon a call some day and see if he was interested in having me find out.

◈ ◈ ◈

I missed Rita. Several times I started to dial her. Each time, I hung up before connecting. A couple times when my phone rang and there was no one on the other end I wondered if she was doing the same thing.

I took time off of work to work around the house. Run at the beach. The city was returning to a semblance of normal. On the surface. Underneath, tension roiled. I tried not to let it bother me. Not that I wasn't concerned. But I figured I'd better work out my own tensions before trying to solve the world's.

One day, I drove down Beverly Boulevard until it turned into Santa Monica Boulevard. I headed toward the beach. A few blocks before the water, I turned up a sidestreet. Parked in front of the Ocean View Rest Home. No ocean view. There was an ocean breeze.

"Mr. Rogers," a nurse said. "It's been ages."

She led me to my father's room. The TV droned. He had been a round, robust man with a ruddy complexion and thick brown hair. He had shrunk to a ghost of himself. His hair was thin and greasy. His cheeks sunken and pale. Eyes dull.

"Hello, dad," I said, taking his hand. It was clammy. He grunted some kind of greeting. But it could have been to anyone. He didn't recognize me. I sat there about an hour. We had never gotten along. He had never been the father I would have picked. I wasn't the son he wanted. If we'd only respected each other on our own terms we might have gotten along. When I left, a sadness hung over my heart. I drove to the ocean. The sun was dying. Golden hour almost over. I watched the sun set over the horizon, a flaming ball of orange amidst bands of magenta, lavender and yellow.

On my way home, a white woman was stopped at a stoplight. A group of black kids, couldn't have been more than ten or eleven years old, were crossing in front of her car. A late model Honda Prelude. She looked nervous. Averting her eyes. The four kids were taking their time crossing the street. When they were in front of her car, the largest of them turned, pounded on the hood three times. "White bitch," he yelled. The others laughed. She looked ready to cry. Rolled her window up all the way. Made sure the doors were locked. I pulled up beside her. The boys moved on.

The light changed. She drove off. On her rear bumper, which the boys couldn't have seen, a sticker said: "If we knew it was going to be this much trouble, we would have picked the cotton ourselves."

Some things never change. And some people never learn.

I remembered Warren's line that I would never understand. I guess I never will.

The End

Coming soon from Paul D. Marks, *Broken Windows*, the sequel to *White Heat*. Read an excerpt:

BROKEN WINDOWS

<u>Prologue</u>

The Hollywood Sign beckoned her like a magnet – or maybe like flame to a moth. The sign glowed golden in the magic hour sun – that time of day around sunrise and sunset when the light falls soft and warm and cinematographers love to shoot. Like so many others, Susan Karubian had come here seeking fame and fortune, hoping to make her mark on the world. And she would do just that, just not quite in the heady way she had anticipated.

She had spent hours deciding what to wear. After all, this wasn't exactly in the etiquette books. She finally decided on a tasteful dress with high heeled sandals.

The young woman drove her Passat down Hollywood Boulevard, turning up Franklin, past the Magic Castle. She turned slowly up Beachwood Canyon, past the low rent area north of Franklin, up through the towering stone gates with their "Welcome to Beachwood Canyon" signs. Past the movie star homes in the hills. She drove in circles, past piles of rubble from the earthquake several months ago, figuring that sooner or later she'd hit the right combination of roads and end up where she wanted to be.

She reached the crest of the mountain – mountain or hill? What was the difference anyway? A small concrete building with an antenna sat just below the road, which crested the mountain. No cars. No one around. It was like the Sherman Oaks Galleria on a Monday morning.

She got out of the car and realized she'd have to hike down to get to the sign. She had thought it would be at the top of the mountain. She rolled up the windows, locked the car, her purse on the floor by the gas pedal. The note that someone was sure to find snug in her pocket.

She treaded toward the edge of the road. The incessant rain of the last couple weeks had broken. The view from up here was incredible. You could almost see Mexico to the south and the Pacific glittering in the west. A beautiful view of the city, shining and bright from up here. Pretty and clean. Millions of ants scurrying this way and that on important business. Oh yes, everyone here had important business all day and all night. Everyone but her. She gazed down at Los Angeles on the cusp of the Millennium. The place to be. Center of the universe.

She hesitated at the edge of the road, her toe kicking some gravel down the hill. It clattered its way down, somehow reminding her of the industrial music in the clubs she liked to frequent.

Should she try to talk to him? What would be the point now? She was talked out. And he wouldn't forgive her. Why should he? She had hurt him. No, it was beyond hurt. There was no way to rationalize it.

She tentatively stepped off the road, pressing on the dirt, testing its firmness. Loose gravel rolled down the hill. After taking off her Jimmy Choo high heels and holding them in one hand, she made her way down. She walked and slid and finally made it to the landing – she didn't know what else to call it – where the sign rested. The city glowed from here, shimmering with hope and desire and people wanting to make their dreams come true. She had come here for the same reason. The Hollywood Dream. The American Dream. She had wanted to be in front of the cameras from the time her parents took her to her first movie-theater movie, The Black Stallion, in 1979 when she was five. After seeing the movie she had wanted a horse, but more than that she wanted to be in a movie. She hadn't yet heard of Hollywood, but by the time she was thirteen she was making plans to come here. And nothing could have stopped her. Everyone told her how hard a career in movies was, how few made it. But she had faith in herself. She was attractive, more than, though she didn't want to be conceited. And she had talent. She had been acting in school plays for years. She was the star, Juliet to popular Paul Bonnefield's Romeo, in middle school. Rave reviews. Fake gold acting awards. What did that mean in the big picture? She had come here gushing with hope and optimism. She still thought she could make it, but what was the point now?

People looked up this way all the time. How many were looking at her now, as she climbed the scaffolding.

Higher and higher.

Her heart pounded through her chest. Her head throbbed.

Was she doing the right thing?

She reached one hand over the other, gripping the steel scaffolding. She held her shoes in her hands and the hard metal bit into her stockinged feet. The pain felt good, like penance.

Would anyone notice? Would anyone care that she was no longer here?

She gripped the scaffolding with all her strength and pulled herself up another rung.

"Don't look down." Her breath came in short bursts. She climbed higher. Warm blood trickled down her right palm.

She worried that the 6.7 quake last January had loosened the sign's footing. Would she fall even before she made it to the top?

Reaching the summit of the 'H,' she pulled herself up and sat on top, balancing as best she could. The wind slammed her, but she maintained her precarious balance. She clutched a piece of scaffolding – warm to the touch. A gust of wind hammered her. She began to topple, holding onto the scaffolding with all her strength. It wouldn't do to fall off. It wasn't deliberate enough.

Her stockings ran. She thought this might happen, but had hoped it wouldn't.

She looked out again – the golden city. Los Angeles. Hollywood. Was that the ocean dancing in the distance?

Sitting on top of the 'H,' a light breeze blew her night-dark hair. She flicked it out of her eyes. She put on her shoes. She talked to God. He didn't respond. If He did, she didn't hear it.

What had she done wrong? Was she just in the wrong place at the wrong time? No, she had chosen her life.

The note she'd written was burning a hole in her pocket. She took it out for one last read. The wind blew up, snatching it away.

"Damn!" There was no time to write a new note and nothing to write it with.

She forced herself into a standing position. The breeze made her unsteady and she billowed in the wind like a sail. Her dress snagged on the scaffolding.

She was scared to death, literally. That wouldn't last long. She held her breath and pushed off as hard as she could. Shrieking. One shoe flew off as she plummeted downward. If she couldn't be famous in life she would be famous in death. But one way or another she'd make her mark. She hoped her fall from grace would be graceful, even if her life had not.

About the Author

Paul D. Marks is the author of over thirty published short stories in a variety genres, ranging from noir to straight mystery, satire to serious fiction, including several award winners. His work has appeared in various anthologies and magazines, including Dime, the Deadly Ink 2010 Short Story Collection, Murder in La La Land, Murder Across the Map, LAndmarked for Murder, Hardboiled magazine and more. He has also published numerous magazine/periodical articles as well as having done film work.

He is also the last person to have shot on the fabled MGM backlot before it bit the dust to make way for housing. According to Steven Bingen, one of the authors of the well-received book MGM: HOLLYWOOD'S GREATEST BACKLOT: "That 40 page chronological list I mentioned of films shot at the studio ends with his [Paul D. Marks'] name on it."

Visit Paul at: www.PaulDMarks.com
www.whiteheatnovel.blogspot.com